For the Love of Heaven

Pamela Jackson

AGAPE
Publishing, Inc

PUBLISHED BY AGAPE PUBLISHING, INC.
12600 Deerfield Parkway, Ste. 125, Alpharetta, GA 30004
United States of America
678-684-1500

www.agapepublishinginc.com

ISBN: 978-0-578-00003-9
Library of Congress Control Number: 2009901857

Printed in the United States of America

Acknowledgments

FOREMOST, I ACKNOWLEDGE that it is by the grace of God that I have written this book. For without Him, I am nothing.

A very special thank you goes to all my readers who have patiently waited for me to finish this book. Without your "gentle" nudging, I might not have completed it! I am most grateful.

I graciously thank my dear friend Judi Collins and all the ladies of my Monday night Bible Study who continually offered prayer that my writing time would be productive. I am most grateful to Andy Stanley for his encouragement, and to Harriette and Joe Bowen for their love and support throughout the years. And, a great big thank you goes to Lynda Furr and Marion Lane for their invaluable editing skills.

My heart bursts with gratitude for those who love me unconditionally and support me unreservedly. Always there for me are my mother, Caroline Allen; my father, Ken Allen; Jo Allen; and Denise Jacob, my very best friend and my equilibrium.

I owe an incredible debt to my children, Juliette, Jeffrey, Cameron, and Annaleigh. Through each of you I have truly learned the power and miracles of our Lord. I cannot wait to see what is still to come. You all have brought me more joy than I can express! I love you beyond comprehension.

For my loving husband, Dale, there are no words sufficient. You are my soulmate and in such the nonverbal is much more powerful, so I will not attempt to minimize what we have together with words. *Thank you...*

Chapter One

BEN MONTAGUE STOOD in the center aisle facing the altar at First Covenant Chapel. The air was silent and the room dark, except for the glow of the emergency light over the door at the back of the pulpit. The red light illuminated the shadowy space behind the altar and cast a rose-colored glow on the wooden Cross which hung on the wall. The members of the tiny white clapboard church in the country were still trying to pick up the pieces after the sudden death of their senior pastor, Bob Buck. Although two months had passed, time seemed to be suspended and hung gloomily over a congregation in mourning. The membership of First Covenant Chapel had been divided on their loyalties; Reverend Bob Buck's death left a mixture of emotions. His charismatic charm had swooned many, but equally as many had been keen to his political panache. Regardless, Reverend Ben Montague, the associate pastor at First Covenant Chapel, was left to deal with much more than just to clean up the fallout of a church betrayed by its leader, even if not everyone knew it. Over the past two months the services on Sunday mornings had stayed status quo, and he and Ashley March, the ever eclectic worship leader, managed to work together on a daily basis and never speak a word. To Ben, the prospect of restoring the church seemed more difficult than climbing Mt. Everest, and an even colder journey.

Grief and mourning are well needed. It is the process by which we get the fuel to restore us and continue living. However, because of the death of both of his parents on the same day, Ben's grief was doubled. He mourned in silence for more than just the loss of both his mother and father; he mourned for the life he never had.

Learning at his mother's deathbed that Bob Buck was his real father was still a knowledge with which he had not come to terms. The situation was made worse by the fact that being Bob Buck's son meant he also had four brothers and sisters. One of his brothers, Bobby, openly despised him, and that was further complicated by the fact that Bobby was such an intrinsic part of First Covenant Chapel. It was more than he could handle. Over the last two months he had learned to shut off his heart from emotion, a place too painful to approach, regardless of who or what was trying to reach it —Sylvia included.

During private moments, he had gone to the altar often over the last several months, mostly to listen. He saved nearly every heartfelt word he had for preaching, which left him drained of anything he had in reserve. Tonight, the altar beckoned him more strongly than before. "I will come," he said out loud with a voice that contained exasperation. Facing the Cross, he slowly walked up the aisle and then kneeled resting his knees on the well-worn pads that nurtured those who came seeking comfort. He leaned his forearms on the altar rail, but did not bow his head. He fixed his gaze on the Cross barely visible in the darkness, although its shadow preeminently filled the room.

"Why me?" he said in a whispered tone which was also pleading, and then he was silent. Again, he said it, this time a little louder, "Why me?" Then, the words began to flow from his mouth. "I do not even know where to begin, God. I feel as though I have been left in a hole of emptiness. I have lost everything dear to me and even things I didn't know could be dear to me. I am alone! I am left facing mountains. I am not confident I can climb these mountains. I don't know how to begin a relationship with brothers and sisters I never even knew I had, or even if I should. I don't know how to lead this church which has been left into my care. This church is so divided on issues and now grief stricken from the death of their pastor." Ben paused and reflected for a moment. "Not only that, I am afraid to let my heart be touched by a woman I feel you might have created just for me." Then, he became silent and let his head drop. His face buried into his cupped hands, his words were muffled, "What do you want from me, God? A clear message is what I need," he said. Lifting his head, his tone became stronger, "A neon sign would be nice. Don't send me a dove with an olive branch right now God, because I can't understand it. Lay it out for me!" His voice had grown intent with anguish. Then, in a whisper, "Please, God, I am begging." He kneeled in the stillness for a moment longer and then quietly stood, turned his back to the altar, and walked down the aisle and out the front door of the tiny white clapboard church in the country and into the darkness of the night.

Chapter Two

HE HAD NOT slept past sunrise for as long as he could remember. But today, Ben awoke to the sunlight streaming in through the bedroom window of the parsonage. He still was not used to living here and it did not feel like home. His own cardboard boxes, along with all the boxes and belongings from his mother's home still remained stacked up in the guest bedroom. He had not the heart to unpack any of them, not even his own things. He had arranged his mother's furniture into the parsonage. There was plenty of space for it, not really having owned any of his own except for his bed, a mismatched dresser, and a few assorted chairs. That is all his little apartment had ever really needed.

Ben did not feel like he was the one who should be living in the parsonage now. He really felt it only right that Peggy Buck should continue living there. It had been her home as much as it had been her husband's. Ben had asked Peggy to stay there and he would find a rental nearby. "It won't be the same without Bob," she said. "Your time has come to lead this church and this should be your home. Besides, I want to live with family." As soon as she was strong enough after Buck's death, Peggy had moved in with her daughter Amy and her husband. That was five weeks ago.

Ben lay in bed letting the sunlight warm his face. It felt good. His mind wandered from one thought to the next. He briefly addressed each with God. Then, the thought of Sylvia seeped in and dominated his thoughts. He had not seen her for two weeks. Between his demands at First Covenant Chapel and her schedule at the hospital, it just had not been possible. They had hardly spoken either. Their voice mails had been their communication, which was impersonal, but that seemed to be par-for-the-course recently. He had looked for her at the hospital when he went on visitation, but that had proved futile too. Ben knew that he was not making too much of an effort to see Sylvia. He just could not. There were too many other things with which his heart had to deal right now, and a relationship with a woman was a complication he could not handle. As much as he tried to convince himself of that, he had a burning desire for her he could not shake.

He rolled over and reached for the cordless phone on his nightstand. Propping himself in a more upright position against his pillows, he lifted his hand and rubbed it across his whiskers. He took a deep breath and let it out. *I hope I'm doing the right thing,* he thought to himself? With a deep exhale he said out loud, "Proceed with caution." He did not know what he was going to say if Sylvia answered the phone. Although she understood that he had been dealing with a lot, he was aware from her voice in their last conversation that she was hurt by his sudden distancing. Now, it had been two weeks since they had spoken.

"Oh, God!" he said out loud as he stared at the phone. Then, looking upward he said, "That's a prayer request, You know." He dialed the phone. Each ring seemed like an eternity; then she answered.

"Hello." Somehow, hearing this one word was like a key unlocking his emotions. Her voice was sweet and it sent a quiver through him that radiated to his feet.

"Hello," he replied softly.

Sylvia pushed herself up to a sitting position and straightened her bedcovers across her lap. "Well, Reverend Montague," she said with a hint of sarcasm. "How are you?"

The salutation stung him. Maybe he deserved it. "I'm well. Thank you for asking," he said a little curt himself. His voice softened, "But, how are you?"

"I'm very well!" she said with over enthusiasm. She began to brush her hair away from her face and straighten her nightgown as if he could see through the telephone.

There was a deafening silence that seemed to last an unusual amount of time. Then at once they both began to speak…

"I was," they said simultaneously.

5

"I'm sorry," Sylvia said, "you go ahead."

"No, I'm sorry, you go ahead," he replied.

"I was just wondering if things were settling down for you." There was definite tenderness in her voice.

"All things come in time. I'm more settled in the parsonage," he said as he looked around the room at the unpacked boxes.

There was silence again.

"I've looked for you at the hospital when I've been there visiting," he said.

"The staff has been busy," she replied. They both knew this was only small talk and not about what either one wanted to be talking. "We have a new chief of staff coming in next week."

"Is that a good thing?" he asked.

"I don't know. It really shouldn't make much of an impact on me directly. My job is to take care of my patients." She paused and then said, "By the way, how is Miss Mary?"

"She is as lively and spunky as ever!"

"You have to admire her," Sylvia commented. "I hope I have that kind of attitude when I am her age."

There was a long pause of silence.

"It's supposed to be a beautiful day today," Ben said, obviously looking for something to keep the conversation going.

"I've heard. I'm looking forward to it. It's the first breath of spring and my favorite time of the year."

"Do you have something special planned for today?" he asked.

Sylvia had missed not seeing him over the last several weeks. Her lips curled into a smile which Ben could not see. *Oh, please ask me to spend the day with you,* she thought to herself. "Well, I haven't really thought about it yet," she replied. "Today is the first day I have been able to sleep in for a long time." She paused and pulled the covers up to her chin in modesty, "Truth be told, I'm still in bed."

Ben smiled, "Shame on you," he said in a jovial tone. "Truth be told, I am too." He wanted to ask her if she would like to do something today, but for some reason he could not make the words come out of his mouth. *Why am I afraid?* He silently pleaded with himself.

"What do you have planned for your day?" she asked.

He wanted to say, *spend it with you, take you to lunch, walk with you in the park, and catch up on the last several weeks,* but he could not make the words form. "I think I will work in the yard here at the parsonage. There's a lot to be done."

Her smile quietly disappeared. Sylvia let her head flop back onto her pillows and her eyes rolled back. *I am not going to wait around any longer for this man,* she thought to herself. Frankly, she was getting a little bored with the conversation. "I hope you enjoy your day," she said with a sharp tone. "I really need to be going now."

"Oh," was the only comment he had.

"Thanks for calling."

"You're welcome. I'll call again soon. Hopefully, I'll run into you at the hospital," he said, wondering how it was possible that he was letting this phone conversation end without asking to see her.

"Sure. Bye now." She was quick and then hung up the phone.

Ben gently set the phone down. He swung his legs around and put his feet on the floor. Sitting on the edge of the bed he stared out of the bedroom window of the parsonage. On one side he could see the little pond that the parsonage shared with the house next door and on the other side he saw the church property, which used to be Edward Tarken's. He sighed, but it came with a real sense of readiness. There were so many things left unsettled after Reverend Buck's death —all things that now demanded his attention. He suddenly felt ready to face them. It was time he started taking charge of his new appointment as senior pastor at First Covenant Chapel, which included some hard decisions. They were soul searching decisions about whether to continue with building a new sanctuary on the property that Edward Tarken had given to the church, and a delicate decision as to whether he and Ashley could work together in the best interest of the church and its people. He needed to, prayerfully, consider how to approach a relationship with his brothers and sisters, who at this point still did not know that he was also Bob Buck's son. And, then there is Sylvia…whom he had no intention of letting slip away from him.

He stood up, stretched his arms and walked to the window. As he peered out a smile came across his face. "Well God," he said, "It wasn't a dove with an olive branch; it wasn't a neon sign either." He paused for a moment then let out a little laugh. "It was more like a rock to the head!"

Ben was ready to make this a new day, indeed. Out loud, he proclaimed, "This is the day that the Lord has made, let us rejoice and be glad in it!"

Chapter Three

BEN WALKED UP to the door of the church offices. He placed his hand on the doorknob and then stopped. Pulling his hand back, he reached into his pocket and took out his handkerchief. Carefully, and with much pride, he wiped a smudge from the window pane in the door and then smiled with satisfaction.

Stepping inside, he saw Margaret, the church secretary. She had been working at the church for three years now. She began in a volunteer position while she was interviewing for another job. Somehow, this became her permanent position and she was good at it. She was young and energetic, quick as a whip, and took no nonsense from anyone. "Good morning, Margaret!" He said in a cheerful tone as he entered.

Margaret was sitting at her desk sorting the mail which had arrived on Saturday. "Well, good morning to you too, Reverend Montague," she replied.

Ben walked over to Margaret's desk, placed a hand on it and leaned to her eye level. "Please, call me Ben," he said in a firm and rhythmic voice. This was perhaps the hundredth time he had made that request.

Looking him in the eyes, she smiled. "Yes, sir."

"Thank you," he said standing up straight again.

She picked up a stack of little pink papers and handed them to him. "Here are your messages."

He smiled at her and began to walk down the hall to his office.

As he was walking, Margaret called out, "Glad to see you so happy today…Reverend Montague."

He shook his head and continued, smiling as he walked along.

When he had almost reached the door to his office, he stopped. "No time like the present," he said to himself, then turned and walked back down the hall to Ashley March's office. He peered in the door. Ashley sat in a perched fashion on the edge of his desk chair. He was peering at a newspaper spread open on his desk; in fact, it was the only thing on his desk. Ben observed the unusual tidiness of Ashley's office. The bookshelves were void of anything except a few pictures of Ashley himself, a porcelain cross and a Baptist hymnal. Ben duly noted that no United Covenant Hymnal existed in Ashley's office, further confirming Ashley's stance that hymnals are full of horizontal songs and are therefore worthless. Ben chuckled when he thought about the day that Ashley had told them that horizontal songs, such as those in the hymnal, where flat, that they did not go anywhere and just stayed here on the earth. When, on-the-other-hand, vertical songs, like the new contemporary songs, went straight up, from our mouths to God's ears. He glanced back at the bookshelf; the Baptist Hymnal must be a remnant of his past, but hardly an oversight in its prominent location.

Ashley, obviously startled, looked up at Ben. He did not say a word.

In a nonchalant voice, Ben said, "Good morning, Ashley. When you have a moment, come to my office. It's time we talk." Without giving Ashley a chance to respond, Ben turned and walked away. He was the senior pastor now, it was time he started acting like it.

Ashley was a little uncertain about what to expect, and he appeared a little nervous. He got up from his desk, walked over to the door of his office and closed it. On the back of the door was a full length mirror. He stared into it straightening his clothes; he gave a little nod of approval. "So, what do you think he wants?" Ashley began to talk to his reflection. "He probably thinks he's going to be able to pull rank on me now that Buck's dead." He reached up, smoothed his finely groomed blonde hair and tugged at his collar, which was a contrasting shade of burgundy to the rest of his shirt. "Well, he's got another thing coming to him if he thinks he's going to push me around. I'm the reason all of these people are coming to this church in the first place. He should be grateful to me!" The mirror gave every appearance of approval to this thought process. "We'll see who's in charge here." He opened the door and began making his way down the hall.

Ashley stopped for a brief moment just before he reached the door of Ben's office. He took a deep breath and quietly let it out. Then he made the final steps and appeared in the doorway. "Brother Ben!" His entrance was well staged.

"Come on in, Ashley," Ben said as he stood up from his desk. "Have a seat," he gestured to a chair as he walked around to the front of his desk to join him.

Ashley seated himself in a delicate manner, crossing his left leg over his right and letting his arms rest on the sides of the chair with his hands dangling off the ends —he wiggled his fingers. He had a distinct air of confidence, and was totally unaware of the large sweat stains at his armpits. "So, what's the worry, Ben, that you felt a need for a meeting?"

"No worries, Ashley. I just thought it was time we begin to move the church forward again. We have been in a much needed state of mourning, but as leaders of this church, you and I, need to start a forward progression." Ben clearly said *you and I* with emphasis.

"Well, I do believe you are right," Ashley said with a guarded and slightly sarcastic tone. "Where do you suggest we start?"

"I thought clearing the air between us would be a good place start," Ben replied. For the three years that Ben and Ashley had worked together under Bob Buck, it was no secret to anyone that Ben and Ashley did not get along.

"Whatever do you mean?"

Ashley's sarcasm irritated him, but he was not about to fall prey to it. "We have not always seen eye to eye, and I don't suspect that we are going to start now. But, oftentimes the best team can be made out of opposites. I do not underestimate your importance here and, in fact I value it."

Ashley began to rapidly shake the foot of the leg that was crossed over the other. "Well, Brother Ben, I'm glad to hear that." He tilted his head and raised his chin. "I think we each have our responsibilities under control. I think we should just carry on." Ashley's message was clear —don't bother me.

This isn't going to be easy, Ben thought to himself. "I don't think it's quite that simple. We need to work for a common goal and that

11

means planning and working together." He paused. "On Wednesday we will start with weekly staff meetings again. Is nine o'clock good for you?"

"Perhaps you're right, we do need a plan," Ashley said with arrogance. "Nine-thirty is better. Bobby and I will get a plan together, and let you know then." He stood up and pushed the wrinkles out of his pants with his hands. "Thank you so much for the meeting. I think it was well needed. We should be headed on the right track now." He pronounced his "t's" hard when he spoke.

Ben smiled coyly. He did not say a word, but was very aware of the challenge he was facing; Bobby would be a totally separate issue. Bob Buck's son, Bobby, had a grave distaste for Ben. And, it would be much worse if Bobby ever found out the truth about his Dad's affair and that Ben was Buck's son too. Bobby had no place at the staff meeting, but making that call now would prove to be fatal, and Ben was well aware of that. Bobby and Ashley had been two peas in a pod and ever since Buck's death, they had become more formidable than ever.

Chapter Four

AMONGST THE USUAL busyness, Sylvia sat at the nurse's station on the third floor of Salem Regional Medical Center poring over a patient file. Intent on work, with her head down and her pen pushing copiously, making notations, she had not noticed that Mr. Hartford, the hospital director, was on the floor with the new chief of staff making introductions.

"Dr. DiLeo?" she heard his voice over her shoulder. She turned.

Mr. Hartford and an extraordinarily attractive man with sandy brown hair dusted with gray were standing next to her. She stood and turned toward them.

"I would like to introduce you to our new chief of staff, Dr. Richard Davies," Mr. Hartford said.

She looked up at Dr. Davies, immediately noticing his well defined jaw with a shadow of whiskers, and even though he was wearing a suit, she could tell his physique was as well defined. She smiled.

"This is Dr. Sylvia DiLeo. She is one of our finest orthopedic surgeons on staff," Mr. Hartford continued.

Richard Davies extended his hand toward Sylvia, "Very pleased to meet you, Dr. DiLeo."

She placed her hand in his with a firm grip. There was something awkward about his touch. "Welcome to the third floor," she said with a smile.

"Thank you," he replied still holding her hand. "I look forward to getting to know you better."

She gave no response, just a slight smile which was obviously uncomfortable.

* * *

BEN WAS ENERGETIC as he walked through the automatic doors of the hospital. He only had two parishioners to visit today, which was a blessing. They were still at the tail end of the flu season. Last year at this time his parishioners nearly took up half a wing of the hospital. He arrived a little early with the intentional hope of running into Sylvia.

The elevator door opened; he stepped in. Mr. Hartford and a well dressed man he had never seen before were already in the elevator.

"Hello, Reverend Montague," Mr. Hartford said in his deep voice.

"Hello." Ben extended his hand.

"This is our new chief of staff, Dr. Richard Davies," Hartford looked toward Davies. "This is Reverend Montague from First Covenant Chapel. He's sort of a regular around here." Hartford smiled. *Ding*...the elevator door open and they all stepped out onto the floor.

Ben extended his hand which Richard Davies firmly grasped in a handshake. "It's a pleasure to meet you," Ben said.

"Likewise," replied Davies.

Richard Davies and Mr. Hartford turned and headed toward the nurse's station. Ben turned the other way and headed down the corridor. The handshake left him cold and uneasy. Davies appeared to be more like an actor playing a doctor on television —just a little too perfect. He shook the thought from his mind. *What did it matter anyway?*

* * *

WHEN BEN HAD finished his visits he headed back to the elevator. He was going to the third floor, the most likely place to find Sylvia. When the doors closed, he straightened himself and smoothed his hands across his hair. He had not seen her in awhile. Right before the doors opened again he got that feeling in his stomach that crept down his legs, the same feeling he had the first day they met and the same feeling he had when he was fourteen years old and asked Cindy Baker to the Valentine's dance. *What's wrong with you Ben,* he thought to himself. *You're a grown man!*

He stepped off the elevator and looked around. The floor was quiet. Walking over to the nurses' station he appeared nonchalant, hoping he would just casually bump into her. He surveyed the area; there was no sign of her.

"Excuse me," he said to a nurse filling out paperwork behind the station desk. "I'm Reverend Montague, is Dr. DiLeo on the floor?"

The young woman looked up with a sweet smile, "If you didn't see her, she is probably in with a patient."

"Oh." He stood there a moment thinking what he should do.

The nurse looked at him, waiting patiently for him to say something else. "Would you like to leave her a message?" she finally said.

"You don't know whether she'll be long, do you?"

"I'm sorry, I don't," she responded with intentional sympathy.

"That's all right. Thank you," he said in a voice that he hoped did not reveal how disappointed he was. He headed back to the elevator.

Ben walked out the automatic glass doors of the hospital and headed toward his car. As he approached the parking lot he saw a man and a woman talking. The woman was dressed in a professional outfit, however her blouse allowed a considerable amount of cleavage to be revealed, which Ben noticed was to what the man appeared to be talking. As he got a little closer he recognized the man as Dr. Davies, the new chief of staff, whom he had met earlier that day. Ben smiled at him in recognition, but Dr. Davies indifferently nodded and gave a half smile indicating that he had no recollection of their earlier meeting.

Chapter Five

HE AROSE EXTRA early. The promise of the sun was barely visible. Ben put on a pair of sweats and an old t-shirt. Walking out onto the front porch of the parsonage in his sock feet, he sat down in one of the rocking chairs. Peggy Buck had left all the porch furniture when she moved. She had told him she had no use for it. Ben liked Peggy and felt sad for her. Somehow, he sensed that her life with Buck must have been hard.

He put on his tennis shoes, walked down the front steps and began to stretch. He would run at least three miles this morning, needing to blow off as much steam as he could before the staff meeting at nine-thirty. Ashley had informed him that Bobby would be at the meeting; it was not going to be a tea party. Bobby Buck, his wife, and their children had continued coming to First Covenant Chapel since his father had died, in spite of the commonly known fact that Bobby detested Ben. Ben sensed Bobby was still coming to church more to make a point that the Buck family was still in control of First Covenant Chapel. On Sunday mornings the church had the feeling of a wedding gathering, with the bride's side and the groom's side. Bobby was always on Ashley's side. Even though Bobby had been constantly present at First Covenant Chapel since Buck's death, he had not spoken a word to Ben.

"Hey girl!" Ben called as his neighbor's big, fluffy, white dog bounded toward him across the front yard of the parsonage. Angel and Ben were friends; she was always a welcomed guest. He petted Angel enthusiastically on the head and then reached down and picked up a pine cone that had become soft with age. Tossing it in the air and catching it again several times, Angel watched with anticipation. "All right girl, are you ready?" Angel moved her head as if to nod; her eyes never left the pine cone. Ben raised his arm and threw it as far as he could into the field which connected the parsonage to the church. "Get it girl!" he cheered her on as she took off after the pine cone. Ben waited for her to return, trophy in mouth. Angel's tail wagged back and forth which spoke volumes —clearly it was saying, "Again! Again!" Ben lowered himself to her eye level and placed both of his hands on her furry face and rubbed back and forth. "I'm sorry girl, I've got to go run. I've got a tough day ahead of me." Angel's eyes pleaded with him. He smiled at her, "Believe me, I would much rather play catch with you all day, than cat and mouse with Ashley March and Bobby Buck." He paused and then added in a whisper, "That's our secret. Okay?" Angel dropped the pine cone from her mouth and then licked Ben across his cheek and nose, as if acknowledging that his secret was safe.

The grass was wet with dew and the dawn air still chilly. Ben took off running, heading south down the street which passed in front of the tiny white clapboard country church. Ben communed with God during his jogs. He breathed in the sweet air letting it fill the very depths of his soul with fuel for the day.

When he returned to the parsonage he was drenched in sweat. The sun had made its presence. He ran up the porch steps of the parsonage and sat down on the top step to catch his breath. He felt well. Lifting the bottom of his t-shirt, he wiped the sweat from his brow. He turned to look across at the tiny chapel. The sun had now risen above the horizon and shone against the little church; the steeple cut through the sun's rays sending a reflection of light in opposing directions. The congregation of First Covenant Chapel was equally divided on issues of all sorts. There are two types of churches —congregation driven churches and pastor driven churches. Ben attributed the majority of the division at First Covenant Chapel to the fact that Bob Buck had created a pastor driven church. Worse than that, Buck had created a dictatorship, and with his sudden death the congregation was lost and there was virtually no leadership to be had.

It is time that the congregation at First Covenant Chapel take ownership of their church, Ben thought. But, it was going to be a challenge because the few that did see themselves as leaders were still walking in Buck's footprints. Those footprints totally neglected the fact that first-and-foremost the ownership of the church belonged to Christ, a fact that Ben had every intention of re-establishing.

* * *

BEN ARRIVED AT his office early. He wanted time to prepare his agenda and thoughts for the meeting; he also wanted time to pray. Closing the door, he shut the world outside. He briefly looked around the office —his office; it still felt unfamiliar. He moved to the bookshelves that filled the entire east wall. Surveying its contents, he ran his hand across the bindings of a row of books. Slowly, it began to dawn on him that these were his father's books. A man he had known all his life yet never known. A sudden burst of anger staggered through him; anger at his mother. "Why did you keep the truth from me?" he whispered. It grieved him. He studied the titles that rested on the shelves. His father was a well-read man. Ben looked forward to a time when he could sit and absorb each book, drawing in their knowledge. As he continued to scan the shelves he came across a copy of D.H. Lawrence's *Sons and Lovers*, which he found oddly out of place among the liturgy and prayer books. Next to it was a much worn copy of the United Covenant Book of Rules. It was obvious from its tattered appearance that Buck was familiar with the rules of The United Covenant Churches of America. *Why had he betrayed them so readily?* Ben wondered what could make a man turn so far away from what he knew to be right. He knew that answer; it was as old as Cain and Abel —greed, plain old greed.

He walked to the chair in front of his desk –the one which he was beginning to frequent as he sat across from church parishioners. This time he did not sit, but kneeled instead, placing his elbows in the seat of the chair; he folded his hands in prayer.

* * *

WHEN BEN ENTERED the Sunday School room, the same room where they held the staff meetings while Buck was still pastor, Margaret was already there. She had placed a tray of coffee and Styrofoam cups in the center of the table. Ben remembered that at the very first staff meeting he attended, Margaret had made a makeshift tray out of the top of a box of copier paper. Today, it was a real tray; one which looked similar to a cocktail tray, one like you would see in a bar, and it crossed his mind how it could have come to make its home in a church.

"Good morning, Reverend Montague!" Margaret said in her usual cheerfulness.

"Good morning, Margaret; and it is Ben."

She smiled at him. "Today is a big step. Are you ready?"

He glanced at her with a curious eye. Ben wondered exactly how much Margaret really knew. "Yes," he said with certainty, and then quoted from one of his favorite poems, "The time has come...the walrus said...to speak of many things."

She stared at him for a moment trying to figure out what that was supposed to mean. Then, deciding not to bother she said, "I just want you to know that I think you are a fine man, Reverend Montague, and I am honored to be working with you."

"Thank you, Margaret," his voice told that he was touched by her comment.

The sunlight was making its full appearance through the windows warming the room that was destined to be chilly once the meeting started. Ben walked to the end of the table and spread out his notes. His jaw was clenched and his shoulders rigid; Margaret could tell he was under a lot of stress. A few moments later Ashley walked into the room with his usual saunter; Bobby followed behind him.

"Good morning!" Ashley began with the intent of making his presence known and dominant. "Hello, Margaret!"

She smiled at him taking particular notice of how impeccable was the ensemble which he was sporting –right down to the laced up oxfords that appeared beneath his extremely well pressed slacks.

"And, how does your corporosity sagaciate on this salubrious morning?" he said with an unusual flair.

Margaret looked at him with a totally blank face. "What?"

Ashley chuckled, "How are you, Margaret?"

She shook her head slightly indicating that her confusion had been clarified. "Oh. I am just fine. And, you?"

"Dandy!" Ashley replied quickly and with nauseating exuberance.

He certainly is dandy, Margaret thought to herself. She smiled.

Ashley turned toward Ben and in a very controlled, emotionless voice said, "Brother Ben?" The words came across as a statement rather than a question.

"Good to see you this morning, Ashley," he replied while giving his head a slight nod, then he turned and looked at Bobby, "It's good to see you, too, Bobby. How are you doing?"

Obviously, Bobby viewed it as a rhetorical question, not responding as he reached to the center of the table and poured himself a cup of coffee.

Here we go again, Margaret thought to herself remembering the staff meetings before Buck's death that verged on the eruption of an all out civil war.

It was only the four of them this morning and frankly Ben thought it should be only three. But, for as long as Buck was pastor, Bobby had attended the staff meetings. Now was not the time to make a change. He also wished that Tom Werner was there.

Tom had been an excellent finance chairman for the church, but he made the fatal mistake of disagreeing with Buck on the proper handling of the church money. Tom had been the first of Buck's causalities, in more ways than Tom knew. Ben winced at the thought that Tom's wife, Lisa, had been having an affair with Buck prior to his death. At the same time that the church was blowing up over the controversy of building the new sanctuary on the property that Edward Tarken had been manipulated to tithe, Tom discovered that Lisa was having an affair. What Tom did not know, and Ben had accidentally found out, was that she was having the affair with Bob Buck. Ben had been counseling with Tom regularly since Tom had learned about the affair. Tom and Lisa were trying to patch their marriage back together. They both agreed that the details of her affair were not important and agreed never to speak of them. With this agreement, Tom would never know that Buck was the "other man"—perhaps that was for the best. But, it made Ben feel like he was betraying his friendship with Tom not to share this knowledge. Ben was in a difficult position, somewhere between confidentiality and friendship – he felt loyalty to both.

Ben opened the meeting in prayer and then addressed the obvious. "Our church has been grieved and in mourning." He looked at Bobby with sincere sympathy. "I know the loss of your father has been painful. I have prayed that the peace of God has sustained you and your family during this time." Ben paused. He hoped the words were coming out right and that his own overwhelming grief and anger were not showing through. "Whatever you need, please know that your church family is here for you –always."

"Thank you," Bobby replied through clinched teeth, unwilling to accept Ben's participation in the healing process. Ben was surprised that Bobby had even acknowledged that Ben had spoken. Bobby continued looking to the others at the table as he spoke, "The people of this church have been gracious and kind beyond any hope or expectation, which has been a witness to the entire Buck family that my father was truly a great man in the eyes of this church. I have no doubt that his name and spirit will remain a legacy here," he paused, "and I intend to see that he is never forgotten."

Ben was dumbfounded by the response and the dramatics of it. And frankly, he did not know whether he should respond to Bobby's statement or not. But, Ashley handled that concern for him.

"Amen, Brother Bobby!" Ashley said as he smacked his hands on the top of the table. "Your father, and my mentor, was an inspiration to this entire community. What he began we all need to pull together and finish!" He turned and looked at Ben, "Right, Brother Ben?"

Margaret watched Ashley and his exuberance. She could just imagine what he would look like in a cheerleader's uniform. She scooted down in her chair wondering how Ben was going to respond to his display and wondered if she needed to run for cover.

Ben opened his mouth to speak, but before any words could come out Ashley continued. "Bobby and I have made a list of where we need to start." Ashley picked up a piece of paper sitting on the table in front of him; Ben looked down at his own list he had compiled. Ashley stood up and, as he spoke, began to pace behind his chair.

21

"First, we must get the building committee back in swing and moving with the construction of the new sanctuary building."

Ben could not believe what he was hearing, but then again, why should it surprise him? This had been Ashley's method of operation since he had known him –the bull in the china shop technique. Actually, it was more like a gazelle, but either way they did damage.

"Ashley," Ben interrupted.

Ashley held up a finger, "Just a moment, let me run down the whole list and then we can have discussion." His voice took command.

I'm the pastor here, Ben thought to himself. *I'm in charge!* But, he also believed that being a good leader oftentimes meant staying quiet and just listening.

Ashley continued, "Bobby and I are going to bring the choir band back on Sunday mornings and liven up the place again. We have our Sunday Supper starting again in two weeks and," he paused briefly but not long enough for anyone to speak, "we have a big surprise for everyone." He looked toward Bobby. "Go ahead Bobby, you tell them!"

"Sure." Bobby stood up. He put his hands together and lifted them to his chin. "As you know, Easter is in three and a half weeks. We have all that beautiful property that Edward Tarken so generously gave to the church in honor of my father." History was being rewritten; forever it would be lost that Edward Tarken had actually tithed the property in honor of his late wife, Beverly. "Ashley and I have planned a beautiful sunrise service for Easter morning as a way of memorializing Dad."

Ben was suddenly consumed with nausea. *An Easter service memorializing Buck? They can't be serious,* he thought to himself. That is what the funeral was for. Easter is the celebration of the Resurrection of Christ. There was no way he was going to allow Bobby and Ashley to make a mockery out of Easter! But, he was also between a rock and a hard place when it came to authority.

"We are going to advertise in the community. We will be the only sunrise service in the area and we have the perfect setting; the way the sun comes up over the little pond, just as it breaks the earth's surface, it reflects the light with radiance only God can create." Bobby was animating with his hands the way the scene would look. "Some of the men in the church have agreed to build a stage right at the edge of the water. Ashley is going to rent sound equipment. Believe me; this is going to be an awesome show. It will draw a ton of people. My father would be proud."

Ben sat quietly, composing his thoughts. This needed to be handled carefully. He was trying to mend fences, not tear them down. He brought his right hand up to his face and rubbed it across his chin. *Give me the words, Lord,* he prayed silently. "I think a sunrise service for Easter is a wonderful idea; it could be just what this congregation needs right now. Easter is a celebration indeed; a simple sunrise service could be very meaningful."

Ashley twitched his shoulder and his lips noticeably puckered. "I detect a hint of disapproval in your tone. What do you mean by 'simple'?"

The muscles in Ben's neck were beginning to ache from the tension. Unless Ashley was to undergo a conversion like that of the Apostle Paul's, Ben's leadership of First Covenant Chapel was going to be one roadblock after another. "Let's table the sunrise service for a moment. I would like to focus our attention on a few basic understandings which we all need to hold in common. One of them is, I have noticed that whenever we are in the sanctuary of the church, it seems as though we are making the congregation the audience." He took a deep breath. "The audience is not the congregation." He paused again and then very firmly and articulately said, "The audience is God."

Ashley cocked his head in obvious distress over Ben's comment. "What are you insinuating?"

"I'm not insinuating anything. I'm just addressing where we need to refocus our attention."

Ashley began to shake both his hands in front of him and in an agitated tone said, "Yes, you are. You are insinuating that Bobby is trying to make his father the audience."

Yes, I think Bobby is viewing Buck, his father…my father…as the audience, but I was more thinking that you, Ashley, use the congregation as an audience, Ben thought to himself.

"Your problem is that you just can't think outside of the box!" Ashley said with indignation.

Ben was growing angry himself. "I have no problem with things in the church being outside of the box," he said and then paused briefly. "I have a problem with things in the church being outside of The Body."

"Very poetic," Ashley said coldly as he dramatically brushed his hand across his forehead in a gesture to brush off Ben's reply.

Ben took several deep breaths trying not to make them too obvious. He calmed his demeanor and in a quiet and compassionate voice said, "I'm sorry. I do not want to be at odds. What I am trying to say is that there is a language to the sanctuary and I feel it is our responsibility as leaders to speak it and to teach it to the people who come here. Call it piety, but the fact is, acts of piety are part of the spiritual life. And, in respect to a sunrise service, I'm sure that we all agree that the focus of such a service is the Resurrection of Christ. I have total confidence that you all will put together a beautiful selection of music for the service, and I will make sure my sermon does it justice." Ben did not want this staff meeting to continue. He did not allow any time for comment. Looking at Margaret, he said with finality, "Is there any other business we need to cover?"

Margaret was ready to have this meeting end too; it was déjà vu. Almost afraid to interject anything she meekly said, "The ladies of the church wanted me to let you know about their new blanket ministry. Julia Matthews is heading it up. If you know of anyone who is suffering from a serious illness, please let one of the ladies know and they will take them a handmade blanket." She flipped the page of her legal pad. "Also, there will be a children's used clothing sale in a couple of weeks to raise money for the homeless shelter over in Salem, specifically to benefit homeless children. And, don't forget Sunday Supper in two weeks." She put her pad down on the table signifying that she was finished.

"I'll close us in prayer," Ben said quickly, not allowing any time for further comments.

Chapter Six

THE WORDS RANG in angelic voices...*Jesus loves me, this I know, for the Bible tells me so!* What child who has ever attended church, Sunday School, or Vacation Bible School, even if only a few times, does not know this song? The children's choir had grown to quite a chorale. Twice a month they opened the Sunday service with the Call to Worship.

Miss Mary sat in her usual seat, donning a wide brimmed yellow straw hat with silk flowers of a contrasting shade which welcomed the spring morning. Although the past year had taken its toll on her, Miss Mary was, without a doubt, the youngest eighty year old lady this side of the Mississippi. Her broken hip had healed well and only bothered her on rainy days. She was able to exchange her walker for a cane. Julia Matthews had given her a lovely one with a Mother of Pearl handle for her birthday. Julia had also graciously taken over the pleasure of picking up Miss Mary on Sunday mornings to chauffeur her to church since Miss Mary was no longer able to drive. Julia and Miss Mary enjoyed each other's company and the wisdom that each had to offer the other.

As the children sang Miss Mary watched with delight. "Who is that little girl in the second row?" Miss Mary whispered leaning toward Julia who sat next to her in the pew every Sunday. "The towhead with curls? She's beautiful."

"They're new to the area," Julia whispered back. She nodded her head to the right in order to indicate the family. "That's her family sitting in the third pew back. I don't know their names yet, but they seem to have three children." Miss Mary turned her head to glance at the family but, she did not recognize any of them.

Miss Mary watched pleasantly as the children sang. Pausing briefly, she looked around the sanctuary. The pews were full. For the first time since Buck's death she sensed newness in the air.

When the children sat down, Ashley March made his usual entrance into the sanctuary wearing a new addition to his wardrobe, a light blue silk Nehru jacket, symbolizing spring. Holding his cordless microphone in one hand and clapping his other against it, he motioned the congregation to stand and sing with him.

"Put your hands together for the Lord!" he shouted into his microphone, "and let us sing Holy, Holy God!"

The congregation stood, including Julia. She adjusted her slightly too short skirt and tried not to noticeably cringe at the sight of Ashley's performance. It baffled her why others did not seem to see through him. She resented him representing himself under the pretense of spiritual leadership and in addition to that, his sway was just a little too feminine for her way of thinking.

* * *

AFTER THE SERVICE, Miss Mary slowly, but elegantly, made her way out of the church into the warm sunshine. The trees were now in full bloom and the newly sprouted jonquils made their appearance at every turn. She saw the little towheaded girl kneeling and looking intently at the ground. A smile came across Miss Mary's face. She walked toward the little girl and as she got closer she saw the little girl was kneeling in a clover patch.

"You sang beautifully today," Miss Mary said in a soft voice. The little girl looked up and smiled. "What are you looking for?" Miss Mary asked her.

"Four leaf clovers," the little girl answered. "Have you ever found one? They bring you luck!" The little girl's voice was full of excitement.

"I have, but it was a very long time ago." The question took Miss Mary back to her childhood. "What is your name?"

"I'm Alex."

"And, I'm Miss Mary."

Alex stood up. "I like your hat!"

For the Love of Heaven

"Thank you." Miss Mary's face was warm and reassuring.

"Here, you can have this one." Alex extended her hand toward Miss Mary and gently placed a perfectly formed four leaf clover into the palm of her hand.

Miss Mary felt lucky indeed. "Thank you, I shall take very good care of this and treasure it forever." She turned to see a gentleman standing next to her.

"Pawpaw!" Alex said with excitement. "I found a four leaf clover for you!" The older man extended his opened hand toward his great-granddaughter. His hand showed his years but it was steady and strong as Alex gently placed the clover into his palm. "Today's your lucky day, Pawpaw!"

"Thank you," he said as he kissed her on the top of her head. "Who is your friend?"

"This is Miss Mary. I gave her a four leaf clover too!"

"I see," he replied.

"Hello," Miss Mary interjected. "It's a pleasure to meet you, and welcome to First Covenant Chapel." As they looked down they both realized that shaking hands was impossible because they each cradled a four leaf clover in the palm of their right hand.

"A pleasure to meet you. I am Leon Jefferson." He smiled. Leon was a tall man, and thin; his shoulders were slightly rounded. His white hair was neatly trimmed, although there was not very much of it. The wrinkles on his face were reassuring.

"Are you new to the area?" Miss Mary asked.

"I suppose you could say that. I moved here from the Baltimore area about six months ago. I'm living with my grandson and his family."

Miss Mary turned and looked at Alex, "How lucky for you to have your Pawpaw living with you." She had noticed that Alex had called him by that name.

"It's the four leaf clovers!" Alex said with enthusiasm.

"I believe you're right!" Miss Mary's enthusiasm was equal to that of Alex's. She looked back at Leon. "Well, I must be going or I will miss my ride home. I certainly hope that you will come back to church again."

27

"You can count on it." His voice was deep and certain.

Miss Mary turned and began to make her way over to Julia who was talking with a group of ladies.

"Are you ready to head home?" Julia asked.

"Yes, ma'am," she replied with a natural but excessively emphasized drawl. When they reached Julia's car, Miss Mary turned back to look at Alex and Pawpaw who were slowly walking in the opposite direction, holding hands.

Chapter Seven

BEN SAT IN his office preparing his sermon for Palm Sunday. He had opened the windows to welcome in the freshness of spring. Planted beneath his windows were tea olive plants offering a pungent aroma of sweetness which seeped into his office in an intoxicating pleasantness. Every gift of beauty through sight, touch, taste, hearing, and smell heightened Ben's awareness of the omnipotence of God. He was at peace. The words that he would speak to his congregation began to flow from his fingers to the paper –an affirmation of what he felt God wanted him to say. Thoroughly intent, his concentration was suddenly broken by the sound of power saws and hammering echoing across the open field between the parsonage and the tiny country church. Ben rose from his desk and walked to the open window. Across the field he could see a group of men next to the pond, clearly being directed by Bobby. Lumber was stacked to the side and men were measuring, cutting, and hammering. The stage was being set for the impending sunrise service, which was scheduled for Easter morning. It had the potential to be a beautifully reverent worship service, or –a fiasco.

Unable to concentrate on his sermon, he picked up the phone and dialed Tom Werner's office. Ben deeply wanted to see Tom return to First Covenant Chapel, not merely to have him back at church, but to see Tom restored to worship and fellowship.

Tom's secretary put Ben's call directly through. "Good morning, Ben," Tom said in a cheerful voice.

"Good morning, to you," Ben replied. "I thought I'd take a chance that you might be free for lunch today."

"Well," Tom said in a solemn tone, "I am scheduled to have lunch with the Prime Minister of England, but," his voice lightened, "I'll cancel for you."

"Don't I feel important!" Ben responded.

Tom chuckled. "How about noon at the Dixie Diner?"

The Dixie Diner was where Tom and Bob Buck met for lunch every week for three years. It had been their weekly meeting to discuss the church finances.

"I'll see you there," Ben answered.

Ben set down the phone and stood up from his desk. He walked out of his office and down the hall which housed the portraits of all the previous senior pastors who had faithfully served First Covenant Chapel. Ben wondered if Buck's portrait would be added to the collection; he was certain that it would be in time.

"How's it going Margaret," Ben said as he entered the reception area of the church.

Margaret looked around startled. "Fine. How's it going with you?" she mimed him back.

"Very well, thank you."

The door opened and Julia Matthews entered. She was wearing a bulky cardigan which was buttoned securely around her.

"Good morning, Julia," Ben said cheerfully.

Julia looked up shocked and obviously nervous. "Ben," she paused, "Good morning."

"Is everything all right?" Ben asked.

"Sure, why wouldn't it be?" Julia responded in a curt voice.

Margaret jumped into the conversation, "What's with the sweater? Did you lose track of the seasons? It's spring, you know."

"Does my outfit bother you?" Julia snapped.

"Sorry!" Margaret replied with a sarcastic voice.

"Time's a wasting," Julia said. "I'm here to stuff and stamp newsletters, not receive fashion advice."

Ben raised an eyebrow, but remained silent. In the few years that he had come to know Julia, he was very aware that she spoke her mind, but she had never been short tempered. "Well, I'll leave you ladies to work." He paused. "Let me know if I can help in anyway."

Julia simply nodded at him.

After Ben had cleared the corner, Margaret looked at Julia and said, "What's going on?"

"Nothing's going on."

"We've been stuffing and stamping these stupid envelopes for four years together," Margaret replied. "Don't tell me nothing is going on!"

"Fine!" Julia said with exasperation and she stood up and took off her sweater.

Margaret looked at Julia with an odd expression. Julia stood there in a soft pink tee shirt, much more appropriate for the weather outside. Something was obviously wrong; Margaret just could not figure it out.

"Well?" Julia said firmly, as if demanding an answer.

"Well what?" Margaret responded.

"What am I supposed to do?" Julia snapped back.

Margaret was not sure what they were talking about, but she did notice that Julia was oddly disfigured. She cocked her head. "What happened?"

"What do you mean, what happened? Isn't it obvious?" Julia said exasperated.

"Well..." Margaret stammered. "What happened?" she asked again.

"It blew up!" Julia said with outrage.

"Blew up?" Margaret's face was covered with question. "How is that possible?"

"Don't ask me!" Julia returned. "All I know is that there was this 'poof' and then it flattened."

A small smile came across Margaret's face and then she began to laugh.

Julia sat back down. It was clear that she did not think this was as funny as Margaret did. She gazed down with a look of embarrassment on her face. "What was I thinking?" Julia began. "I was in my early twenties and I thought if I had bigger boobs it would help me meet a man." She shook her head dumbfounded. "A lot of good that did me, I'm forty-five now and still haven't gotten a man. And, now I'm lop-sided! I'll never get a man!"

Margaret looked at Julia with sympathy but could not help but continue to giggle. "It's only half as bad as you think it is," she told Julia, not intending the pun.

"What do you mean, only half as bad?"

Margaret smiled cautiously, "Well –you still have one left," and she began to laugh again. "Maybe you'll meet half a man!"

"This isn't funny!" Julia demanded. "What am I going to do?"

"See a doctor, of course." Margaret suggested the obvious.

* * *

BEN WALKED INTO the Dixie Diner. Tom was already seated in a booth and looking at the menu. When Ben reached the table, Tom stood up and shook his hand.

"Good to see you, Tom," Ben said.

Tom smiled, "Good to see you too." Tom appreciated the fact that Ben did not use the word "brother" when talking to someone. "Brother Tom," Buck used to say. Not that being brothers was bad, it was just that it seemed insincere, especially coming from Buck.

A young lady approached the table carrying a pad of paper and a pencil. She had a sweet face and pleasant smile which immediately recognized Tom.

"Hello, gentleman!" she said with enthusiasm.

Tom smiled with great sincerity, "Hi, Sandy. Long time, no see. You look wonderful."

Sandy was the waitress who served Tom and Buck lunch nearly every Tuesday for several years.

"This is Reverend Montague," Tom said, gesturing toward Ben.

"Hi!" Sandy replied in a cheerful voice. "Sure is too bad about Reverend Buck. Did you know him?" She directed the question to Ben.

Ben smiled with a sense of sadness. "I did know him," was his simple answer.

"What'll you have?" she said nonchalantly.

The gentlemen ordered their lunches and set into conversation.

"So what's the purpose of this impromptu meeting?" Tom asked.

"I wanted to check in on you. And, I wanted to invite you and Lisa to come back to First Covenant Chapel," Ben's voice was sincere. Tom remained silent. Ben continued, "Tom, I know that you and Reverend Buck had a falling out, and the whole financial situation with the church is a mess. But, you know as well as I do that Buck created that situation, and you were only trying to protect the church." Ben paused to gather his thoughts. "However sad and difficult were the events that unraveled, what you were trying to achieve in stopping the rush into a building project that the church couldn't afford, has been accomplished. At least for the time being. When you left the church it was because of your conflict with Buck, not with God. God is still there. First Covenant Chapel is your home. We are your family."

Tom smiled. "Lisa and I have talked about the church. We haven't been to church in months."

"How are things with you and Lisa?" Ben asked.

Tom looked sad. "We are trying. We still love each other." He paused. "But, how do you put back the pieces after an affair?"

Ben nodded with empathy, "It helps you understand the depths of forgiveness that Christ has offered us."

Tom gave a slight smile, but his face was pained. "May I share something else with you, Ben?"

"Anything."

There was a very long pause before Tom began to speak. "Lisa," he said and then stopped. "Lisa is pregnant."

Ben did not know how to respond. He reached within his heart and to the guidance of God. "How do you feel about that?" was all he could say.

"Well, if it is mine then I am ecstatic." They were both aware of the realities.

"And, if it is not?" Ben asked.

"She said she would get an abortion."

Ben swallowed hard. It was not his place to pass judgment. He just nodded at Tom offering him a continued listening ear.

"I can't let her get an abortion."

Ben let out the breath he had been holding. *Thank God,* he thought to himself.

Tom continued. "When we decided to fix this marriage and make it work, we agreed to never speak of her affair again. That had been working well until we discovered she was pregnant. Now, there are all kinds of questions that need to be asked. Like who was the other man? He has the right to know that this might be his child?"

Ben wished that he could tell Tom that he did not need to worry about the other man —that he was dead. As he was struggling with what to say, it suddenly dawned on him that there was a distinct possibility that the child which Lisa was carrying was his own brother or sister. This angered Ben. *How many little Buck's are running around out there,* he thought to himself?

"Could you love this child even if it wasn't yours?" Ben finally asked.

Tom shook his head slowly. "I can't even think about that right now."

"This may be little consolation to you right now," Ben said, "but remember, nothing comes to you that has not come through God first."

Chapter Eight

AN HOUR NORTH of Wakefield was the small mountain town of Crimson. It was a town that could not have been quainter if it had come out of a fairy tale book. In the middle of the town square was the courthouse circled by the original cobblestone street. With just a little imagination, one could hear the clip clop of the horses' hoofs that at the birth of this town were the only means of transportation. Still today there are a few horse and buggies that take tourists for rides around the tiny town. On the other side of the cobblestone circle are shops and restaurants.

Ashley March sat on the bench outside The Fudge Shop. He came to Crimson frequently to get away and relax. Usually he came with his good friend Guy Turner. They had worked together years ago when they both were trying to squeak by, singing jingles for commercials. Guy had gotten a huge break with a prestigious ad agency in Salem. It was another year before Ashley took the worship leader position at First Covenant Chapel. Even after they had both gone their separate ways Ashley and Guy had remained close. Crimson was a peaceful town where they both liked to go as a stress reliever. It was also a place where nobody knew them.

"I got us some strawberries dipped in chocolate!" Guy said as he walked out of The Fudge Shop. Guy was a fair looking man. His features were well defined and he was impeccably groomed; right down to his manicured fingernails.

Ashley smiled. Guy sat down next to him on the bench and handed him a strawberry on a white paper napkin. They both sat quietly for a moment letting the warmth of the spring sun soak into their cheeks.

"How are things at the church?" Guy asked. He knew about the strain between Ben and Ashley, even before Buck had died. Plainly put, he knew that Ashley despised Ben and felt that he was a pious idiot with no talent for leading a church.

"Well," Ashley said with a sigh, "time will tell." He twisted to face Guy as he continued to speak. "Buck couldn't have chosen a worse time to die. We were just beginning to really take off with this church. We were moving forward with building a new sanctuary, we were developing some really dynamic shows for Sunday morning services," he paused. "Buck and I were on the same page," he looked at Guy intently. "You know what I mean?"

Guy smiled and nodded in acknowledgement.

Ashley continued, "Ben and I couldn't be more opposite. Frankly, he's a stick in the mud. He has no idea about what the modern day church needs. I think he really believes that hymns and sermons are all it takes." Ashley paused with more silence and obvious contemplation. "I'm going to fight for this church; it is what Buck would have wanted."

They stood, tossed their napkins into the "Keep this City Clean" container next to the bench, and began to stroll past the stores, window shopping as they went along. It was a lovely day and they were happy to spend it together.

Chapter Nine

BEN WALKED INTO the church office shortly after eleven o'clock. He had begun a habit of staying at the parsonage on Monday mornings to work on his sermons. He liked the small study on the second floor of the house. It was quiet and had a lovely view of the pond from its window. It was especially beautiful at this time of year as the trees were filling out and the rebirth of life was abundant.

"Good Morning, Reverend Montague." Margaret said.

"Ben," he replied in an exasperated, but sweet tone.

She looked up. "Been where?"

He shook his head and smiled. "No. Call me Ben."

She pointed her index finger and nodded with acknowledgement.

"So, what's going on around here?" he asked.

She handed him a stack of pink telephone messages. "You've been in demand this morning." This reminded him why he liked the study at the parsonage. "The ladies are in the Sunday School room planning the Sunday Supper coming up next week and Ashley's in his office," she paused, "doing...whatever Ashley does."

"Thank you, Margaret." He headed down the hallway toward the Sunday school room.

"Hello, ladies!" Ben said cheerfully as he walked in the room. "How is everyone?" He was pleased to see such a large group, but especially pleased to see the lady who sat at the far end of the table – Peggy Buck. He looked at her and smiled; she smiled back. Ben walked to her and took her hand in his. "It is so good to see you here. How are you?"

"I am well. Thank you," she replied.

"You look well. And, how is all of your family?" he asked.

"We are all moving in the right direction. That's why I'm here. It's time I start living again." Peggy smiled sweetly. She had aged years over the last few months since Buck's death. She was a widow now and her appearance showed the grieving she had done. Her face was drawn and she was much thinner, but Peggy had an unusual gift of dealing with adversity. She somehow always guided situations to land on the positive side, no doubt which was where she was leading herself now.

Ben smiled back. "Make sure we have lots of fried chicken!" he proclaimed as he headed out of the room.

As soon as he walked out of the door Julia Matthews spoke up in her usual non-discrete way, "I need to find a man just like that, only ten years older."

"Don't you mean fifteen?" Susan said under her breath, audible to only the few around her.

Miss Mary smiled. Yes, things were getting back to normal.

* * *

PEGGY HAD PRAYED about Ben over the last several months. Somehow, she felt responsible for some of his pain. Ben had lost both his mother and father on the same day, which was also the day that he learned the truth about who his father was. She had known all along that Buck was his father, but, she had never even let Buck know that she had been aware of his affair with Ben's mother, Katrina; and she did not blame Katrina either. Early in their marriage Peggy had learned what kind of man Buck was, but she loved him and had also learned to forgive him even when he did not know she was aware of his transgressions.

When the ladies meeting ended, Peggy walked the hallway to Ben's office; the office which had been her late husband's. She knocked lightly on the open door.

Ben looked up. "Peggy!" He was a little startled. "Please come in." He stood and walked to greet her by the door. "Come sit down with me." They walked to the chairs which sat in front of his desk. "I am so glad to see you." He voice was deep with sincerity.

"It looks as if you are settling in well." Peggy looked around.

"Well, it's not as well put together as Bob had it." He paused then said, "But, it serves me well." They both smiled trying to become comfortable with each other. "I have left all of Bob's books where they were. They may stay here for as long as you like and when you're ready, I'll pack them up for you."

"I am ready," she said in a steady tone, "and I would like for them to stay where they are and become yours."

"Peggy..." he began to speak, but she interrupted.

"You are a fine young minister and every minister needs a well appointed library. It would mean a lot to me for you to keep them." Looking to the side she saw sitting on the corner of the desk her husband's Bible that she had given to Ben the day he came to visit her after Buck had died. It was the day that she had told Ben that she had always known that Buck was his true father. She reached out and rubbed her hand across its worn leather cover.

"I don't know what to say, Peggy," Ben replied.

"You don't need to say anything to me Ben, but use them in serving this church and its people. You have a gift and I believe that you have the ability to bring this church back together."

Ben took in a deep breath. He could not remember ever knowing anybody who exemplified the life of Christ more than Peggy Buck. Even in the light of adversity, she loved, forgave, and served.

"Your confidence means a lot to me." Ben seemed to feel at peace with Peggy. He had worried about how she truly felt about him. After all, he was the progeny of her husband's illicit affair.

"There's something else Ben." Peggy paused.

"What is it, Peggy?"

"I would like to join this church. I never officially joined while Bob was pastor. I don't know why, I just didn't. But, I am ready now."

"I am so glad, Peggy. You are such an important part of this church."

"Ben?" Peggy said with a definite hint of reservation. He did not speak, but acknowledged that she had more to say. "I have spent a lot of time thinking and praying, and there is something that lays heavy on my heart."

"What is it?" he asked.

"Well, you are my husband's son. Technically, that makes me your stepmother. I would like to openly take on that honor; if you will allow it."

Ben was stunned and did not know what to say. In fact, he did not know how to feel. A rush of confusion ran through his body and settled in his chest, powerful enough to take his breath away.

"Ben?" Peggy whispered.

"I'm sorry, Peggy." Ben was clearly choked up and trying to shake the confusion from his head, "I don't know what to say. I am touched, but there are so many complications around this. What about your children? They would most certainly be furious with you."

"Why should they be furious with me?" she said in a matter of fact voice. "I did not do this to them; their father did this. Now, I intend to make it right."

"Right?" Ben questioned, his face was quizzical.

"You have a rightful place next to David, Bobby, Amy, and Elaine."

Ben was shaking his head in a slow and steady motion. "We cannot do this. Some things are better kept quiet."

Peggy smiled slowly, "Did Joseph deny Jesus? Did they hide who he was?"

While she was speaking, she picked up the Bible resting on the corner of his desk and opened to the family tree page. She then picked up the pen from the desk set. She wrote something in the front of the Bible and then closed it and set it back on the corner of the desk.

Ben took a deep breath and blew it out. "Have you told your children who I am?"

"No. That is not my place to do alone. This is not about me. I am a bystander. This is about you and your brothers and sisters. It is up to you when the time is right, and when that time comes I will stand with you."

"My God, Peggy, you are truly an angel of kindness." He knew nothing else to say.

"Think about it," she said as she stood up to leave.

Ben stayed seated, his eyes focused on nothing in particular; he maintained a slow and steady nod.

Chapter Ten

SUZIE BLALOCK EYED him from the distance. She sat at one of the round tables, covered with a red and white checked tablecloth, which was set up under the oak tree in front of First Covenant Chapel. Her husband sat across from her; their three children had headed for the dessert table.

Suzie and her husband, Jim, had been married for seventeen years; only two of them happily, as far as she was concerned. Nothing was horribly wrong with their marriage. It was just when their first child was born things somehow became routine and mundane in their lives. Jim worked long hard hours and she cleaned, cooked, and carted kids around. At the end of the day neither had anything left, which made the evenings a bore…eat dinner, do the dishes, put the children to bed, and then drop dead, just in time to get up at the crack of dawn the next morning and do it all again.

Sunday morning was the highlight of Suzie's week. She loved going to church and seeing Ben Montague. There was something about him to which she was drawn. He made her feel new and fresh. His sermons were deeply meaningful to her; and on occasion she had been wakened in the middle of the night by a dream of him so vivid it seemed real. He was always standing in the pulpit wearing his clergy robe, which was unzipped and she was the only one in the pews.

Ben was talking with a group standing next to the table that had come to be known as the "Chef's Altar". Sunday Supper had become a huge competition among the women of the church, and even a few men. Macaroni and Cheese, some of which included butternut squash, had been taken to a new level. Chicken was no longer just fried. There was braised chicken with herbs, baked chicken with onions and mushrooms, and chicken so smothered that the chicken itself was secondary. Green beans were offered in all degrees of tenderness, from al dente to slow cooked with ham. One lady had renamed her "Church Salad" to "Cathedral Salad" because of the elaborateness of the ingredients.

Suzie watched Ben from the distance. She lifted her glass of iced tea from the table and took a sip as she continued to focus on him. From where Suzie was sitting she could not hear what Ben was talking about, but he was smiling and laughing, and that made her smile too.

Julia had filled her plate with fried chicken, mashed potatoes and one of her own delicious gooey, double chocolate brownies. She sat down next to Miss Mary who appeared quite elegant, wearing a natural straw hat with silk daisies circling the brim; her cane leaned against the table next to her.

"I'm starved!" Julia said as she set her plate on the table.

"It would appear that way," Miss Mary replied, eyeing her plate.

The weather in March was always uncertain, however this particular Sunday morning it could not have been more perfect if it had been special ordered. It was the kind of day that simply beckoned you to commune with nature. The slight breeze mixed with just the right amount of warmth from the sunshine provided the perfect temperature.

"There must be one hundred-fifty people here," Julia commented, while brushing a strand of hair from her face. She was quickly interrupted.

"Miss Mary!" Little Alex's voice rang out as she ran toward the table. "I have another four leaf clover for you!"

Miss Mary grinned and held out her hand, "For me? Another!"

"Look at it, it is perfect!" Alex traced its leaves with her tiny fingers.

"Just like you," Miss Mary replied as she touched Alex on the tip of the nose with her index finger.

"Pawpaw!" Alex shouted. "Come here!"

Leon Jefferson was carrying two plates piled high with desserts. He looked toward his great-granddaughter, who was standing next to Miss Mary, and smiled. When he reached the table he set the desserts down. He bowed dramatically toward Miss Mary and boasted a definite smile and sense of jolliness as he said, "I come in peace and I have brought you these gifts of sweets as a ransom for my young great-granddaughter. I sincerely hope that she has not been a bother to you."

Miss Mary smiled and let out a shy giggle.

"I'm not bothering Miss Mary!" Alex proclaimed, "I'm making her lucky!"

"Well then," he replied, "in that case, may I join you?"

"Please do." Miss Mary answered as she motioned to the plates Leon had just set on the table and said, "You see I have all these desserts to eat and I simply cannot do it by myself." She tucked a curl of hair behind her ear and tried to sit up a little straighter.

Leon pulled out the chair next to Miss Mary and sat down. "It's a lovely day, wouldn't you say?"

"Lovely, indeed," Miss Mary responded and then turned to Julia. "Have you met Julia Matthews?"

"I don't believe I've had the pleasure," Leon said as he started to stand again.

"Don't get up, please!" Julia said quickly and then added, "Nice to meet you," while swallowing down a bite of chicken. She wiped her hand on her napkin and then extended her hand across the table toward Leon.

Miss Mary looked at her disapprovingly for her clumsy manners.

"Julia is one of my dearest friends. I think of her as my granddaughter." She smiled at Julia.

Leon studied Miss Mary for a moment. "Why you could not possibly be old enough to have a grown granddaughter," he said with the intent of a serious compliment.

"You flatter me, Mr. Jefferson," Mary returned in a tone that said caution.

"Should I apologize?"

"Not at all, I shall take it as a compliment even if I think it is due to the lack of your wearing eyeglasses."

They both smiled. Julia was watching as if she was at a Sunday matinee theater show. *Was Leon Jefferson flirting with Miss Mary,* she thought to herself? And, what was more, *Miss Mary was flirting back.* It was certainly obvious that Leon and Miss Mary had totally forgotten that Julia and Alex were even at the table. She finished the last of her own gooey, double chocolate brownie and decided that she would go mingle among the rest of the crowd.

Ben stepped away from the group, to whom he had been speaking, carrying a hand full of dirty paper plates and plastic utensils. Suzie watched him as he walked toward the trash can. She quickly gathered up the plates on her own table, which had been left behind by her children when they headed to the field to play kickball. She walked toward the trash can at a rapid pace. Ben had his back to her and she stepped just close enough so that when he turned around he would bump into her; the plates she was holding spilled to the ground.

"I am so sorry!" Ben exclaimed embarrassedly.

"No, it was my fault," Suzie replied, looking at the ground, she stooped to pick up the litter. "I wasn't paying attention to what I was doing."

Ben reached down to help her.

"I am so sorry, Reverend Montague; I've had so much on my mind."

Ben noticed shakiness in her voice.

"Are you all right Suzie?" he asked.

"Oh, I'm fine," she said in a tone that definitely said she was not. She leaned a little further making sure her blouse spilled open just a bit.

He smiled at her as they cleaned up the last of the trash. "I am so glad that you and your husband have joined the church. I hope this feels like home to you. And, I hope you know that I am always available to you."

"Thank you, Reverend Montague. I may take you up on that. I have so much on my mind that I just can't seem to sort out on my own."

"My door is always open."

"You are so kind, Thank you," her voice was low with a slight hint of seductiveness. Ben did not notice.

Leon and Miss Mary seemed to be enjoying each other's company very much. They had not stopped talking and neither seemed to notice that most everyone had gone home except for a few, mostly those who were on the clean up committee, which included Leon's grandson and his wife. Little Alex was content in the clover patch, seeking her treasures.

Julia approached the table, "Excuse me, I hate to interrupt, but I must be leaving."

Miss Mary looked up smiling cheerfully, "Then, I must be going too." She turned back to Leon. "Julia has been so kind to drive me to and from church every Sunday." She paused and looked down slightly with embarrassment. "When I broke my hip I had to give up driving."

Leon stood and pulled Miss Mary's chair out for her. "I have thoroughly enjoyed our conversation," he said. "And, thank you for sharing your desserts with me."

Miss Mary smiled shyly. "It was my pleasure."

Julia and Miss Mary headed to the parking lot and Leon walked toward Alex and the clover patch.

Chapter Eleven

HE PICKED UP the phone and dialed. There was no doubt about it, this time he was not going to make small talk. He was just going to ask her to join him for dinner.

"Hello." Sylvia's voice had something about it that made his entire being react to its sound.

"Hi," his voice was soft and cautious.

Hearing his voice made her sit up straight. "Well, to what do I owe this pleasure?"

"I believe I am long overdue in taking you to dinner. I was hoping that you would be able to join me."

A smile broke across her face. "When did you have in mind?" she said in a matter of fact tone that would not reveal her glee.

"This evening?" his tone was questioning, but hopeful.

"Why Reverend, it is Sunday evening, is that allowed?"

He was relieved; that old familiar sarcasm was back in her voice. "Yes, ministers are allowed to eat dinner on Sunday evenings. Are doctors?"

They both laughed together.

"You aren't going to try to 'save' me, are you?" she said in jest.

"Even if I wanted to, God hasn't empowered me with that ability. So, if you want to be 'saved' you'll need to go to dinner with a Baptist."

"You're bad," she said with a giggle in her voice.

"However, there is the issue of that comment you made when we first met."

"Comment?" she said with a confused tone. "You'll have to enlighten me. I not sure I remember."

"Well, you asked me what denomination I was and I told you that I was a minister in the United Covenant Churches of America. Then, I asked you what your faith background was. Do you remember what you told me?"

"Ah, that comment," she replied, remembering well. "Didn't I say something like outwardly I was Presbyterian, inwardly Buddhist and intellectually Agnostic?"

"That was it!" he said with a definite exclamation.

"And, you wanted to know if that had something to do with the kind of clothes I wore," she came back. They were both flirting again –and it felt good. Their conversation flowed in rhythm as it did before. "Are you sure you not trying to save me?"

"Well, maybe only from yourself," he said in a sly tone.

"And, here I thought you wanted me to save you from yourself." The conversation had become subliminal and neither was really sure what the other meant, but hoping they did; and, both were afraid to find out.

"Well?" he said.

"Well, what?" she answered.

"Will you join me for dinner?"

"Dinner...I almost forgot. Let me check my calendar," she said with total sarcasm and then paused for a moment of silence. "I can fit you in at seven-thirty, but not a moment before."

"I'll see you at seven-thirty. In the lobby of your building?"

"I'll see you there."

* * *

BEN WALKED INTO the lobby of The Sheridan Towers at seven-twenty. It had been several months since he had been there. The last time was before Buck's death. And, at that time he was certain he was in love with Sylvia DiLeo. He was still as certain, but Ben was a man who took things slowly. He had seen too many people make mistakes in their lives because they did not have the patience to truly follow their heart or look to God for guidance. While he waited he walked over to the large window at the back of the lobby. He gazed out at the last of the rosy shades in the sky that were left as the sun had just disappeared beyond the horizon. He began to pray...*Dear God, I believe I have fallen in love with Sylvia, but I need to know that it is Your will. Please guide my heart, my mind, and my thoughts. Thy will be done, on earth as it is in Heaven. Amen.*

He stared intently into the empty space of the evening, lost in thought and feeling. Then again, as a reminder to himself he whispered out loud, "On earth, as it is in Heaven." He turned just as the elevator doors opened. Sylvia stepped out. The sides of her long hair were pulled up with a clip and the rest fell softly over her shoulders. He felt something new as he looked at her –desire.

He opened the front door of the Sheridan Towers and held it for Sylvia. She offered a smile and nod of thanks as she exited the building. Ben followed her; a smile across his face —he was looking forward to this evening.

A new French restaurant had opened on the square in Salem — Chez Louis. It was very elegant, but moderately priced, which was good because that was all he could afford on his pastor's salary.

The Square in Salem was becoming quite a popular place. It was quaint, but elegant; the gas streetlights glowed on the brick sidewalk below. Speciality shops and restaurants were opening adding new life to the old area. The shop owners were taking special pride in the ambience they offered. There was almost a European flair to the square. Several of the restaurants had created patios on the sidewalk, with tables and chairs. Gas tower heaters provided warmth on a chilly night. It was a lovely evening.

"Would you like to sit inside or out?" Ben asked Sylvia.

"Let's sit outside!" she replied with excitement. "I've been cooped up for so long. I could use the fresh air."

Ben smiled. "Two for the patio, please," he said to the hostess.

A young lady dressed in a clingy black outfit led them to their table. Ben pulled Sylvia's chair out for her. She brushed against him slightly as she sat down; Ben felt a rush inside of himself.

Sitting, he looked around, observing the busyness of downtown Salem. "Wow! This is a happening area," Ben commented.

"It's growing," she replied. A mischievous smile came across her face. "So, what do you folks do for entertainment out there in the country? Watch the cows graze."

He smiled, "Hey, cow grazing is an art form."

"Sure it is," she returned.

"What do you know about cows?"

"What do you?"

They smiled at each other as the waiter interrupted them to take their drink order. Afterward, there was a moment of silence and the mood shifted to more serious.

"So, how are you?" Ben asked with a gentle voice.

"You sound concerned. Don't I look well?"

Ben smiled with unintended innuendo, "You look very well."

"I'll take that as a compliment."

"As you should. But, I guess what I meant is how have things been for you?"

His question warmed her. "I have been fine. Nothing to write home about. Just the same old routine everyday —which is a good thing."

"How about you?" she asked.

"It's one day at a time," he replied with a slight sigh. He paused and then spontaneously said, "I've missed seeing you."

She smiled and responded in kind, "I've missed seeing you too."

There was an awkwardness as they looked at each other. They were both relieved when the waitress came with their drinks.

"So, how are things at the hospital?" Ben asked as soon as the waitress left.

"About as usual." She grinned, "A bunch of sick people and arrogant doctors. You know how it is."

Ben returned the smile. "Speaking of which, how is the new chief of staff?" He paused and then added, "Dr. Davies?"

Sylvia raised a suspicious eyebrow. "Time will tell."

"I'm sure," Ben replied under his breath.

Chapter Twelve

SYLVIA STOOD IN the hallway outside a patient room talking with an elderly lady. She wore green scrubs and her long hair was pulled back neatly, away from her face. Her surgical mask still hung at her neck. Richard Davies watched her intently from a distance. Her eyes spoke volumes of compassion and the drawstring of her pants told the story of her small waist and the curve of her hips. He watched as she looked down at the cell phone clipped to her waistband. Gently touching the elderly lady's shoulder, Sylvia smiled and turned as she removed the cell phone from its clip. Davies strained to hear what she was saying into the phone, but he could not make it out.

Richard Davies was new to Salem. Most recently he had served as the head of emergency services in a hospital in Atlanta. He had an impressive background in medicine and his schooling was equally impressive, Harvard Medical School and a residency at Johns Hopkins. When the position of chief of staff opened at Salem Regional Medical Center, he was recruited by the hospital's administration. Along with being handsomely compensated, Davies knew that this was an impressive position for a thirty-eight year old and did not hesitate in accepting the position.

His colleagues in Atlanta respected him as a physician; they also saw him as a playboy and certainly a man not likely to ever settle down with one woman. He was never lonely when it came to women, but he did not consider himself a man destined to never marry. He had just never met a woman whom he felt was equal to him. Until she came along, why not play the field? He was good at it and he enjoyed the game. Once, he juggled three women in a single weekend, and none of them was the wiser.

Sylvia entered the nurses' station and sat down in front of a computer. She stared blankly at the screen for a moment and then began to type. She put her hand on her face and rubbed it across her forehead as if to release stress.

"Dr. DiLeo?" His voice startled her.

"Dr. Davies, I'm sorry, I didn't see you standing there." She smiled at him with a tired face.

"Are you all right?" he asked with a compassionate voice.

She sighed, "I'm fine. It's just been a long hard day."

"I've had more than a few of those in my career," his face was tender as he looked at her. "Is there any way I can help?"

"Can you play God?" she responded with a jovial tone.

"I've tried a couple of times, but wasn't very successful."

They both laughed.

"It never becomes easy," she said. "I don't care what anyone says; you can't be in this profession and not become personally involved with your patients." She paused for a moment; he stared at her, keeping his eyes fixed directly on hers. "I have a patient who is not doing well. Things don't look very good. His wife is one of the sweetest people I have met. They have been married for sixty-eight years. If he dies, she will lose the very heart of herself."

He smiled at her with compassion but all he could think was, *how can anyone spend sixty-eight years with just one person?* "Love is a hard thing. It's like vertigo –it takes two to keep the boat balanced." He thought he sounded profound.

She looked at him deeply, not really sure of what he had just said or what it meant, but she could see a kind spirit in him. "Are you settling in? Here in Salem," she asked.

"Well, I'm learning my way around the hospital; Salem is another story," he replied. "Any suggestion on where I should take my laundry."

She wondered if that was a serious question, but responded none-the-less. "Just about any shopping center you pass will have a dry cleaner." Beginning to feel a little uncomfortable, she looked away from his eyes and directed her focus back on the computer screen.

"Thank you," she said. "I appreciate your concern for me. I need to finish up here; I'm meeting a friend in the cafeteria for a late lunch."

"Anytime." He smiled at her and then he placed his hand on top of her hand which was resting on the counter next to the computer keyboard. His hand was warm and strong; he gently squeezed. "That's what I'm here for. My door is always open." Standing, he walked in the other direction.

Sylvia took a deep breath and let it out, then softly bit down on the side of her bottom lip and smiled to herself.

* * *

SHE WALKED INTO the cafeteria and looked around. It was late in the afternoon and most of the tables were empty. The janitor was mopping the back portion of the cafeteria which was closed off with a yellow 'wet floor' sign. She saw Ben sitting next to one of the few windows that allowed what natural light was available in the large room. She was struck by how handsome he appeared even when dressed in a more casual blue oxford button-down shirt and khaki slacks. When he saw her, he stood. Just the sight of her made him feel complete. Even in scrubs and with her hair pulled back, she was the most beautiful woman he had ever seen. She joined him at the table.

"Hey," she said in a tired voice.

"Hey, yourself. How are you?" he asked.

"I'm tired and hungry. I hope you haven't been waiting long."

"No, not too long. Besides, I always enjoy a few moments of quietness." In actuality he had been waiting more than an hour. The one parishioner he had come to the hospital to visit had been discharged that morning. But, he had decided that for Sylvia it was worth waiting a lifetime. "How has your day been?"

"It's been hard. I have a patient I don't think is going to make it and I feel so helpless. He and his wife have been married for sixty-eight years. She just sits next to him, holding his hand."

"Sixty-eight years," Ben replied. "What a gift. If only everyone could be that blessed."

Sylvia and Ben fell into a comfortable conversation.

* * *

DR. DAVIES SLOWLY approached the door of the cafeteria –he did not want to be noticed. Looking through the glass on the door, he recognized the man who sat with Sylvia as someone he had met, but could not place him.

"Hi, Dr. Davies," came a voice from behind him. He startled and turned quickly.

"Hi."

A cute, shapely, young blond in a nurse's uniform was looking at him. He smiled at her, with his perfect white teeth.

"You probably don't remember me. I'm sure you have met a ton of new people in the last week. I am Leigh Ann Myers. I work on the surgical floor, usually the night shift."

"Yes, I remember," he lied, not even being able to recall the number of shapely, young, blond nurses he had met in his career. "I'm still trying to get my bearings around here. I was just wondering how late the cafeteria stayed open," he lied again.

She smiled at him. "Well, it was good to see you. I've got to get up to the second floor."

"I'll walk with you. I am heading that direction myself," he said as he sized her up.

They walked the corridor making small talk. The hallway was quiet except for the echo of their footsteps and laughter. Entering the elevator, he pushed the number two. When the doors closed he extended his hand toward the young nurse. She placed her hand in his with what appeared to be a professional handshake. "I am delighted to have had the opportunity to get to know you better," he said, and then placed his other hand against the back of her hand which he was already holding. He looked straight into her eyes. "I hope we will have another opportunity soon."

She smiled. He let go of her hand and the doors opened. They both stepped out.

"Have a good evening," he said in a cheerful voice and then walked in the opposite direction.

Chapter Thirteen

"REVEREND MONTAGUE?" HER voice was soft at the door. Ben looked up from his desk. Suzie Blalock was standing slightly off center in the doorway. She was wearing a black skirt which addressed her mid-thigh and a blouse of animal print.

"Suzie?" he said with a tone which was slightly questioning. He stood up. "Please come in." He walked around and greeted her at the front of his desk.

Her eyes looked sad. They were filled with an emptiness that was transparent. She lifted her hand to tuck her hair behind her ear and then shifted her focus toward the floor as if battling shyness.

"Is everything all right?" Ben asked.

"May I sit down?" she asked very softly.

"By all means, yes, please sit down."

Ben began to sit too, but before he was fully seated she spoke up, "Would you mind closing the door? Please."

He nodded and then returned to a standing position and walked to the door, gently closing it. When he returned, he sat across from her. It was obvious that something was deeply troubling her. He also noticed how long and slender her legs were. She had them crossed at an angle which forced the eye to follow them upwards. How could he not notice?

"What is it Suzie?" he asked in a compassionate tone.

She lifted her head and fixed her gazed directly on his eyes. "Do you ever feel like the world in closing in on you?" She paused. "And, do you ever feel that God has abandoned you?"

Indeed, he knew the feeling exactly. "I have." He responded.

She watched him. His eyes appeared kind and his mouth sweet when he spoke. She let her mind wander for a moment to what it might be like if they were somewhere more intimate and she sat closer to him allowing her sadness to be held in his arms. She knew his touch would be soft and his care genuine.

"Suzie?"

She shook her head and returned her focus.

"What exactly is troubling you?" he asked directly.

"I don't really know, Reverend Montague." She let out a small laugh. "Reverend Montague? That sounds so formal. Do you mind if I call you Ben?" She was smiling now.

"Please, call me Ben," he responded.

"I pray to God all the time," she began, "but how do I know He is listening?"

Ben nodded his head to acknowledge that he was listening.

"I have been so lonely for so long. My husband is rarely home. We don't really have a relationship. We are two ships that pass in the night." The volume of her tone was increasing.

She paused as if waiting for Ben to respond, but frankly Ben did not know what to say. He was not really sure what she was trying to convey. Again, he nodded in acknowledgement.

"Do you ever get lonely, Ben?"

The question made him a little uneasy, but as a pastor, he had been asked many questions that made him uncomfortable. He had also been told a lot more information than he really cared to know. That was simply part of this job; people would pour their hearts out, confessing things which they would never usually admit, simply because he bore the title "Reverend" before his name. Laity has an illusion that it somehow meant he had a more direct connection with God, and that he was less of a 'normal' man himself. He took the question in stride. "Of course, I get lonely. It is part of being human. Do you think that Jesus was never lonely?"

She shifted her gaze and smiled. "When would Jesus have been lonely?"

He was startled by her question; he rather thought his had been rhetorical. "Well, I am certain that there were numerous times, but foremost, when He hung on the Cross."

She appeared untouched by his statement and redirected the conversation. "What should I do?" Her stare was piercing.

He had witnessed this scenario before, with both husbands and wives. One would feel estranged from their spouse and somehow they connected that to God abandoning them. "Are you allowing your disappointment with Jim to effect your relationship with God?" he asked.

"I don't know," she stammered a bit. "I don't think so."

"Have you talked to Jim and told him how you feel?"

"Jim doesn't care how I feel! He doesn't want to listen to me!" Tears began to well up in her eyes. She looked a Ben; her eyes were pleading. How desperately she hoped that he would understand what her eyes were saying, and that he would feel the same way too. She wanted him to kneel down next to her and take her hands in his. She wanted him to reach his hand to her cheek and tenderly wipe away her tear. She wanted him to speak softly to her and say, *Jim doesn't know what he is losing; you are the most sensual, beautiful woman I know. He is a fool to let you go. Jim should be guarding you and protecting you...like I am.*

She heard Ben begin to speak. "I am terribly sorry for your pain, and I am quite certain that God has heard your prayers. I also strongly recommend that you and Jim talk." He really was not quite sure what else to say.

"Thank you," was her disappointed reply.

"May we pray?" Ben asked.

"I would like that."

Ben scooted to the edge of his chair and extended his open palms toward her. A soft smile came across her face and she placed her hands in his. He closed his large strong hands around hers and she felt his warmth radiate through her.

He prayed, as he would with anyone.

Chapter Fourteen

IT WAS LATE. Sylvia headed toward the main lobby exit doors of the hospital. She passed the security guard seated behind a glass window. "Goodnight, Johnny." She waved as she passed him. She headed into the parking garage which was well lighted. It was quiet, except for her own footsteps. As she was approaching her car, she heard a voice call out her name. She turned to look.

"Dr. DiLeo?" It was Richard Davies.

"Dr. Davies," she returned with a startled voice.

"I hope I didn't scare you. I was on my way out and wanted to catch up with you."

She stopped and waited for him to catch up to her.

When he reached her, he smiled softly at the sight of her face. "How is your patient?" He paused for a moment and then realized he needed to clarify further. "The elderly gentleman."

She returned his smile, and was touched that he cared. "Thank you for asking." She paused to reflect, "He's about the same. No change really. I still do not think he will make it."

There was sadness in her eyes that he noticed. "I am so sorry. But, I am certain that the very reason you feel so strongly about him is the exact reason you went into this profession in the first place."

Davies appeared to be a kind and intuitive man. She liked this. "I suppose you are right," she said. "But, I tend to disillusion myself and live for the perfect world...you know, where nobody dies and everyone lives happily ever after."

"Now, that is a fine fairy tale, isn't it?" His smile was charming. "Have you had dinner?" The question came out in a blurt.

She was slightly taken back by his question. "Dr. Davies, I..."

He interrupted, "Forgive me. Let me rephrase that so you don't misunderstand my intentions. To the best of my ability, I am trying to have "one-on-one" time with every doctor in the hospital, in order to build a stronger network. Would this evening be convenient with you? We could have dinner and chat; kill two birds with one stone."

She looked at her watch. She was tired, but probably could use a diversion. "I suppose that would be all right."

"Wonderful. You take your car and I'll get mine. Let's meet at Rosemary in fifteen minutes."

"That will be fine," she said and turned to make the last few steps to her car.

* * *

WHEN SHE ARRIVED at Rosemary, Davies was already seated at a table. *That was fast,* she thought to herself. She walked to the table; he stood to greet her.

"Please, sit down," he said, helping her with her chair. "I took the liberty of ordering a bottle of wine. Would you like some?"

"Thank you," she said with a slight uncertainty in her voice.

There was a moment of dead silence as he lifted the bottle and poured a little into the wineglass which sat in front of her.

She looked at him curiously.

Understanding her expression he said, "You must taste it first." He picked up his own wineglass. He placed his nose at the top of the glass and breathed in deeply. "First, you take in the aroma." He gestured to her to follow. "Then, you swirl it to perfection." Quickly, he placed the glass beneath his nose again and breathed in deeply. "Ahh. Now, you taste." Sylvia copied him, unsure of herself. Davies let the wine roll across his tongue in an exaggerated manner. He smiled. "Typically, we would chew the wine at this point," he paused and then added with inuendo, "but, I'll save that for our next lesson."

"So tell me, Dr. Davies, have your meetings with the other docs included dinner and wine? If so, you must have been afforded quite a large expense account."

Rosemary is an extremely nice restaurant in Salem which caters to the nuevo riche. One could hardly enter the establishment without it costing at least a hundred bucks.

"Hardly!" he said with a laugh. "If I tried to turn this in on my expense account I'm sure I would have seen my last days as chief of staff." He lifted his wineglass and took a sip. "I simply wanted to do something special for you because I know how hard you have been working recently and I wanted to give you an opportunity to relax and enjoy yourself."

She smiled shyly.

"So tell me, how long have you lived in Salem?" Small talk was Richard Davies' specialty.

They ordered dinner, conversed and laughed for the better part of the evening. She enjoyed herself and had more wine than she would have normally.

"You are a remarkable woman, Dr. DiLeo." He paused. "May I call you Sylvia?"

"May I call you Richard?" she responded.

"You may," his voice was sultry.

"Then, you may call me Sylvia."

"Anyway, Sylvia, you are a remarkable woman. I have never met an orthopedist as beautiful as you."

"In that case, may I have a raise?" she said in a joking tone.

The adolescent boy trapped inside of him wanted to tell her that she had already gotten one, but he just smiled instead. "Sorry, that is not within my jurisdiction."

For the second time her cell phone was ringing. She glanced at it; it was Ben again. She felt bad; they had talked about getting together after work and grabbing a quick bite at Leo's.

Sylvia and Richard finished their dinner, and the bottle of wine. It had been nearly two hours.

"I really need to be heading home," she said.

"It is getting late." His response was cool. "Thank you so much. I have enjoyed getting to know you better."

They both got up and headed toward the door together. As they walked past the bar area, Davies glanced in and saw Leigh Ann Myers, the cute blond nurse from the cafeteria hallway. She was sitting with several other women. They were laughing and obviously enjoying themselves.

Davies walked Sylvia to her car. "Be safe going home," he said. "I will see you tomorrow. He watched her drive out of the parking lot, and then headed back toward the restaurant. Once inside again, he sat down at the bar and ordered a beer. Casually, he swiveled his stool and surveyed the crowd. He had seated himself in a place which would be obvious should Leigh Ann look up —and she did.

Leigh Ann steadied herself against barstools as she made her way over to him. "Dr. Davies, wh..what are you doing here?" A few of her words ran together as she spoke.

He smiled coyly, "Leigh Ann…right?"

"Yes!" She was pleased that he remembered.

"I just stopped in for a beer after work. It's been a long hard day." His voice was cool.

"Tell me about it!" she said.

They talked and shared a few more beers. By this time, the other ladies with whom Leigh Ann had been sitting, had all stopped by and said goodnight. It was very apparent that Leigh Ann should not drive home and Davies offered to take her. She gladly accepted, not really caring to whose home he took her.

* * *

THE LIGHT WAS flashing on the answering machine when Sylvia walked in her door. Without listening to the message, she scrolled through the caller id. She looked at her watch. It was ten-thirty. She really felt it was too late to return Ben's calls but she felt obligated, and she wanted to.

"Hello," Ben answered.

"Hey." She felt guilty, *but why?*

"Hey!" he said, excited to hear her voice. "You must have had a long day."

"It was." She paused to collect her thoughts. "I'm sorry, I know we discussed having dinner, but I ended up having a business dinner." She felt she needed to give more of an explanation, being overcome by guilt. *Why should she feel guilty? She did not do anything wrong.* "The new chief of staff is arranging meetings with each of the doctors; he asked me to join him for dinner to talk business."

"Oh." There was a hint of concern in his voice. He had seen the way Dr. Davies eyed the other females at the hospital. He did not want him setting his eyes that way on Sylvia. "Well, I hope it went well." His voice was sincere.

"Yes, it was fine."

Chapter Fifteen

BEN STOOD ON the front porch and stared at the lawn of the parsonage. Spring had only been present for less than three weeks and the grass was already knee high. Lawn maintenance was not his forte, although he certainly had enough practice as a kid. With no father around when he was growing up, he was the man-of-the-house. His mother expected that all chores considered masculine, were handled by him. He knew them all –but he did not like them.

He walked over to the little shed which sat on the backside of the parsonage. The door creaked as it open. It was the first time that Ben had been to this little shed since he had taken up residency here. Peggy Buck had told him that she left all the garden tools and the lawn mower for his use.

The push mower, which sat in the far corner, was covered with plastic. A shovel rested across the top holding the plastic in place. The shed was damp and cool in spite of the warm weather outside. Ben stood silently in the middle of the cramped space and took in the surroundings. He breathed in deeply, struggling for oxygen; his chest was heavy. His father had stood here. This was his father's mower — and his father's shovel. A pair of gloves rested on one of the exposed cross studs of the wall. Ben picked up the gloves and held them in his hands. He inspected them closely and gently rubbed them between his own. Slowly, he separated them and carefully slid his hand into one and then the other. He held his gloved hands in front of his face and stared at the palms. These were the gloves which protected his father's hands. Fixated on the gloves he was filled with a rush of emotion. *Did the gloves protect or conspire with his father?* Ben thought to himself, feeling anger well up within him. These gloves had cradled the hands which strangled the life out of the Body of

Christ. Quickly, he ripped them from his hands and threw them on the floor of the shed dragging the wheels of the lawnmower across them as he pulled it out the door. Outside again, he took a deep breath, determined not to let the past bring him down.

He twisted the top on the gas tank and peered inside –empty. He stood up straight and looked around. Having lived in an apartment for so long, he was rusty in the process of cutting grass. He returned to the shed and picked up a gas can and slightly shook it —empty as well. He turned and headed toward his car. Stopping short, he shook his head. "I'm not putting a gas can in my car," he said out loud, as if he were giving himself a lecture. As he stood there feeling totally defeated in this task, he saw Angel lying asleep in the sunshine in his next door neighbor's yard. Ben set down the gas can, and headed across the yard through the knee high grass.

Stopping shy of the sleeping dog, Ben reached down to the ground and picked up a well aged pine cone. "Psst," Ben whispered.

Angel lay silent offering no recognition except for a noticeable twitch in her ear.

"Angel," he whispered.

This time Angel lifted her head and gave every appearance of smiling. Ben tossed the pine cone in his hand several times and then said, "You want to get it?"

Angel continued to lay still except for her eyes that moved up and down carefully following the pine cone as Ben tossed it in his hand. Turning, Ben threw the pine cone as hard as he could back across the yard of the parsonage. With one fluid motion, Angel bounded to her feet and took off after the pine cone as it sailed through the air. Angel was Ben's friend, but even more, Ben was Angel's friend. She quickly retrieved the pine cone to him and begged for more, which Ben happily obliged.

"Reverend Montague," Ron called from the front porch. "How are you today?"

Ben turned and waved at his neighbor and headed toward the front porch to join him. Angel followed in disappointment.

Ron Silver and his family had been neighbors to Bob and Peggy Buck and now to Ben. They were nice folks and typical for the area –

young professionals, two kids and a dog. They did not attend First Covenant Chapel even though it was in their backyard. Betty, Ron's wife, and the children usually went to Uriah Jonah's church, which was always a point of contention for Buck when he was still alive. Ron had been raised in a Jewish home.

"How are you, Ron?" Ben asked. "And, please call me Ben." He extended his hand and they shook.

"I'm just fine," he responded. "Angel seems to have adopted you."

Ben reached down and petted her on the head; she still held the pine cone in her mouth. "She lifts my spirits," Ben replied. "I sure hope we haven't been disturbing you with all the hammering and sawing out back."

"Not a bit," Ron answered. "Looks like your sunrise service is going to be quite a production."

"It does, doesn't it?" Ben had no other response. Considering the source –it was sure to be a production.

Ron moved to a chair sitting on the front porch of his home. He gestured to another, "Please, join me."

Ben smiled and took the seat next to him. Angel set the pine cone down, joined him at his side, and laid down resting her chin across Ben's feet –keeping one eye fixed on the pine cone.

The two men sat silent, enjoying the spring air.

In a moment Ron spoke, "Do you mind if I run something past you?"

Ben turned and looked at Ron, "Sure."

"My son's having a hard time at school." Ron paused briefly. He breathed in deeply signifying the depth of his concern.

"I'm sorry to hear that," Ben responded.

"It's not his grades. His grades are great, although that might be part of the problem. He's smarter than most of the other kids."

Ben listened trying to figure out what exactly was troubling Ron.

"The kids pick on Mark," Ron continued.

Ben began to nod his head; he was getting the picture now. "He's is sixth grade, right?" Ben asked.

"Yep."

Ben remembered his sixth grade year well –probably the worst of all his school days. "That's a hard age."

"Sure is. The problem is that Mark is the one getting in trouble," Ron said with an agitated tone.

Ben's expression turned puzzled and his curiosity peaked.

"There is a group of kids that taunt and tease him beyond belief. They are a manipulative bunch of boys. They know how to fly below the radar so the teachers don't see what they are doing. Last week they teased Mark so much that he turned around and shoved one of the boys against the wall and told him to leave him alone."

Good for him! Ben thought to himself.

"Problem is," Ron continued, "a teacher saw what Mark did, so he's the one in trouble."

"I am so sorry to hear that," Ben responded. "It's pretty unfair. I'm sure Mark feels that."

"Yeh," Ron sighed and then his tone changed slightly. "I don't mind that so much. It is part of learning to deal with the world, which is unfair."

Ben smiled. "You got that right! When I was young and would complain about something being unfair, my mother would look me in the eyes and very sternly say, 'Nothing is fair on this side of heaven; deal with it.'"

Ron laughed, "That's what we all need to be teaching our children. When I was a kid if we had this problem, we would handle it ourselves in the afternoon behind the school. We'd sort out the pecking order on our own and the problem would be over."

Ben nodded in agreement.

"How are boys nowadays going to learn to be men?" Ron asked staring off in the distance –deep in contemplation. A smile broke across his face in obvious amusement of his thought. "I just had an interesting vision of these boys grown and trying to defend our country. I can see them grabbing the enemy and dragging them to a nearby chair and telling them..." Ron sarcastically lifted his hand and pointed his finger toward Ben's face. Shaking his finger rapidly he said, "You have a timeout and if you don't start being nice, we're going to take your guns away from you!"

Ben laughed at Ron's dramatic gestures; and he was in every bit of agreement with him. Ron was obviously distraught and was venting.

"We overprotect our children in America. We have damned seat belts on swings." Ron turned in embarrassment realizing he had cursed in front of a minister. "I'm sorry."

Ben smiled thinking about the Apostle Paul's Technicolor use of language. "You are damn right!" he responded.

Ron looked at Ben, he liked this man. Continuing, Ron said, "If we let them fall off the swings once or twice they learn how to hang on!"

A silence came across the porch for a moment. Angel rolled to her side, stretching her legs and settling into a more comfortable position, her head still across Ben's feet and one eye still on the pine cone.

Ron took a deep breath and let it out. "What I really wanted to talk with you about is what happened yesterday."

Ben focused his attention toward Ron.

"Yesterday, these boys were teasing Mark again. This time because he is half Jewish."

Ben's eyes narrowed. "Tell me about this," he said.

Ron shifted his focus. "They told Mark that everybody hates Jews. They told him he needed to get off the planet since he was a Jew –that he should go home and commit suicide."

Heat ran up Ben's spine and then splintered into his shoulders. *I'd like to meet these boys' parents behind the school and settle this problem!* Ben thought to himself. "Unbelievable!" Ben said.

"I addressed this with the principal," Ron continued. "He appeared to be sympathetic. But, since none of the teachers heard it, there wasn't a whole lot he could do about it."

"That's a load of garbage," Ben said with disgust.

"That's what I thought," returned Ron, "but, it's hard to fight city hall. And, this is the Bible Belt."

"Being in the Bible Belt has nothing to do with that kind of thought process. Ignorance is the key factor here." Ben's voice was enraged. He turned and looked at Ron. "I hope you know that kind of thinking has nothing to do with Christianity."

"I know," said Ron. There was not even a hint of hesitation in his voice.

It saddened and frustrated Ben to think of a world under so many misapprehensions. *On what basis does anyone think they have a better vantage point with God?* Ben thought to himself. Ben had seen too many people who confused their roles on this earth. "Where light is concerned there are two possible choices. One can be the light or the mirror which reflects the light. The job of the Light has already been filled." *All I can hope to be,* Ben thought to himself, *is the mirror which reflects the light.* There are too many trying to be the Light – and constantly failing.

The sun rose higher over head and the temperature was rising as the morning dissipated. The only sense of busyness was from a couple of house wrens, whose sense of urgency brought peacefulness to the two men sitting on the porch. The air was light and sweet and in spite of the world at large, all was well. Ben leaned his head against the back of his chair and closed his eyes.

Disrupting the peace was a sudden barrage of hammering, sawing, and Ashley March's voice giving stage directions; all which were amplified by the natural acoustical property of a body of water. Ben opened his eyes and focused on the white ceiling of the porch, dismayed that the peaceful moment was gone. Ron sympathized, but neither man commented.

Looking across the yard of the parsonage, Ron saw the gas can sitting in the knee-high grass. "You are welcome to borrow some gas."

Ben lifted his head with excitement. "Thanks!" He paused. "Do you think Mark would like a job? I'll pay him labor plus gas to cut the grass at the parsonage every week."

"I think he'd love it. How about if I send him over to talk to you in a little bit? You all can work out the details."

Chapter Sixteen

"MARGARET, I'M HEADING over to the hospital to visit some folks," Ben said as he walked past her desk on the way to the door.

"You sure do spend a lot of time at the hospital," Margaret commented in return.

He stopped and turned to look at her not really sure what to say. "Thank you for noticing."

"Don't forget you have a three o'clock finance committee meeting," she reminded him.

"I'll be here." Then with a hint of sarcasm added, "I wouldn't miss it for the world." He opened the door. At the same time Julia Matthews was walking in.

"Hello, Reverend Montague," Julia said in a cheerful voice. "What a creative way to raise money for the church." Her usual tone of sarcasm present.

Ben returned to her a confused look; he had no idea about what she was talking. "I'm sorry, but what is creative?"

"According to the sign out front, our church is selling children this Saturday —all sorts." Her humor was dry. "What does one go for anyway?"

Ben stepped out the door and then turned, looking back toward the church. Stretched across the church was a big white banner with bold black letters. It read:

CHILDREN SALE
ALL SORTS
THIS SATURDAY 9-4

He shook his head, turned back toward the parking lot and headed for his car.

* * *

HE HAD QUITE a few visits to make in the hospital, and he was hoping to be able to finish in time to catch Sylvia for lunch. He did not want to take any chances on missing her. His first stop was to the nurses' station on the third floor. He looked around hoping to see Sylvia sitting there. No such luck. He walked over to a nurse sitting at the station. "Is Dr. DiLeo on the floor?"

The young girl looked up and smiled, "She should be back in about twenty minutes."

Richard Davies was sitting on the opposite side of the station. When he heard Sylvia's name, the conversation drew his attention.

Ben took his business card out of his pocket and wrote on the back of it. He handed it to the nurse. "Would you please give her this when she gets back?"

"Sure." The nurse took the card and set it on the counter in front of her. Davies watched her set it down.

Ben headed back toward the elevator. As soon as he had entered and the doors had closed, Davies got up and walked over to the nurse.

"Would you mind getting a warm blanket for the patient in 307?" he asked nonchalantly.

"Yes, sir."

When the nurse was around the corner, Davies picked up the card and read what Ben had written on the back. It said:

Lunch? 12:15 - Cafeteria

He turned the card over and read the name *—Reverend Ben Montague.* He had a vague recollection of meeting him. Sticking the card in his pocket, Davies returned to his work.

* * *

BEN HEADED TO the cafeteria a few minutes after noon. He grabbed a sandwich and some iced tea and sat at the table where he and Sylvia sat the last time he had dined with her in this lovely establishment. He sipped his tea and waited.

Richard Davies went through the food line selecting tuna salad and a diet cola. He held his tray and looked around until he saw the man he vaguely recognized. He walked over to the table where Ben was sitting.

"The cafeteria is crowded today. Do you mind if I join you?" Davies said to Ben.

Ben would never turn anyone away who requested to share a meal. "Certainly, please sit down." He extended his hand, "Good to see you again, I'm Ben Montague. We briefly met in the elevator on your first day here."

Davies shook his hand, "I hope I'm not disturbing you. Are you expecting someone?"

"I was hoping a friend would meet me, however, the plans weren't firm. But, either way, I am delighted to have you join me."

Davies sat down and placed his napkin in his lap. "Do I remember correctly that you are a minister?"

"Yes, I am."

"Over at First Covenant Chapel...correct?"

"You have a very good memory, Dr. Davies."

Davies smiled, thinking about the card in his pocket. He made no comment to that statement, but simply replied, "Please, call me Richard."

They chatted for a moment. Ben glanced at his watch; it was already 12:30. He picked up his sandwich and began to eat.

"I'm still quite new to the area," Davies began. "I would be interested in visiting your church." Although it clearly came from his mouth, that was a statement as foreign to Davies as if he were speaking a different language.

"We would be delighted to have you." Ben took another business card from his pocket, wrote the times of the services on the back of it and handed it to Davies.

"Thank you." Davies took the card and put it in his pocket with the other one.

They finished their lunch. There was no sign of Sylvia.

"Well, I guess my friend couldn't make it." There was an air of disappointment in Ben's voice. "But, I have certainly enjoyed breaking bread with you. I hope to see you at church."

"You can count on it," Davies confirmed.

Chapter Seventeen

HE SORTED THROUGH his messages. He had two from Suzie Blalock and they were both marked urgent. Dialing the phone, he had a sense of uneasiness. When Suzie answered it was obvious that she had been crying.

"Oh, Ben," her voice quivered. "I just don't know how much more I can take."

He did not really know how to respond to her or what she was expecting him to do, but he did know that simply listening was a great service to her.

"I am so tired of being isolated. I tried to talk to Jim, like you suggested. He told me that I place too many demands on him." She was silent for a moment.

"I am sorry, Suzie, that you are facing these difficulties." He paused. "Do you think you place too many demands on him?"

"Well, you tell me," her voice became soft and almost sultry. "Do you think it is too great of a demand for a wife to want to be kissed good morning each day and kissed goodnight each evening?" She carefully spoke the words insuring the full potential of each. "Ben, you're a man. Do men not have the same need for affection as women do? Do you like to be kissed?"

He shifted in his chair. He knew she was hurting and looking to him for counseling, but this was out of his realm of expertise, additionally it made him uncomfortable. The church takes a very strong position on the sexual ethics of their pastors and this was a conversation which bordered on danger. He was sure that she had no wrong intentions but he had no desire to find himself in a place of scrutiny.

"Suzie," his voice was calm and reassuring, "have you considered a marriage counselor? I could recommend a few. Perhaps that would help you sort this out."

"Counseling? With someone else?" her voice sounded startled. That was not where she intended to go with this. Her marriage was not that bad. Jim was a good husband; he provided well and did not mistreat her. She had just come to a lull in her life. Jim was too familiar and there was no longer any romance or element of surprise. *With what could a counselor help?*

"Of course my door is always open," he paused, "to both you and Jim."

"Thank you," her voice was quiet and sad.

"This will be in my prayers."

Her words replied again with, "Thank you," but other thoughts raced through her mind. *Your prayers? I want more than your prayers.* She desperately wanted to be alone with him and she often fantasized about what it would be like —his strong arms wrapped around her. He was such a kind and gentle man, she knew his touch would be equally so.

The conversation ended.

Chapter Eighteen

THE SUN WAS setting. Ben stood at the window at the back of the parsonage and gazed out across the pond. This was perhaps the most beautiful pond he had ever seen regardless of how tiny and insignificant it might be. God had perfectly placed it so that it was the center reflection for both the sunrise and sunset. The hues of orange and pink glowed through the sky at the point of the horizon. His heart swelled at the glory and he could not help but say out loud, "Look there's God!" The very vision of His power displayed before him. *This would be a lovely place for a Sunrise Easter Service – Ashley and Bobby are correct about that.* His thoughts then shifted to Sylvia. It seemed as natural to think about her as it was to think of himself. He had waited far too long to invite her to come to church at First Covenant Chapel. He wanted to protect her. He knew how brutal some of the people could be. Laity oftentimes sees the pastor of the church as theirs alone. To think that he might have a life separate from the church is incomprehensible to many of them. But, he was beginning to no longer think of Sylvia as separate from himself and he wanted to see her there on Sunday mornings. He turned and walked to the telephone. Picking it up, he dialed her number which he had committed to heart.

"Hello," her voice had power over him.

"Hello," he returned, "I know that it's a little late, but I haven't had dinner and I was hoping that maybe you haven't either."

Her tone of voice revealed that she was smiling, "As a matter of fact, I haven't even had lunch."

"Well, then I guess I'm glad that I missed you for lunch, I much prefer to have dinner with you if I can only choose one meal."

"You were at the hospital for lunch?"

"I was doing visitations and I was hoping that I might have snuck you away to the cafeteria for some gourmet dining."

She laughed, "Gourmet? You must get out more often and educate your taste buds. I am sorry, I wish I could have joined you, but it was a busy day." In all honesty she wished she had known he had been there, because she would have made the time to have lunch with him.

"Well, then how about dinner?" he asked again.

"It's not past your curfew?" she teased as usual.

"Curfew?"

"Yes, don't ministers have a curfew? So that you have plenty of time to count your sheep at night."

He laughed, "Very funny." In an extremely jovial tone he continued, "You are highly disillusioned. It might surprise you to know that a minister puts his pants on the same way every other man does. And, be prepared for what I am about to tell you," he paused to add suspense to his drama, "I have had a speeding ticket."

"Well, in that case I better cut my losses now," she said. "You are way too fast for me!"

"We can continue this banter over dinner; I can tell it will not be an easy feat to convince you that I am perfectly human."

"I am honored to have dinner with a "perfect" human; I didn't know any still walked the earth. Where shall I meet you?"

Her humor and discourse made her all that much more desirable to him. "Leo's?"

"I'll see you there."

* * *

LEO'S WAS IN downtown Salem. It was a quaint little Italian restaurant, and lively. It was always busy and rather noisy, but the noise provided the ability for intimacy by preventing anyone from being able to overhear a conversation.

It was past eight o'clock when they arrived and the waiting area was still packed. Ben added his name to the waiting list and, despite its appearance, the hostess promised him that the wait would not be more than fifteen minutes. They squeezed themselves into a space at the side of the waiting area and chatted about their day.

As promised, the hostess called their name within a relatively short time. They tried to weave their way through the crowd, which was far easier for Ben because of his size. In an effort to help Sylvia, he reached back and took her hand. Initially unaware of what he had done, within moments he was fully aware, realizing that this was the first time he had ever touched her. He felt warm and his heart began to beat more rapidly. When they had made their way through the crowd he had no desire to let go, but reaching their table, he slowly released her hand and helped her with her chair.

The waitress came over to ask for their drink order.

Ben looked at Sylvia, "I would like a glass of Chianti, would you?"

Sylvia's eyes became wide and she gave him a look of question, but before she could say anything, Ben leaned forward across the table and whispered, "Even in His perfectness, Jesus drank wine."

She smiled and nodded.

Ben looked at the waitress, "We'll have two glasses of Chianti."

The waitress smiled and turned to walk away.

"So," Ben said suddenly uncomfortable.

Sylvia waited for him to continue, before she replied with hesitation in her voice, "So?"

They both laughed.

"I'm really sorry I missed you for lunch," Sylvia offered with sincerity.

"Don't worry about it," he relied. "Although, I would have enjoyed your company more."

Sylvia looked at him with question.

"Dr. Davies joined me instead."

"Oh," she responded quickly.

"He's an interesting man," Ben's tone had skepticism.

"What do you mean?"

He caught himself being judgmental. "I didn't mean anything negative. Actually, I enjoyed his company very much. He may come to a service out at First Covenant Chapel."

Sylvia raised her eyebrows with surprise. "Oh?" She felt a bit of hurt since Ben had never asked her to visit his church.

* * *

THEY ENJOYED THEIR dinner and were never at a loss for things to talk about. Slowly, they walked to the parking lot. When they reached her car it was obvious that neither one of them really wanted the evening to be over, but it was late. There was still one very important thing that he wanted to ask her and he was not going to let the evening get away without having done it.

Her car lights blinked as she unlocked her door with the clicker in her hand.

"Sylvia?" His voice was soft and clear.

She turned around to face him, "Yes?"

He smiled, "Would you like to come to church this Sunday –Palm Sunday?"

They were standing unusually close. Each was uncertain but neither sure about what. The moment of quietness was deafening and neither moved. Sylvia finally spoke and broke the silence.

"I would love to."

Ben smiled, "Wonderful."

The air was filled with stillness again. He leaned toward her slightly. Sylvia waited in anticipation. The moment seemed like an eternity. Her whole body was tense.

"Thank you for a wonderful evening," he said softly. Stepping away from her he added, "Drive home safely."

She smiled shyly and then got into her car. He closed the door and then turned to walk toward his.

Sylvia started her car and then leaned her head against the backrest and sighed with frustration. It was by far the most fabulous evening she had ever had, *but why doesn't he kiss me*, she wondered?

Chapter Nineteen

THE SUN SHONE warmly as the parking lot at First Covenant Chapel filled. Julia let Miss Mary out of her car at the front of the church. It was difficult for her to maneuver with her cane through the parking lot. Today, Miss Mary was dressed in a navy blue silk suit, which was in striking contrast to the ivory reveres of her blouse. Her navy hat was simple and had only a grosgrain ribbon of contrasting ivory.

Miss Mary stood in the narthex and did not rush to her pew as usual. She looked about in anticipation. People were passing beside her; she smiled.

An usher stopped and offered, "May I help you to your seat?"

She responded nervously, "No," and then smiled with embarrassment and repeated in a very soft tone, "No, but thank you so much for your kindness."

A voice came from the other side, which startled her. "Are you looking for someone?"

Startled Miss Mary turned. A slight smile came across her face as she saw Leon Jefferson standing behind her.

He repeated himself, "Are you looking for someone?"

"No. No, I was just admiring the beauty of the church this morning. The way the sunlight comes through the windows." She paused and looked around. She pointed to her left, "Do you see the small crack in that window and how it creates a prism? That crack has been there since I was a child." She lowered her voice to a whisper, "Eddie Martin hit it with a baseball. There were only three of us who ever knew. We all took an oath and promised to keep it secret. But, that was seventy-one years ago and Eddie passed away last year." She smiled sadly. "The other with us was Eddie's brother, but he was killed long ago in the Normandy invasion."

Leon leaned toward her. "I promise, I'll keep the secret safe —for Eddie's sake." He smiled at her. "May I escort you to your seat?"

"Thank you. That would be lovely."

He placed his hand on her elbow as she turned to make her way into the sanctuary.

Ben, who normally was making last minute preparations for the service, stood in the doorway greeting people as they arrived. He was slightly anxious, and he knew why. Sylvia would be walking into his church for the first time. They had known each other for more than a year now and this was the first time she was coming to church —it was the first time he had invited her. He had wanted to protect her, but now he wanted her to be here as well. He would keep his distance and not alert anyone that she was there with him.

"Good morning, Reverend Montague," Julia said as she entered the narthex. "What a surprise. Are you our new greeter?" She stepped back a little and took an unusual look at him. "My, but you look exceptionally handsome, if you don't mind my saying so."

Julia and Ben did not question each other. Everyone knew that Julia said whatever was on her mind at any given moment. She had also let Ben know that she thought he was extraordinarily handsome. However, their ages and personalities were amiss, thus it was a comfortable relationship; all comments were accepted for just what they were and nothing more.

"You must have a hot date after the sermon," she added.

Ben chuckled and then out of the corner of his eye caught a glimpse of Sylvia approaching from the parking lot. The last thing he wanted was for the first person she saw to be Julia Matthews. Nervously he said in a whisper, "If you'll excuse me, I see some children that we could put up for sale."

She laughed as she finally moved toward the sanctuary.

Ben let out a sigh of relief as he moved closer to the door. He greeted several more people trying his hardest to give them the respect and attention they were due, but he found it very difficult when his real desire was to keep his eye on Sylvia until she reached the door.

When she approached him a smile broke across her face like the sun rising in the morning. "Good morning, Reverend Montague," she said in a charmingly mischievous voice, as if they had never met before.

"Good morning, Dr. DiLeo," he replied in a like manner of obscurity. "What an honor to have you join us this morning." He was glad to have her at church and had not realized until this moment how nervous he really was.

She continued to smile. "Thank you. I heard about your church through a friend of mine," she paused, "and since he was busy this morning, I thought I would come on over and check it out myself."

Ben played along, "Too bad he couldn't come too; he'll never know what he missed."

Ben introduced Sylvia to several people then led her into the church to help her find a seat. Sylvia glanced around the tiny chapel. It was warm and inviting. A sense of peace came over her instantly, and upon seeing Miss Mary she smiled. "Well, there is Miss Mary," she said. "I'd like to sit with her."

"She will be delighted to see you," Ben responded and they headed up the aisle.

Miss Mary was comfortably seated between Leon Jefferson and Julia Matthews. When they reached the pew Ben realized that the only available seat was next to Julia. This made him extremely uncomfortable. Sitting next to Julia was like sitting next to the entire Associated Press.

"Dr. DiLeo!" Miss Mary said with delight. "How lovely to see you here."

"Hello, Miss Fletcher," Sylvia replied. "How are you doing?"

"I am very well, dear. And, please call me Mary."

"We call her Miss Mary," Julia interjected. "Hi, I'm Julia Matthews," she said and extended her hand toward Sylvia. "You probably don't remember, but, we met in the emergency room when Miss Mary broke her hip."

Sylvia shook her hand and said, "Yes, I remember. It's very nice to see you again, Julia." Turning back toward Miss Mary she said, "And, Miss Mary, will you please call me Sylvia?"

Mary nodded and then turned toward Leon Jefferson and introduced Sylvia to him.

"Take a seat!" Julia said to Sylvia as she shifted slightly to her left in order to make room.

Sylvia looked around the church; it was crowded and still more were arriving. She felt a sense of familiarity and comfort. Sandy, the pianist, had begun the prelude. The chattering of the congregation became hushed and Sylvia was suddenly overcome with a reverence she had learned as a child and not felt for so many years –it was unmistakable. She visibly smiled as Ben stood and welcomed the congregation.

Ben surveyed the crowd, and it was a crowd indeed. Looking across the pews, he felt honored to be a servant of God. He especially liked seeing Sylvia sitting among the other people he had come to know as family. After offering the Call to Worship, Ben paused and intuitively smiled before moving back to his seat.

With his usual dramatic flair, Ashley leaped to the center of pulpit area as if it had been choreographed. "Man! It is good to be alive!" he shouted into his cordless microphone. "Are you feeling it with me brothers and sisters?! Are you feeling it?!" Ashley looked sleek. He was garbed in his usual Nehru jacket and black slacks. "We have got a surprise for you this morning," he continued with enthusiasm. "The band is back!"

Ben was suddenly overcome with sickness in the pit of his stomach. *Oh my goodness!* Ben thought to himself fearing that his expression shared his private thought of having forgotten to factor Ashley into the equation of inviting Sylvia to church. He looked over at Sylvia. Her eyes were noticeably wide with startle. He wondered exactly what her expression meant.

The side door which leads from the back of the church into the pulpit area opened and four men walked out; two were carrying electric guitars, one a bass, and the fourth man walked over to a set of electronic drums which were already in place. The men were all dressed alike –in Nehru jackets of a lighter shade than Ashley's.

The band members moved to their assigned positions. With a subtle hand signal from Ashley, they began to play one of the popular Christian contemporary songs. As the first few chords began to unfurl over the audience, Ashley began the show.

"Everybody stand up and put your hands together for the Lord!" Ashley shouted as he reached his hands above his head and began to clap with rhythm. The band became louder and the congregation, standing and joining in with clapping, began to sing.

Ben stood and began to sing along uncomfortably; he was ashamed. It was Palm Sunday and this was by far the biggest spectacle Ashley had created –by a long stretch. For a moment, Ben stopped singing. Quietly, he spoke as the music continued, "I need help Lord. I need direction. Please show me what to do."

Julia leaned over to Sylvia and whispered, "This is the best entertainment you'll find this side of Charleston."

Sylvia smiled. She certainly was not accustomed to this type of music in church but, it had been quite awhile since she had been to church. Maybe this was normal now. She looked around and the majority of the people seemed to be enjoying it. She actually enjoyed it a little herself, even if it was too loud. After the music ended, Ben stood and and offered the pastoral prayer. He then asked the congregation to pray as Jesus had taught us to pray and in unison they recited *The Lord's Prayer*. Sylvia had not said that prayer since her mother's death, nearly six years ago. She was glad that she had come to church this morning for more than just the reason she had thought.

"Our Scripture reading this morning is from the Gospel of Matthew, chapter twenty-one, verses one through eleven." Ben's voice was deep, clear, and distinguished. He read with passion the story of Jesus riding into Jerusalem on a donkey and the town's people laying down palms as He entered.

"Think about it," Ben said, prompting the congregation into thought. "The King of kings, the Lord of lords was riding on a donkey. How much more humble could His entrance have been?" Sylvia thought about how humble Ben was; a smile appeared across her face. Ben continued, "A donkey was the least royal of all the animals on which He could have ridden. It is a work animal for the common folk and yet that was the animal that Jesus chose on which to make His triumphal entry into Jerusalem. We know Jesus was the one who chose the donkey because Scripture tells us."

Sylvia intently listened as Ben spoke. His clergy robe set off his dark hair and she thought that, by far, he was the most attractive man she had ever seen. She was mesmerized as Ben continued. "I started thinking about the choice of a donkey, and then I started thinking about it from the donkey's point of view. Here's this donkey," Ben's face was full of expression, "he's tied to a fence post, probably in some beautiful lush, green pasture, munching on sweet grass, soaking in the warm rays of the sun. I imagine life was pretty good for that donkey. Didn't have any worries except for himself and along came these two guys who start dragging the donkey off." Ben was gifted at preaching. He continued, "I can imagine that, that donkey looked at those two disciples and said, 'Ho, ho, what are you all doing? I'm quite happy where I am. I've got my juicy grass, I've got my sunshine, and besides that, I'm really not up for a whole lot of work right now.'" Ben paused for a moment, "What do you think the disciples told that donkey?" He posed the question to the congregation and then offered the answer. "We know what the disciples said, because Scripture tells us. In verse three of Matthew twenty-one, Jesus is speaking and He tells the disciples, 'If anyone says anything to you, you tell them that the Lord needs them.' I think Jesus even meant this for a donkey that might ask. So off goes the donkey, probably with a pretty sour attitude. Then, to add insult to injury, this guy hops up on his back. And, you know what happens next?" Ben paused for a moment allowing people to think. "The donkey is told to walk. Walk! Can you believe that? After all this, the donkey is now supposed to do work. I can just envision that donkey. He starts to walk, but I imagine that his head is dragging the ground." Ben's whole body is in animation of the donkey. "He's probably got his lower lip sticking out pouting. But, he walks. And, as they move along, the donkey's probably feeling a little sorry for himself, but as they begin to enter the city, there is cheering and shouting." Ben smiled and radiated joy. Sylvia was enticed by his sermon. "I bet that donkey lifted his head and began to look around and smiled. And, as the donkey got closer, I bet he held his head high, because the people were cheering as that donkey entered the city. I bet that donkey was thinking, 'Man, they're cheering because I'm walking in.' You see," Ben said in a matter of

x

fact tone, "the donkey had a new perspective. I think that he stopped looking at it as though his comfortable life had been interrupted and now saw it as he had been chosen to carry Jesus to the people. The donkey was the messenger that carried Jesus to the people. What a privilege!"

Julia leaned toward Sylvia and with overt sarcasm whispered, "Ashley would do well to recognize that he's just an ass carrying the message too!" Sylvia lifted her hand to her mouth and covered it to keep from laughing out loud.

They finished singing the final song, a similar version to the others, loud and overbearing. When the electric instruments stopped, Sandy began to play the piano and Ben walked up the center aisle to offer the Benediction. "Go forth from this place as a messenger for Christ. And friends, I don't care what the calendars on your office desks say, Sunday is still the first day of the week! It is a day of rest! Be Blessed."

Ben walked up the aisle and the ushers opened the doors to the narthex as people began to collect their belongings. She watched Ben as he exited and then turned to begin greeting people as they filed out. This was a side of Ben she had never imaged; a warmth was kindling inside of her.

The narthex was crowded after the service. Ben patiently bid adieu to each person, but anxiously was looking for Sylvia. As Miss Mary and Julia approached Ben, he saw Sylvia was with them. A smile broke across his face, which did not go unnoticed by Julia who turned to see that the smile was intended for Sylvia.

Chapter Twenty

SYLVIA PICKED UP the phone on the third ring, recognizing the number on the Caller I.D. She immediately knew the deep voice on the other end.

"I am calling from First Covenant Chapel," Ben began in a jovial tone, "and we want you to know that we are so glad you visited with us today." Sylvia giggled as Ben continued the shtick. "We hope that you will join us again soon and in-the-meantime, if you have any questions, I would be delighted to answer them over dinner this evening."

"I've heard about pastors like you. Let's see," Sylvia paused for emphasis, "I think it was on *20/20* and maybe *World News Tonight*."

"We're a dime a dozen. What can I say?" Ben responded with humor. "So how about dinner?"

"I'd be delighted," she answered quickly.

"Shall I pick you up at seven?" he asked.

"I'll be in my Sunday best."

* * *

THEY DROVE TO a quaint little seafood restaurant on the river called The Boathouse which was best known for its dining porch on the backside of the restaurant. It extends to the river's edge, viewing the romantic ripple of the water. They took a table for two which was perfectly placed next to the railing. The table was dressed with a white linen cloth and a tea-light candle illuminated the center. The early spring air was still rather chilly but tall outdoor heaters were amply placed around the deck creating a comfortable atmosphere.

Ben looked affectionately at Sylvia. She was elegant in a simple fashion. He noted how her rose-colored cashmere sweater perfectly accented her cheeks.

"I am so glad you came to church this morning," Ben said. "I hope that everyone made you feel welcomed and you felt the presence of God."

Sylvia nodded and gave a slight smile.

Ben waited for more of a response. "Well?"

"It was lovely."

"Lovely?" he repeated after her.

"Yes, lovely," and she tipped her head forward.

He raised an eyebrow indicating that he did not fully understand. He so badly wanted her to feel comfortable at First Covenant Chapel; he so badly wanted her to be there every Sunday.

She smiled playfully, "You know it has been awhile since I have been in church. Things have changed."

"Changed?" he questioned. "What do you mean?"

"I was rather used to church being boring," she responded. "Your service was certainly not boring."

"Is that a good thing or a bad thing," he asked with concern in his voice.

"Well, a good thing —I guess."

He was relieved.

"Ashley certainly does have energy," she commented cautiously.

"There's no question about that," he returned.

"Your sermon was fabulous. You have a real gift."

Hearing her say that made him feel warm inside. He never preached with a desire for recognition, but he had to be honest, it did wonders for his ego that the woman he was courting was so impressed.

She giggled.

"What so funny?" he asked.

"I'm not sure if I should repeat it," she said.

"Oh, go ahead," he encouraged.

"When you were talking about the donkey being just a messenger of Christ, it seemed to have struck a cord with Julia Matthews."

"What do you mean?" Ben queried with a curious face.

"She leaned over to me and whispered that Ashley would do well to recognize that he is just an ass carrying the message of Christ."

Ben laughed, "Welcome to my world!"

Sylvia's face shifted to serious. She spoke softly and sincerely. "It was really wonderful to be in church today. I truly had a feeling of being at home."

Ben smiled.

Chapter Twenty-one

THE SUNDAY SCHOOL rooms at First Covenant Chapel were small. The Celebration Class now consisted of twenty-six seniors. None ever missed an event, including the opportunity to sit around on a Tuesday morning and stuff colored plastic eggs with candy for the egg hunt after the Easter Service. Most everyone from the group was already hard at work when Miss Mary arrived, Julia following closely behind her. When Miss Mary entered the room the first person to catch her eyes was Leon Jefferson, who was sitting on the opposite side of the room –and his eyes caught hers.

"Good morning," one of the ladies called out. "Glad you could make it."

"Thank you," Miss Mary replied, "I'm glad I could too. Thanks to Julia who has so graciously taken on being my personal chauffeur." Using her cane she carefully stepped further into the room.

Julia smiled, "It's my pleasure," she said. "Now, I've got to run. I'm skewing the age bracket in here!"

A collective chuckle came across the room.

As Julia turned to exit the Sunday School room, Leon quickly made his way to Miss Mary. "May I?" he said as he extended an arm to her. She smiled shyly and accepted his offer.

The room was cozy and every seat was taken. Leon led Miss Mary to his seat and gave it to her. "Thank you, but where will you sit?"

He turned slightly, steadying himself on the back of her chair. "Ah," he said. "I shall return!" He made his way back across the room and exited the door.

The group was chattering as they stuffed candy into eggs. "What time is sunrise anyway?" asked one of the men.

"What time is sunrise?" came an exasperated rhetorical reply. "It's about two hours after my old body says it can't stay in bed any longer!" Sounds of laughter replied in agreement. "What I'd like to know is what time is sunset?" There was a mutual understanding in the room.

"The service is going to start at six-thirty," Peggy offered. She turned to Miss Mary and handed her a sleeve of plastic eggs and a bag of candy. "You are looking exceptionally well," she said gleefully.

"I'm feeling quite well for an old lady," Miss Mary responded. "But, the more important question is how are you, Peggy?"

It had been nearly six months since Buck had passed away. Peggy was a strong lady and she was an inspiration to the rest of the group. She never became angry or bitter at life's events. She never wore her heart out on her sleeve.

Miss Mary glanced up to see Leon carrying a red plastic chair through the door to the Sunday School room. Due to the size of the chair, it obviously was from the children's classroom. "Excuse me," he said as he made his way around the room determined to make it to the other side. Miss Mary pretended not to be paying attention. She appeared intent on the task at hand of filling the eggs with candy –but a smile crept across her face.

"May I?" he said. Miss Mary looked up trying to seem startled. "May I sit next to you?"

"Certainly," she said. "Pull up a chair."

He smiled mischievously. "It's my lucky day. There just happens to be a chair right here. I don't mind if I do!"

It was all Miss Mary could do to keep herself poised, but as Leon sat down in the child-size chair the sight was so humorous that she broke out in a definite giggle.

"You find this funny, do you?" Leon said with sweet irritation. "I may never get up again!"

"I'll lend you my cane," Miss Mary replied coyly.

"I am sorry," he replied, "but a man of my reputation cannot be seen with a lady's cane."

They both laughed and acknowledged the humor as they set into work on the Easter Eggs.

"Did you all hear what they are doing over at that church of Uriah Jonah's?" Roy Macy spoke loudly so the entire room could hear. A few heads raised and looked at him, but no one spoke a word.

Uriah Jonah was the preacher at the Spring Rock mega-church over in Salem. It was common knowledge at First Covenant Chapel that Bob Buck was modeling the new sanctuary, which he had intended to build, after Spring Rock. Buck had admired Uriah Jonah and envied him at the same time. Much of the worship at First Covenant Chapel now was patterned after Spring Rock Community Church.

"Okay, I'll bite. What are they doing at Spring Rock?" someone finally responded.

"This isn't a joke," Roy said sharply.

Leon shifted in his chair which moved him slightly closer to Miss Mary, who was very aware of his presence. Frankly, it flustered her a bit, but she secretly smiled.

Roy Macy continued, "They are passing around catalogues that are selling chickens, donkeys, cows, and such. You can buy them for your family and friends for Christmas and the money goes to help third world countries."

A quizzical look came over most of the room. "What do you mean you can buy a donkey?" someone asked.

"I don't know," Roy replied. "That's just what I've heard. My neighbor goes to Spring Rock, he was trying to explain it to me."

"How much does a donkey cost?" came another voice.

"Somewhere around fifty bucks," he replied.

"And a cow?"

"About the same, I guess."

"What do you do with the animal?"

"I don't know," answered Roy. "Keep it in your backyard?"

"This must be a joke," Leon responded as he slyly stuffed a pink egg with an extra piece of candy for some lucky child.

"No joke," Roy said with absolute certainty. "My neighbor showed me the catalogue. Some group called Heifer. He asked me if I wanted to buy one." His face was covered with an expression of disbelief.

"What did you say?"

Roy paused for a moment and rubbed his forehead. "I told him I divorced one twenty years ago. Why'd I want another?"

The men in the room let out a collective laugh as the ladies shot darts with their eyes.

"How many people do you think will actually buy a heifer?" another asked.

"And what is somebody going to do with a donkey in their backyard?"

"Or a goat or chickens, for that matter?" Roy piped back.

Miss Mary giggled, trying to absorb the nonsense. She looked out of the corner of her eye toward Leon who also had a combined look of humor and disbelief across his face. He caught her glance. "Are you buying this?" He asked.

"It seems a little odd," she replied, "certainly there is more to this."

Peggy who had not said a word until this point spoke up. "I think there must be some kind of confusion. Certainly they are not really selling animals as a fundraiser."

"It's this young generation," Roy snapped back.

"I tell you, this community has way too much money," came another.

"They have become too indulgent," Roy continued.

"I'll have Bobby find out what this is all about," Peggy responded. "He knows a lot of the folks over at Spring Rock. I know they are cutting-edge over there. What do you call it?" She paused for a moment to think, stuffing another piece of candy in an egg. "Out of the box!" She paused. "No, it's outside of the box! That's it! Bobby says that church is outside of the box!" She paused again and changed her demeanor. "But, even so, this donkey thing is a little off the wall." She smiled.

The group continued to chatter and fill plastic eggs.

Miss Mary turned slightly toward Leon, "So how is that precious little Alex?"

"Ah," he replied, "she is the apple of my eye."

"I can certainly understand why," Miss Mary replied.

Miss Mary reached up and smoothed the lapel on her beige silk blouse. She pushed back her shoulders and tried to sit up a little straighter. Carefully crossing her legs at her ankles, she delicately tucked them to the side of her chair.

The eggs were nearly completed and the room was becoming less crowded as people began to leave to go home for lunch. Leon was puttering about stacking chairs that others had left behind. Miss Mary took her cane from aside her and slowly stood, letting herself steady before she attempted to move. She glanced at Leon as he was stacking chairs. Gripping her cane tightly, she took a deep breath. She felt slightly light-headed and her stomach mildly queasy. Leon was an extremely attractive man –and so kind. He took her breath away.

"Are you all right?" Peggy Buck said as she touched Miss Mary on the arm.

"Oh, yes. I'm quite fine," Miss Mary replied trying to hide her embarrassment. "Quite fine, indeed. And, you, Peggy?" She was trying to divert the attention away from herself. "You are looking so well."

"I am well. Thank you," Peggy responded.

"I am so glad that you decided to stay at First Covenant, even after Reverend Buck's death," Miss Mary's face was full of compassion and understanding. She knew very well the changes in dynamics that a church undergoes when there is a change in leadership. Miss Mary had seen more than fifteen ministers come and go at First Covenant Chapel during her life. With every change at least one group of people is displaced. But, to be the pastor's wife –when he is gone, this is an entirely different type of displacement.

"You know Miss Mary, in all my years of being a pastor's wife, this is the first church where I have felt at home."

"I know what you mean," Miss Mary replied. "We may be full of faults here, but we are a family."

"Do you need a ride home?" Peggy asked.

"Thank you so much, but Julia is coming back for me. I brought my book," she patted the side of her pocketbook; "I'll sit and read until then."

Miss Mary and Peggy continued to talk as they walked out of the Sunday School room. Leon watched Miss Mary closely as she left. He stopped his work for a moment and sighed. Leon Jefferson was eighty-two years old and had been a widower for the last fourteen years. He and his wife Nancy had been married for forty-six years when she suddenly died in her sleep from a heart attack. Moving in with his grandson Art and his family was a tough but good decision. It had concerned him at first, he felt as though he would be an imposition on them. But, Leon had his own apartment in the basement, which was lovely; and, being in a home that was lively with three small children made him feel more alive and certainly less lonely. Watching Miss Mary right now made him feel very full of life too.

Miss Mary slowly made her way down the Sunday School hall into the narthex. She settled herself into a Queen Anne chair which sat in the corner and took her book out of her pocketbook and laid it on her lap. The room was quiet and still and overcome with a serenity that radiated from within the walls. She thought about all these walls had seen, and in recent times the sadness they beheld. The thought of Bob Buck left her stirring with confusion. She might be old, but she was not blind, nor deaf, and certainly not dumb. So much that transpired prior to Buck's death did not make sense. It still pinched her with bitterness that he had never so much as said "thank you" when she gave him her dark blue Mercedes for his last birthday. It pained her even more that it had been her car in which he died.

"A penny for your thoughts?"

Miss Mary jumped. Turning she saw Leon standing to the side of her. "You frightened me," she said with a startled voice, but maintaining her usual composure. Their eyes met for a brief moment and then she shyly moved hers away.

He stood there nervous, like a teenaged boy. He had planned to ask her if he could buy her lunch, but at this particular moment he was not sure he could make the words come out. The narthex was deathly quiet. The afternoon light broke through the side lights and transom around the door. He took a deep breath. "Would you care to join me for some lunch?" He could not believe the words came out.

Miss Mary smiled. She had beautiful high cheekbones, and they glowed. Her eyes sparkled like a child's. "Julia will be coming for me in about forty minutes."

"I'd be happy to drive you home," he replied.

She would really like to say "yes". He is such a kind man and she did enjoy his company. "Perhaps another day."

"Yes, perhaps," he echoed. Trying not to show his disappointment he changed the subject. "So, what are you reading?" he said as he looked at the book with a picture of a church on the cover which was resting in her lap.

Chapter Twenty-two

SYLVIA WAS SITTING at the nurses' station on the third floor of Salem Regional Hospital making notes in a patient's chart. Although the sun had just made its full appearance, she had been at the hospital for quite sometime.

"I've been looking for you," an energetic voice came from behind her.

She turned to see Richard Davies. She did not miss the fact that he looked exceptionally fine this morning.

"What can I do for you?" she returned.

A lot, an awful lot, he thought to himself. "I have some ideas I wanted to run past you about our orthopedic department." He looked straight into her eyes as he spoke. "Are you free for lunch? We could meet in the cafeteria."

She smiled, "Sure. About twelve-thirty?"

"Very good." His tone was professional. Without another word he turned and headed down the corridor.

* * *

BEN DREADED THE staff meeting this morning. They would be finalizing the details for the Sunrise Service that would be taking place this Sunday. It had the potential to be such a beautiful time of worship, but in his gut he felt that it was more inclined to be a spectacle. Bobby and Ashley had been working endless hours building a stage and preparing the area at the edge of the pond. It was equipped with lights and sound. There was going to be nothing simple about this event.

He rested his elbows on the desk which used to be Bob Buck's. He was beginning to feel settled and his surroundings were beginning to feel like home. He glanced at the picture of his mother which sat on the corner of his desk. He missed her. His mind then slipped to Sylvia. He was anxious for the staff meeting to go quickly; he wanted to get to the hospital to do his visitation. He hoped that he would be able to sneak in lunch with Sylvia at the hospital cafeteria.

Taking a deep breath he lowered his head until his forehead was resting on his hands. Silence filled the room, and then his words came forth. In a very soft voice he spoke aloud. "Father, how thankful I am that I do not have to rely on myself. I certainly would botch it all up if I did. Thank you for being with me and giving me strength. And, thank you for having confidence in me." He paused and a smile came across his face. "Frankly, I'm not sure it was Your wisest decision, but then again You never asked my opinion." Through the years Ben had learn to pray as if God was indeed his best friend. Often he felt that the two of them could just sit around and shoot-the-breeze. He continued, "Just in case Ashley and Bobby have not thought to invite You, I would like to extend my personal invitation to You to this Sunrise service." His voice broke into pleading, "Oh God, please be there! You've got to help me with this. Direct me. Whatever You ask of me Lord, I will follow. Show me the way to lead this little church of Yours." He was silent for a moment more and then raised his head. Standing, he collected his papers and then headed out of his office and down the hall to the Sunday School room where the staff meetings were held.

"Ben!" came a voice as he was passing the front office.

Ben turned. Standing in the reception area was Tom Werner. "Tom!" Ben walked in and extended his hand. "So good to see you," he said as they shook hands. "What are you doing here?" Ben asked and then realized that his question probably came across as rude. "I didn't mean it that way," he quickly corrected. "I am glad you're here. What brings you?"

"Well, I thought if it was all right with you I would sit in on the staff meeting. This is the day, isn't it?" Tom asked.

"It is. Yes, please come and join us. Does this mean you're thinking about coming back?"

"I'm thinking about it," Tom smiled.

"Great! You should probably know that Bobby will be at the meeting," Ben informed him.

The last time Tom was at First Covenant Chapel was at the meeting where the members were voting on approving the $8.5 million loan to build a new sanctuary –only days before Bob Buck died. Tom stood in front of the entire congregation and spoke against approving the loan, claiming it a financial disaster for the church. The whole meeting turned into a "Bob Buck" popularity contest. Bobby was the ring leader.

"Bobby doesn't scare me," Tom said with confidence.

"Good. Let's go." Ben turned and led the way.

As they approached the room they could hear chattering, which turned into dead silence when they entered. Everyone's attention was drawn to the doorway where Ben and Tom stood.

Lord, have mercy! Margaret thought to herself.

"Good morning everyone," Ben said as he moved to his seat. "I hope everyone is well this morning."

The room remained silent. Bobby shifted in his seat, turned his head to stretch his neck, and was obviously uncomfortable. As much as Ben did not want to acknowledge it, it did give him some sense of satisfaction to see Bobby squirm. Ashley remained poised, cool, and collected.

"Good morning," Tom said in a quiet voice. He nodded his head toward the table as he moved around it to take a seat. Bobby's eyes followed him.

I might as well start by acknowledging Tom, Ben thought to himself. *Although, the sport of watching Bobby was entertaining.* "I'll open us with prayer," Ben's tone was straightforward and very direct. "Please bow your head." They prayed.

If staff meetings exemplified the general state of a church, then by all accounts First Covenant was in a constant state of pre-war. Thankfully, staff meetings have very little to do with the actual heart of the church; and for this Ben was grateful.

Ben opened his mouth to begin the meeting, but Ashley's voice sounded first. "Tom, so good to see you." Ashley spoke with purpose. He sat straight and his hands rested on either side of the notepad which lay on the table in front of him. "I hope you are well. What can we do for you today?"

I'm the pastor here, Ben erupted inside his head. *I'll run the meeting, thank you very much.* "I invited Tom here," Ben said firmly. "I have asked him to come back to his position as financial chairperson for the church."

The room was cold in spite of the sunshine outside. Margaret shifted in her seat.

Bobby visibly chewed on the inside of his cheek and stretched his neck from side to side.

"I believe a move like that would need to go before the church council," Bobby spoke up with certain curtness in his voice. "This is a staff meeting. I think it is entirely inappropriate for someone who isn't staff to be here. We discuss sensitive issues that need to remain in this room."

Ben could not believe he was hearing this from Bobby. Did Bobby forget that he was not staff, yet had been attending the staff meetings for the last four years? He looked at Bobby and the reality set in for the first time –this was his brother, his flesh and blood. Even Ben could see the resemblance and it was unnerving. "With all due respect, Bobby," Ben said in a controlled tone, "may I remind you that neither are you a staff member, yet you have been attending these meetings for years. Tom was never *officially*," he said with exaggeration, "removed from his position and therefore this *move*," he said with exaggeration again, "does not require a vote from the church council." Ben looked Bobby square in the eyes so that there would be no misunderstanding that this was his final statement on the issue. "You are here and Tom is here, we'll make the best of it."

Ashley suddenly stood up. He smoothed his hands down his shirt pushing out any wrinkles. "Very fine," he said. "Let's move on to the task at hand. Easter is only a few days away. We need to discuss the final details of our Sunrise Service." He glanced at Bobby and decided that now would not be the right time to ask Bobby to speak. It was obvious that he was seething with anger. "We are almost all set. It will be a musical extravaganza! And, the talk of the town for weeks to come. This will be our best show yet."

Margaret's eyes widened. She had come to know Ben well enough that anytime Ashley used the words "show" and "church" in the same sentence there was going to be intense discussion.

Ben sat still. He felt the heat rise up the back of his neck and bit together the inside of his lips with the front of his teeth in order to keep himself from speaking, there was no point; it was not going to change what Ashley and Bobby had already planned. He looked at Ashley, *he's just an ass,* he thought to himself remembering what Sylvia had told him. "Fine. Let us know how we can help," was all Ben could offer.

Margaret squinted her eyes and peered at Ben. *What's the deal?* she thought. These staff meetings were too much for her. When she took the job as church secretary it was because she wanted a low stress job. She interned with a securities company while in college and without a doubt, church secretary was far more stressful and less predictable than the stock market.

Ben turned to Margaret. "What's next on the agenda?"

"Uhhh," she scrambled to collect her thoughts. "Budget. The budget."

Ben turned to look at Tom, "I would like to start reporting the weekly budget with receipts and debts in the bulletin. Tom, what do you think?"

"It's customary. I'm all in favor of it," Tom responded.

"My father was firmly against that!" Bobby spoke up quickly.

"Our father" was trying to hide the truth, Ben thought to himself as he watched the heat rise in Bobby's face.

"The congregation has the right to know the church budget –good or bad. This is their church and their money." Tom paused for a moment and scratched his temple. "It encourages the congregation to take on the responsibility of the church."

"It also opens the door for conflict in the church," Bobby retorted sharply. "Something that is much better kept out of the church."

"We are not running a nursery school here," Tom's voice was becoming tempered with anger. "These are intelligent adults. You can't fool them by trying to hide the truth from them."

Bobby's eyes were piercing with anger. "I don't know what your problem with my father was. You were determined to destroy everything for which he worked so hard. He always treated you as a friend."

Tom shifted his position. "I was never against your father," he said slowly. "I am for the church. There is a difference. Please don't confuse the two."

Ben felt an uncomfortable presence come across the room. He had more knowledge than he really wanted. Looking at Bobby, he knew that Bobby thought he was the only son of Buck's sitting in the room. What Ben knew that Bobby didn't, was that Ben was also a son of Buck's, and if that were not enough, what Ben alone knew was the child that Tom would soon be raising might also be a child of Buck's. Ben shook his head to clear the painful thought. He decided it was time that he spoke up. "I ran this idea past the church council. They are in approval of adding the financials to the bulletin every week." He turned to Margaret, "Margaret will you take care of getting those numbers from Tom each week?"

Did that mean Tom was officially back? She thought to herself.

"Tom," Ben continued, "may we consider you officially returned to your position as financial chair of First Covenant Chapel?"

"You may," he responded.

"Margaret, will you also make sure that gets announced in the bulletin this week?" Ben asked. That answered her question –Tom was back. "Meeting adjourned." Ben looked at his watch. He still had plenty of time to get to the hospital, visit a few parishioners, and hopefully find Sylvia in the cafeteria for lunch.

Bobby collected his things from the table and briskly walked out of the Sunday School room without a single word spoken, even as he walked past the others. Ashley followed with an even saunter, but stopped in front a Tom. He extended his hand toward Tom. "Welcome back," he said, his "c" sounds clicking as he spoke. Tom extended his hand to meet Ashley's. They shook.

"Thank you," Tom responded.

* * *

WHEN ASHLEY ENTERED his office, Bobby was pacing back and forth across the floor. Ashley stopped for a moment and watched Bobby with compassion. He knew that Bobby was still suffering the loss of his father. So was Ashley. They had worked so hard to bring the tiny white clapboard country church to a certain level. He knew what Bobby was feeling –like the waves were washing the sand from beneath their feet. Their footing was loose and their spirits were shrinking. "Why don't you go talk to Ben, one on one," Ashley said.

Bobby looked up and stopped his pacing. He took a deep breath and released it. "He's a pompous idiot! What's the point?" Bobby snapped back.

"You won't know unless you give him a chance," Ashley responded.

Bobby glared at Ashley. "Are you kidding me?"

Ashley moved toward Bobby and placed both of his hands on his shoulders and stared him directly in the eyes. "We have got to maintain control here." He tilted his head in exaggeration. "You get more bees with honey. Do you know what I mean?"

"Fine!" Bobby responded in a gruff voice. But, he had little confidence in himself to produce "honey". Bobby was short tempered and he knew it. For some reason, Ben Montague set off that temper. He rubbed his hands across his whiskers and neatened his blue oxford-button-down which was tucked into his blue jeans. Bobby was a tall man and solidly built. He overshadowed Ashley's delicate build. They were an unlikely pair because of all their differences, but...they worked well together.

"I'll be praying for you, brother," Ashley said as Bobby walked out the door.

"Pray for Ben!" Bobby responded in a sarcastic manner as he disappeared around the corner.

Bobby walked down the hallway which led to what used to be his father's office. He stopped short of the door and scanned the portraits on the wall of the previous senior pastors that had served First Covenant Chapel. He would make sure that his father's portrait was added. When he reached the closed door, he opened it and walked in without knocking. Ben was sitting behind the desk and immediately looked up when he heard the footsteps coming closer. "I'd like to talk," Bobby said sharply.

Ben was startled and taken totally off guard. He smiled with reserve. "Certainly." He stood up and walked around to the front of his desk. The air in the room was thick and movement was slow and cautious. "Please sit down." Ben gestured to one of the two chairs which sat in front of the desk. Ben sat in the other one without waiting for Bobby. It took Bobby a few minutes to decide if he really wanted to sit with Ben, but finally conceded. Darkness filled the room. Bobby stretched his neck from side to side to release the tension. Ben unknowingly was doing the same thing. "What would you like to talk about?" Ben asked.

"This church," Bobby answered point blank.

Ben waited assuming there was more to that statement. Bobby did not say another word, but glared deeply at something. "What about this church?" Ben asked.

"What is your intention here?" Bobby's chin lifted upward as he addressed the question to Ben.

"My intention?" Ben shook his head as he spoke indicating that he did not fully understand the question.

"What are your plans with my father's church?"

For a moment Ben thought about how to respond. Coolly he replied, "I assume by 'Father's' you are referring to 'God's' church, in which case it would be 'our Father's' church."

"I think you know exactly what I mean," Bobby said in a low and steady voice, though the muscles in his neck were noticeably tightening.

Ben took a deep breath and nodded his head. He was beginning to understand. "Bobby," he said in a voice that he hoped did not come across as patronizing as he intended. "My intention is to lead this church into being a spiritually sound House of God. And," he paused and thought about his words carefully, "with that being said and with all due respect, this is not your father's church. It is God's church. We must all keep that in mind."

"Of course, it is God's church," Bobby responded with a voice that implied, *you idiot!* "But, that is not what we are talking about." He pointed his index finger with great gesture toward the floor. "My father poured his heart and soul into building this church to the point which it is today. I am not going to sit by," he now pointed his finger toward Ben, "and watch you destroy all his work with your piety."

Piety? Ben shifted his eyes with confusion. Did Bobby not know the meaning of piety or was he seriously suggesting that acts of piety would destroy his father's work? But, now was not the time to correct Bobby. Never-the-less, while Ben was in charge, piety would be in full swing. In his best pastoral voice he attempted to pacify Bobby. "I know that the loss of your father is still grieving you tremendously. I also know that what he accomplished here is very important to you."

Bobby cut him off mid-thought. "You know nothing of how I feel!" he said through clenched teeth. He stood. From the corner of his eye Bobby caught a glimpse of a familiar book sitting on the corner of the desk. He turned to take a closer look. It was his father's Bible. *His father's Bible? Why was it on Ben's desk? How did it get there?* "That's my father's Bible."

Ben was not sure if it was a question or a statement, but either way he remained silent.

"Why do you have my father's Bible? Who gave it to you?" Bobby was firing questions rapidly not giving anytime for response. "That is mine now. You have no right to it."

What was Ben to say? Should he stand up in defense and shout back, *it's my father's Bible and your mother gave it to me!* Ben had as much right to that Bible as Bobby. Ben slowly stood still forming his response. He made the few steps necessary in order to reach the Bible, and he picked it up. He held it firmly in his hands and then stretched it toward Bobby. "Here, take it."

Bobby grabbed it out of Ben's hands then turned and stormed out of the office.

Ben stood there for a moment to absorb what had just transpired. He ran his hands across his face and blew out a deep breath. "Lord, I have nothing to do but to place this in Your hands," he whispered aloud. Looking at his watch, he walked across the room to the wall of bookshelves. On the far left side was a single shelf where he had begun to place a few of his own books. He reached for a tiny leather bound Bible and placed it in his coat pocket and then headed for the door. He looked forward to reaching the hospital –it would be a far more peaceful and happier place.

* * *

BEN LOOKED AT his watch; it was twelve twenty-three. He had finished visitation and was heading toward the cafeteria. Seeing Sylvia would be a delightful relief to this day. Just the thought of her made his spirits soar. He walked through the swinging doors into a line which was backed up to the vending machines that offered feeble nourishment for those who would pace the hospital halls when all else was silent. The cafeteria was noisy at the lunch hour. His eyes sifted through the sea of white medical coats offset by a regular interlude of green scrubs. He glimpsed Sylvia at a small table toward the back corner. He smiled and began to walk in her direction. She was sitting alone, squeezing a lemon into her iced tea. He made his way through the maze of tables. Sylvia looked his way and then right past him. Suddenly, she whipped her head back in his direction and a smile broke across her face, which was enough to tell him that she was glad to see him. When he reached the table, he smiled down at her. "Hello," he said in a somewhat sultry voice.

"Hello," came a deep voice from behind him.

Startled, Ben quickly looked over his shoulder. Richard Davies was standing there with a lunch plate in one hand and the other on the chair in which Ben had intended to sit.

"Hello, Dr. Davies," Ben replied in a far more professional voice. He extended his hand.

Davies appeared reluctant to remove his hand from the chair, he was obviously claiming, in order to shake Ben's, but eventually the two hands clasped in a rigid grip. "Would you like to join us?" Davies offered.

Us? Ben thought most silently. "I'm sorry," he said. "I just wanted to say hello. I don't mean to intrude."

"You're not intruding," Sylvia spoke up. Her eyes were glowing as she looked at Ben –something which Ben could not see, and Davies did not miss. "Please, grab another chair." She shifted her plate around. "There's plenty of room."

Ben looked at Davies for approval –a gentlemanly thing to do. "Yes, please join us," Davies said without any enthusiasm at all.

"Thank you," Ben said as he pulled a chair from the table behind him. He sat and had no intention of moving, even if it was a bit odd that he had never gotten any lunch.

Sylvia took a clean napkin from the holder and spread it out on the table. She took half her sandwich and placed it on the napkin and then moved it in front of Ben. "Please, take half my sandwich. I can't possibly eat the whole thing."

Ben smiled and graciously accepted. He looked at Davies. "So," he began, "are you settling in to being chief of staff?"

"Yes," Davies replied. "It's coming along. I have a few ideas I'm trying to run past some of my doctors. In fact, that is why I am having lunch with Sylvia today." There was an undertone in his voice which indicated he had been interrupted. "So, how is church life, Reverend?"

"Very blessed," Ben responded coolly and then added, "Please, won't you come and join us sometime?" He turned and looked at Sylvia, "Sylvia came out last Sunday."

Davies raised an eyebrow at her. *So, that is why she was not at the hospital this past Sunday morning,* he thought to himself. He had made a special effort to be at the hospital on Sunday mornings because he had noticed Sylvia was always there at that time. The pace at the hospital was a little slower on Sunday mornings and he learned that if he sat at the nurses station next to Sylvia and looked busy, it gave him the opportunity to get to know her a little better, and for him to let her know what he wanted her to know about him.

"It was a lovely service," Sylvia added. "You really should come sometime."

Going to church was an awkward thought for Davies. He could not imagine why he would want to waste time on such a thing, unless of course the pews were crowded and that might give him the opportunity to let his thigh push up against hers. "I just might do that," he replied. "I've been thinking that I should start visiting churches around the area. I just haven't had the chance since I moved here. But, I definitely would like to find a good church."

"This Sunday is Easter. We are going to be having a special sunrise service," Ben offered. "Would you like to come?" He knew it was right to invite him, but there was something about Davies that left him terribly uneasy.

Davies shifted his eyes toward Sylvia, "Will you be there?"

"Well, I haven't gotten an invitation yet," she answered in a teasing voice directed toward Ben.

"The doors of the church are always open to everyone. No invitation is ever required." Ben smiled back at her.

Davies realized that there was a conversation taking place of which he was not a part. "What time?"

"Six-thirty," Ben answered quickly.

"In the morning?" Davies answered with shock in his voice.

"It is a sunrise service," Ben reaffirmed.

Davies had attended church fewer than five times in his entire life, two of those were for a funeral. He guessed he would be classified as a Christian, but he was not really sure what that meant.

The conversation lulled as they each focused on their food.

"So what's your idea?" Sylvia spoke up, addressing the question to Davies.

He returned the look with a quizzical expression. "Idea?"

"You wanted to run an idea passed me. That's why we're having lunch," she reminded him.

"Oh!" He had entirely forgotten that was his excuse to invite her to lunch, which had been thoroughly disrupted by The Reverend Ben Montague. "I am sorry. I got caught up in the church talk. Let me get with you on that later. I've got to get back to my office." He glanced at his watch. "I didn't realize it was getting so late. I have an appointment that will be waiting for me." He stood and extended his hand to Ben. Ben half stood from his chair, with his napkin in his left hand, he grasped Davies' hand with his right. The grip from each man was firm and controlling. It was a handshake full of unspoken boundaries, which they both understood meant that there would be a winner and a loser. Davies turned to Sylvia and smiled as if his vision was x-ray. "Dr. DiLeo," he paused for emphasis, "I will see you later."

Chapter Twenty-three

ASHLEY SAT ON the stool at the breakfast bar swirling his Merlot in a goblet. Holding the glass up to the light, he watched the legs trail down the inside of the glass. On the other side of the counter Guy stood over a cutting board chopping onions, red peppers, and garlic. Extra virgin olive oil bubbled in a wok pan on the Viking professional gas range which was in the center island of the kitchen.

"You look as dour-faced as an old woman!" Guy said firmly.

Ashley looked across at him, "That's supposed to make me feel better?"

"Look," Guy's voice became more sympathetic, "it is what it is. What's stewing going to accomplish?"

"Stewing?!" Ashley said in an agitated voice. "Why can't you be more sensitive to my needs?"

"Ashley," Guy's voice was calming. He set the knife down and directed his focus on Ashley. "I am sensitive to your needs. But, this situation calls for action, not fretting. Let's focus on a solution."

Ashley took a deep breath and let it out. "You're right. I'm sorry. I didn't mean to snap."

Guy smiled, "I know I am right." He returned to his chopping. "So, is Tom definitely back in action?"

"It appears that way." Ashley lifted the bottle of wine and refreshed both his glass and Guy's. "How he can show his face in that church again, I don't understand. Everyone knows that his wife was having an affair. And, Buck was doing his best to help Tom and Lisa keep their marriage together. He spent hours counseling with them." Ashley put the glass to his lips and took a dainty swig, letting the wine settle across his tongue before he swallowed. He thought about the last church meeting, before Buck had died. It was a heated meeting. "And, how does Tom repay Buck but to show up at that church meeting and suggest that Buck was mishandling the money. He flat out accused Buck of wanting to build the new sanctuary as a monument to himself!"

Guy tossed fresh shrimp in with the vegetables. He shook the pan back and forth across the flame and then lifted it and began to toss its contents into the air in a very chef-like manner. "It is all in God's hands, Ashley –all in God's hands. Now go light that candle on the table. Dinner is served."

Chapter Twenty-four

HIS ALARM WENT off at four a.m. Rolling into a sitting position, his feet touched the floor at the same time that his hand hit the button to shut off the piercing beep. It took him a moment to gather his senses before he stood and shuffled toward the bathroom feeling quite like an old man. It was Easter morning. Ben paused and stared at his reflection in the mirror. With contemplative thought he looked deep into his own eyes and wondered what part of Christ could he see there? Did he reflect the love? Did he even understand it? Did he truly know those who had walked before him; those who first appeared at the tomb? Did he really fathom the depth of the events of the first Easter morning?

Showered and dressed, he made his way to the kitchen in the parsonage. It was still pitch black outside. He looked out the window over the sink as he filled the little one-cup coffee maker with water. The moon hung eerily in the sky and illuminated the steeple of the tiny white clapboard country church. Something rested uneasy with Ben. The steeple, refined to a sharp point at the tip, was a symbol of the house of God. But, at this moment what crossed his mind was, how many people had it actually pierced? He had seen pain walk into the church and be healed, but he had also seen pain walk out of the church and never return. His conversation with Ron Silver flooded back into his mind. He had summed up the boys who were teasing Ron's son about being half Jewish as just boys being boys. But, it suddenly dawned on him that he was wrong. Those boys represented a larger group of misinformed. Here is where hatred begins. He recalled a conversation he had overheard years ago in a Bible study he attended while still in college. One of the young men in the group boldly made the statement that the Jews worship Lucifer. What was more disturbing than the statement itself was the fact that this young man seemed to actually believed that statement.

As he sipped his coffee he looked at his sermon notes that were sitting on the breakfast room table. He felt it was a good sermon –on love *–appropriate for Easter*, he thought. He stared off into nothingness, lost in thought. After a moment, he stood and headed toward the door, leaving his sermon notes on the table. It was not the right sermon for today. Today, Easter, he would preach on hate.

He stepped out onto the front porch; he breathed in the crisp air. "This is the day that the Lord has made!" he said out loud as a prayer of thanksgiving.

As he made his way across the field which divided the church and the parsonage, a sudden flash of light illuminated the sky. "One more time!" he heard a voice echo. He turned and looked toward the pond just in time to see the little waterside stage become fully illuminated. Even from a distance he could recognize Ashley's figure in the center of the wooden platform. His arms flapping stage directions. "Bravo!" Ashley shouted. People were scurrying about setting up rented plastic folding chairs and arranging Easter lilies in the outline of the walkway which led to an aisle that divided the folding chairs. Ben watched the scenario from the distance. Whether it was what he envisioned or not, it was community working together for Christ.

Ben decided to detour to the area of action and lend a hand. He still had plenty of time to gather his clergy robe.

"Brother Ben!" he heard from across the green space.

A chill ran down Ben's spine. He turned to barely see Ashley in the still darkness. He was dressed in black slacks and a black dress shirt, only his outline was visible against the midnight sky. *Can the man say "resurrection"?* Ben thought to himself, confused by Ashley's choice of attire. "Good morning, Ashley," Ben responded to the call.

"And, a glorious one indeed!" Ashley was obviously already in performance mode.

"Things are looking good. What can I do to help?" Ben offered.

"You just get yourself focused on your sermon. We have this under control," Ashley responded.

Ben was not sure how to interpret that statement, especially with his own knowledge that he had just left his sermon sitting on the kitchen table in the parsonage and decided on a new topic for which he had not written a word. Ben nodded at Ashley in affirmation. "I'll mingle with the crowd then." He looked at his watch –five fifty-five a.m. Sylvia should be arriving in the next twenty minutes. When he glanced up he saw Bobby on the far side of the tiny stage arranging two chairs. One was certainly his, and the other Ashley's. Bobby set a book in one of the chairs; Ben recognized it as Buck's Bible. A sting pierced through him.

"Quit looking so glum, He is risen, you know!"

Ben turned to see Suzie Blalock standing next to him. "Good morning, Suzie," Ben replied. "Indeed, He is risen. I didn't realize I looked glum. Forgive me. I must still be a little foggy due to the time of day."

Suzie was dressed unusually precisely, especially for the crack of dawn. She was flawlessly tailored in a white flounce gauze skirt and pale pink blouse which tails lay on the outside of her skirt. Her blouse was gathered at the waist with a silk scarf of patterned pastels. She stood exceptionally close to Ben.

"Where's Joe?" Ben asked, inquiring about her husband.

Suzie's face transformed to sadness. "Too early for him. He's still sleeping."

"He doesn't know what he'll be missing," Ben responded. He thought he saw a tear well up in her eye. "Are you all right?"

"Oh Ben," her voice was cracking, "I just can't take it anymore! Do you have time to talk?"

Ben looked at his watch. He felt compassion for her, but people always seemed to think that pastors can heal anything. He did not really know what he had to offer her in this situation. But, he knew that most often it was just knowing that somebody cared was the important thing. "I must go get ready for the service right now. I could meet for a few minutes afterwards. Would that be all right?"

Her face suddenly transformed from sadness; she gleamed up at him. "Oh Ben," her voice was sultry, "you are so kind."

He smiled innocently, "Come by my office after the service."

* * *

WITH HIS CLERGY robe on and his white stole around his neck, Ben stood at the front of the Easter lily aisle and greeted a steady stream of people who were arriving, mostly faces he did not recognize.

"Wow!" Leon Jefferson commented. "How many people do you think we've got here so far?" Leon was standing next to Ben. He had volunteered to be a greeter this morning. First Covenant Chapel had become his community. He enjoyed the people and loved the way he could be so involved in the activities. He fit in and the church gave him a sense of belonging and purpose. Leon also felt that maybe God led him here just in order to meet Miss Mary.

"I'd say several hundred so far," Ben replied.

"What a great outreach to the community. Great idea you had, Ben."

A twinge of guilt ran through Ben. It was not his idea and he had not actually believed it was such a good one either. "I can't take the credit, Leon," he confessed. "Ashley and Bobby put this together. And, I think you are right, it is proving to be a great idea."

As Ben was talking a smile the size of Texas broke across Leon's face and it was obvious that he had not heard a word Ben said. Walking toward them were Julia and Miss Mary, who was wearing her usual Easter bonnet of a simple khaki straw encircled by tiny baby pink roses. Ben looked back at Leon and smiled. "That is a true southern lady," Ben said. There was no response; Leon just kept smiling. Close behind Miss Mary and Julia, Ben could make out Sylvia approaching. A smile of equal size broke across Ben's face and his heart skipped at least two beats. As she moved closer it was clear that she was walking with another person –and it was Richard Davies. For a moment the smile disappeared from his face. Why was Ben surprised? After all, he, himself, had invited Davies.

"Good morning!" Sylvia called. As they reached Ben she rephrased the statement. "Or, should I say good 'daybreak'?"

"Happy Easter," Ben returned with a cautious smile. He turned toward Davies and offered his hand. "Welcome, Dr. Davies. So glad you are joining us."

"Thank you," Davies paused. "I believe this is just what I might need."

There was no misunderstanding what was happening between the two men. It was an unspoken language which defined that they were both vying for the same thing and there would only be one winner in the end.

"You look beautiful this morning," Ben said uncharacteristically to Sylvia, which took her totally off guard. However, Ben did not really say it for her sake, but more for Davies. And then, Ben felt like an idiot after realizing how inappropriate the statement was right then. He disappointed himself that he was stooping to such a low level. But, she truly was beautiful.

"Thank you," she replied with a voice which implied *are you all right?* "We better find a seat. Looks like it's filling up." As Davies and Sylvia headed off, Ben shook his head with embarrassment –and anger.

Clouds drifted across a gray sky which was just on the verge of promising a diffused light. It was eerie and serene at the same time. The weather had not called for rain, but as the sky was becoming faintly visible the threat was lingering. The band began to play. Ben turned to look toward the rather professionally built make-shift stage. The music pulled him. It was surprisingly reverent. Ben headed toward the front while the rest of the folks were trying to find a vacant seat. Ashley and Bobby sat on the opposite side of the stage from where Ben was sitting alone. Although dressed more for a funeral, in solid black, Ashley looked unpretentious. No Nehru jacket, no gold ring. Ben wondered if he had forgotten to dress.

Rays of pink light began to pierce through darkness and fluffy gray clouds floated in front of them. The vastness of the canvas was overwhelming and the precision with which the pastel colors began to rise from beneath the visible surface of the earth was breathtaking. No earthly artist could create this masterpiece. Still, the heaviness of the gray clouds remained offering the contrast of battling forces. The beauty was breath taking and chilling at the same time.

Ashley stood and lifted the microphone to his mouth. All he said was, "Join me." He closed his eyes and began to sing. In unison the congregation joined, the words were familiar.

Christ the Lord is risen today, Alleluia!
Earth and heaven in chorus say, Alleluia!
Raise your joys and triumphs high, Alleluia!
Sing, ye heaven, and earth reply, Alleluia!
Love's redeeming work is done, Alleluia!
Fought the fight, the battle won, Alleluia!
Death in vain forbids him rise, Alleluia!
Christ has opened paradise, Alleluia!

The band played along as if harmonizing. It was beautiful! Ben was awe struck —a hymn. He looked at Ashley, demure in simple clothing, letting the music fill the air; he was not drawing attention to himself. Ben looked out among the congregation which was now visible through the diffused sunlight filtering through the gray clouds that seemed to be rising from the earth and blowing ominously in the sky. Tom and Lisa Werner sat with their two boys to the left. Lisa rested one hand on her slightly swelled tummy, significant of the life that was growing inside. On the opposite side was the Miles family, faithful members on the third row every Sunday. Miss Mary, in her Easter bonnet, sat next to Julia Matthews. Although it was a friendship divided by two generations of age, it was a bond of common ground defined by the love of Jesus Christ. Next to Miss Mary sat Leon Jefferson. Ben smiled. He wondered if Miss Mary realized that Leon was falling in love with her. *How wonderful it is that love has no age boundaries,* he thought to himself. He thought of how he felt about Sylvia, most certain now that he was indeed in love with her. He looked at Sylvia sitting in the row behind Miss Mary. His heart fluttered. Next to her was Richard Davies, his body inclined toward Sylvia in a way which said their interpersonal space was a unit. Ben felt a bite of anger and unconsciously tilted his head in the opposite direction as if his own body movement could direct that of Davies. Nothing changed. Ben continued to survey what was definitely a crowd. Families stood together, a father held a sleeping baby on his shoulder, teenage boys crowded a row, perhaps more interested in the girls in the row in front of them than the music which was being sung. A young couple held hands in the far back and three rows closer and to the other side of the aisle an elderly couple held hands with the same kind of passion which told the story that they shared things in this world that only the two of them knew. Ben continued to smile and thought, *all of this is for the love of heaven.* He questioned now whether he should have stayed with his sermon on love. However, as beautiful as the scene was, he still felt compelled to preach on hate. You cannot really preach on one without preaching on the other because there is such a fine line between love and hate. The defining line is the angle at which you approach the topic.

After *The Lord's Prayer*, offered by a young man who had recently joined the church, Ben stepped up to the podium to begin his sermon. He had prayed silently that God would fill him with the words. It was the first time he had ever approached a lectern without notes.

Silence fell over the open space. Light now fully filled the sky, but the presence of threatening clouds still lingered. A rumble could be heard in the distance, making the threat even fiercer. Ben placed the small leather bound Bible on the stand, opened it, and began to read. From the corner of his eye he could see Bobby flipping through the Bible which had been his father's; seemly trying to make a point that he had it and not Ben. After Ben finished the Scripture reading he closed the little Bible and the words began to flow forth from his lips. Ben was passionate about the love of Christ and he wanted that point to be clear this morning.

Bobby continued to leaf through the Bible, knowing that it was visible to Ben. It was obvious that he was purposeful in his actions. Part of his purpose was that he was not the least bit interested in what Ben had to say. *So be it,* Ben thought and continued with his sermon.

Ben spoke from his heart about hate, in light of love. As he spoke he was not certain what his next words would be, but faithfully, God filled his mouth with the words. Ben thought of his conversation with Ron Silver. "If you are using the name of Jesus Christ in order to hate, then you have no understanding of whom the man Jesus, the Christ, is!" Ben's voice was strong. "I would like to leave you with this thought. A Jewish friend came to me recently, distraught because his son was being teased and bullied at school for being half Jewish. A group of children had been telling this boy that he needed to go home and commit suicide because he was part Jewish and they proclaimed that everybody hates the Jews." Ben paused. "My goodness, people!" Ben said with firm anger, "What is wrong? These children were from so-called Christian families right here in this community. How have they been so misled? Have they not been taught that Jesus the Christ, Lord of lords, was in fact —KING OF THE JEWS!" Ben was practically yelling, a style of preaching which was not familiar to him. But, he wanted to be heard in case anyone in his congregation was so misdirected. "People, know this. When you proclaim yourself a Christian, then you are, in fact, claiming the Jewish faith. Christianity does not stand alone, People. It is a movement within Judaism! The One that hung on the Cross and those at the foot of the Cross were Jews! And, God did not forsake them, you have no right to either. Nor, do we have a right to forsake any of His other children. Jesus Christ is the name in which we love, not hate. Please don't confuse it."

Thunder rumbled in the distance. Ben was emotionally drained. Silently, before offering a closing prayer he looked at the faces which looked at him. Faintly he heard a voice to the left side of him, "Oh my God!" He recognized the voice as Bobby's. He shifted his eyes so that he did not draw attention to what was probably not heard any further than the tiny stage. Bobby sat in the chair holding the Bible open. His face was white as a ghost and his mouth hung open. Ben could faintly see that the Bible was open to the page with the family tree. Suddenly, Bobby looked up and met with Ben's gaze. Ben was consumed with a rush of remembrance of the day that Peggy Buck had come to his office and told him she wanted to stand beside him as Buck's son. That day she had picked up the Bible and included Ben's name in the family tree as one of Buck's sons.

* * *

THE WOMEN'S GROUP had set up an elaborate table of doughnuts, cinnamon buns, and coffee. People gathered around filling their plates and chatting. Ben could see Sylvia in the distance talking with a group of people which included Richard Davies. Ben kept trying to make his way to Sylvia through the crowd, but as usual, everyone wanted to speak to the preacher. "Great sermon today!" A gentleman said as he shook his hand. Ben looked around to see if he could see Bobby; although if he did see him, he did not know what he would say to him. He saw Ashley standing with another group. Ben was still not sure exactly what transpired this morning. Ashley was gentle, subdued, and almost reverent. Ben liked it; he just did not know how to decipher it.

"Look, Pawpaw!" Leon Jefferson looked in the direction his great-granddaughter, Alex, was pointing. "It's a rainbow!" The gray clouds still filtered the sun, but directly above it was a perfectly arched rainbow displaying its beautiful colors. "Isn't it beautiful?" Alex exclaimed.

"Absolutely beautiful." Alex turned to see Miss Mary standing next to her. "Did you know that is love from heaven?" she asked Alex.

"It's God's promise to us!" Alex smiled. A rainbow is an incredible sight to behold; nearly everyone had turned their attention toward the sky. Alex grabbed Miss Mary's hand and then she grabbed her Pawpaw's with her other hand. The three stood there and viewed the sight with anticipation. "Miss Mary?" Alex said, in the form of a question.

"Yes?"

"We're having a big Easter brunch at our house. Want to come?" Alex asked.

Miss Mary tilted her head and smiled.

"Is it okay, Pawpaw?" Alex turned to ask him.

"Well, it's more than okay with me, Sweetie, but your Mama's cooking. Shouldn't we ask her?" Leon said through a chuckle.

"I'll go ask!" Alex dropped both of their hands and ran toward her mother who was across the grassy field.

Miss Mary and Leon were suddenly left alone. They stood there – uncomfortable. They both had feelings that neither one had felt in quite a long time.

"I really shouldn't," Miss Mary replied shyly. "This is a day for your family. I would be intruding."

There was a moment of silence, and then Leon turned toward Miss Mary. His heart was beating rapidly and there was a heat which ran through the center of his body. He looked her directly in the eyes and there was nothing she could do but look back. "Mary," he said softly, his deep voice was comforting. "I would really like it if you would join us." His eyes told her more than she wanted to know right then, and her biggest fear was that in her eyes he could see the same.

She began to tremble and she felt light headed, although not like an illness. Her body was reacting to an unfamiliar emotion. She tried to steady herself with her cane. She did not want him to notice. Softly she replied, "All right."

It was crowded around the refreshment table. Everyone was certainly brushing shoulders with everyone, it could not be helped. But, by Ben's way of thinking, Richard Davies was standing closer than necessary to Sylvia. In fact, to Ben, it almost looked as if Davies hand, which was unnaturally dangling to his side, was brushing against Sylvia's thigh. When Ben finally reached them he forced himself between Davies and Sylvia, separating the two. He extended his hand again to offer another handshake and make small talk. "Hope you enjoyed the service!" Ben's voice was over zealous trying to compensate for his nervous reaction. His statement almost came across as *here's your hat, what's your hurry?*

"Hey!" Sylvia said. "What a wonderful service! Ben, it was beautiful." Her voice was full of admiration, which stung Davies.

Ben moved closer to Sylvia. "God inspired, that is all I can say," he said softly to imply that his words where only for her to hear.

"Quite a crowd you had today, Reverend Montague," Davies said. His words were accurate but the tone was insincere.

"I had nothing to do with it." Ben did not mean to sound snide; he just had no intention of ever taking credit for a church service. It was by the effort of a lot of people and all for the glory of God as far as he was concerned.

Sunshine had now made its full presence and the rainbow was but a memory. Children were running around antsy with baskets of colored grass. They were ready to be turned loose into the field where the Celebration Class had scattered hundreds of candy stuffed, colored, plastic Easter eggs.

Julia Matthews poured another cup of coffee. "Next week, on Friday," she said to Margaret. "Does that work for you?"

"Sure. Not a problem," Margaret replied. "What time should I pick you up?"

"The surgery is set for nine-fifteen. I need to be there by seven-thirty for prep." Julia was still irritated. "Can you believe I spent all that money on a boob job that went bust!"

Margaret broke out into laughter. Obviously, Julia did not recognize her own pun.

"Look, I appreciate everything you're doing for me," Julia snapped, "but I could use a little more sympathy!"

Margaret straightened her face and tried to act serious. "So what's the recovery time?" she asked with a compassionate voice trying to conceal her sniggering.

"Well, I've decided to have them just deflate the other one," Julia said as she shook her head with disbelief that she was even in this situation. "I'm not wasting my hopes on this anymore. It was stupid in the first place. I figure it's kind of like painting a house. You can't just paint one room –the freshly painted room makes the one next to it look shabby, so then you have to paint it." Julia took a deep breath. Margaret's face appeared confused, not understanding Julia's analogy. Julia continued, "If I get a new set of boobs, then I'll need to get my butt done and before you know it I'll be walking out of there with glass eyeballs!" Margaret giggled. Julia still not amused said, "Nope. From now on, what you see is what you get from me. What's further," Julia was on a soapbox, "they don't tell you when you go in for these things that they require maintenance about every 20,000 miles!"

"Maintenance?" Margaret shook her head with question.

"Yeh, can you believe that?" Julia asked. "They don't tell you that you'll probably have to have your boobs re-inflated every ten years or so. And, look at me now," Julia glanced down toward her chest, "I've been walking around for the past two weeks looking like Flopsy and Mopsy." As Julia was talking a doughnut hole whizzed past her nose. She turned to see Donny Phagan, an eight year old little boy with dirty blonde hair that hung below his collar.

Donny, his mother, and little brother had come to church a couple of times. They lived on the far side of Wakefield, where the poorer community still resided –at least those who had not yet been displaced by the new developments being built. His mother was a single mom. Donny was a sweet little boy, but lacked direction. When he saw that he had almost hit Julia square in the face with the doughnut hole with which he was trying nail his little brother, his eyes opened wide with shock. Julia smiled at him, giving him comfort. He lowered his eyes and walked toward her.

"I'm sorry," he said slowly.

"No harm done," Julia replied. "You didn't hit me, but why do you want to hit your little brother?"

"He threw one at me!" Donny said.

Julia smiled. She loved the innocence. "Well, I know it's only Easter, but remember Santa Claus is still watching." Donny laughed. Curious about his laugh, Julia asked, "Don't you believe in Santa Claus?"

"No ma'am," he said with his thick southern accent. "I don't believe in Santa Claus." He turned and headed off to the field of Easter eggs, calling back over his shoulder, "But, don't worry, Miss Julia, I still believe in both the Easter Bunny and Jesus!"

Margaret looked at Julia and said, "Remind me to mention at the next staff meeting that we might want to work on the children's Bible study program!"

* * *

"How ABOUT JOINING me for brunch after the children finish the egg hunt?" Ben asked Sylvia.

"Sounds great!" She paused, leaned toward Ben and whispered, "I rode here with Richard, should we ask him?"

No! No way! Ben was thinking, but of course the words which came out of his mouth were, "Of course." *Why did she ride with him anyway? Couldn't he drive by himself?*

Ben turned to Davies. "How about joining us for brunch today?"

"Sounds great," Davies replied as he side-stepped a group of children making their way to the field scattered with eggs. His side-step intentionally placed him on the other side of Sylvia. Now, she was between the two men.

A whistle blew, the noise of children increased to a crescendo, and within moments the field was cleaned of any trace that an egg hunt had existed. Families began to pack into cars and slowly the crowd began to dwindle. "How about Sandler's for brunch?" Davies suggested.

It struck Ben as odd that Davies was familiar with the small, remote restaurant in Wakefield when it was his first time on this side of town. "I was going to suggest that," Ben began to reply, but was interrupted before he could finish.

"Ben?" Suzie Blalock walked up and joined them.

Oh no, Ben thought to himself. He had forgotten about Suzie.

"Suzie." He had to think quickly. "Please let me introduce you to Dr. Sylvia DiLeo and Dr. Richard Davies."

"So nice to meet you," Suzie said nodding her head toward both of them. She placed her hand on Ben's forearm. "Do you have time now?" Her voice was soft and sultry. Sylvia cocked her head with suspicion. She could tell that Suzie's intent was not pure –women's intuition.

Not now, he thought. But, he had promised; and Suzie was troubled and needed him. He would do it for anybody. "Yes, now is fine." Trying to hide his disappointment, he turned to Davies and Sylvia. "I'm sorry, but I am going to have to bow out of brunch."

Suzie's eyes gleamed. "I'm sorry, if it weren't so important I'd reschedule."

Sylvia recognized the game. Truth be told, she played it herself before. What woman has not –the damsel in distress? Could Ben not see what was going on? Ben looked at Sylvia. Both could read the disappointment in each others eyes. *What was he to do?*

* * *

"I REALLY SHOULD be heading home," Miss Mary said to Leon. Brunch at the Jefferson's home had been delightful —more fun than Miss Mary had had in years. Their home was so full of life –and busy. Leon's grandson Alan and his wife, Janie, were a lovely young couple. Janie had made a beautiful, comfortable home and it was obvious that great-grandpa Leon was very much a part of that home. Miss Mary was happy for them. She often wished she had more family. That was one reason First Covenant Chapel was so important to her. It was not just her place of worship, it was her family. For all of her years, the front door of First Covenant Chapel was always open for her. Over those years the door had changed colors –from white to black to red, but no matter its color, it always welcomed her. Whether she came bearing gifts or in need, the door never cared, it always beckoned her home. Inside there was always room for her, even now as the membership of the church was growing beyond the capacity of the old walls –there was still room for her. Even in the days when only seven faithful people were all the tiny church had to hold, the walls still cradled them tenderly, and they remained family.

"I'll drive you home," Leon responded.

Miss Mary smiled in acknowledgment. Not being able to drive anymore was probably one of the most difficult things she had faced in growing older. It took away her independence and added to her confinement. "Thank you," she replied.

"Miss Mary! Thank you for coming," Alex's voice was loud, full of excitement, and positively angelic.

"You are a little angel," Miss Mary said, leaning down toward Alex. "I have never had a better Easter!"

"Really?" Alex questioned.

Miss Mary could feel the presence of Leon standing closely next to her. She looked Alex straight in the eyes and with a smile that even a four year old could understand. Miss Mary said in a very soft voice that only Alex could hear, "Really."

Leon opened the passenger door to his dark green Honda Accord and offered her his hand to help. She paused for a moment, nervous for the first time to accept his gentlemanly offer. But, in only a moment she placed her hand in his. Gently, he closed his fingers around her delicate hand and it felt as if this is where her hand had always belonged.

The ride to her home was short; it seemed extra short because they were enjoying each other's company so immensely. "Will you be going to Bible Study on Wednesday morning?" Leon asked.

"Yes, I wouldn't miss it for the world," Miss Mary answered.

The Celebration Class at First Covenant Chapel had become a very close group. They were all over seventy years old, retired, and had made the decision to flourish in their advancing years.

"I'd be more than happy to pick you up and take you," Leon offered as he parked his car in Miss Mary's driveway. "I know Julia doesn't mind driving you, but I'd be more than happy to."

"Oh, thank you," Miss Mary said sweetly, "but, I don't want to put you out. It is very kind of you to offer though."

He turned and looked at her. "Mary," he said in a firm voice, "I want to pick you up and drive you."

She smiled softly. She wanted him to pick her up too. "All right then."

He helped her out of the car and saw her to her front door. "Thank you for a lovely Easter," she said, her voice was slightly nervous.

"Thank you." He reached for her hand and lifted it to his face; he gently kissed the back of it. "I will see you Wednesday morning." Releasing her hand, he turned and walked away.

Chapter Twenty-five

WEDNESDAY MORNING WAS bustling at the church. Margaret was the unofficial greeter to all who entered through the office side of the church, which was everyone who came to the church on a Wednesday.

"Good morning, Margaret," Tom said cheerfully.

"Morning." She smiled up at him.

"How about that sunrise service?" he asked as if he was referring to a sporting event.

"Go Jesus!" she responded jovially.

"Ben in?"

She tilted her head toward the hall indicating that he was that way.

Tom headed down the hall. The floor creaked beneath him as if to complain about its age; the sound comforted him. When he reached Ben's office he entered, as a neighbor through a backdoor.

Ben looked up. "Good morning, Tom."

"To you too." Tom easily settled into one of the chairs in front of Ben's desk. "Well, I have the decision of the finance committee," Tom said confidently.

Ben's face beckoned the answer.

Tom cleared his throat and spoke firmly, "We all agree that more space is needed. But, from a financial standpoint this church cannot take on an $8.5 million loan to build a new sanctuary. It would be financial suicide for the congregation."

Ben nodded his head. It was as he had expected.

Tom continued, "We would like to recommend that the church look into building a multi-use structure. For $1.5 million we could build something very nice –and still be able to pay the rest of our bills and fund our missions programs." Tom paused, letting Ben absorb the recommendation. In a moment Tom asked, "Would you like me to break the news at the staff meeting?"

Ben's face appeared stern and very business like. "No Tom. I've been thinking about the staff meetings. We have been running them like council meetings. That is changing today. The only ones in the staff meeting that this will be profoundly affect are Ashley and Bobby. Ashley is our music director. Finance and building are not in his job description." He paused for a moment. "Bobby is a member and of course has a voice, but he is not staff and technically should not even be at the staff meetings. The finance committee has a recommendation and the proper forum for that is a church council meeting. Therefore, we won't mention this at the staff meeting today at all."

Tom nodded. His face said it all. *All right!*

Ben really would rather Bobby not be at the staff meeting today. He had not seen nor heard from Bobby, or any of the Buck family, since the Easter Sunrise service when it was obvious that Bobby had seen Ben's name written in the family tree in Buck's Bible.

Ben changed the subject, "How are you and Lisa?"

"One day at a time," Tom replied, but the grin that crossed his face told a better story. "Actually, things are really fine." He paused for a moment. "I love her more now than I have ever loved her." Suddenly the joy in his face dropped again. "It's just getting past the hurt, and the unknown." Tom sat silently for a moment —deep in thought. His gaze was distant. In a moment he continued sharing with Ben what was fraught within. "She assures me this baby is mine and that I don't ever need to worry about the other man coming to bother us." He paused in reflection. "I don't want to fall in love with this baby and then have some other man come make claim to it. I don't know Ben," he blew out a deep breath, "I just somehow feel this other man has the right to know that it might be his child." His voice became stern, "Yet, if I ever find out who he is, I just might kill him!"

Ben wished that he could tell Tom that he was wasting his time with his fretting. "I hear you." Ben shook his head with empathy. "Come on, we better get down to the staff meeting."

* * *

MARGARET LOOKED UP. Through the glass on the office door she could see Leon and Miss Mary approaching from the parking lot.

That's curious, she thought to herself. Julia always brings Miss Mary. She wondered if something could be wrong. But, as they reached the door Margaret could see the way in which Leon Jefferson was looking at Miss Mary and the way in which he was so carefully protecting her as she walked up the steps. A smile broke across Margaret's face. The sight of a budding romance warmed her heart.

"Good morning, Margaret," Miss Mary said as she stepped in the door. She was as light as a feather on her feet as she glided in, barely using her cane for support. A rosy glow spread across her cheeks and her eyes sparkled with the youth of a child.

"And, a good morning to you too, Miss Mary," Margaret replied with a voice that implied, *so what do we have here?*

Miss Mary smiled, her cheekbones high. "You look lovely today, dear," she said breezily as she walked on by.

* * *

As BEN AND Tom walked toward the Sunday School room where they met for the staff meeting, Ben caught a glimpse of Margaret still sitting at her desk. He popped his head through doorway. "Are you going to be joining us this morning?"

Margaret glanced up. "Oh my goodness! Is it that time already?"

The door from the outside opened again. Peggy Buck and several other members of the Celebration Class entered. Greetings were offered. The church was buzzing this morning.

"Let me grab my things," Margaret interjected among the other communications.

Ben, too, was caught up in the frenzy of community that made church a home. Seeing Peggy he could not help but take the opportunity to ask her about Bobby. "Peggy, may I speak with you for just a moment?" he asked.

She thought he looked serious. "Certainly."

He turned to Margaret, "I'll be to the meeting in just a moment."

"Take your time!" Margaret called as she, Tom, and the elderly folks made their way down the hall.

The front office fell quiet. "Is everything all right?" Peggy asked.

"I don't know," Ben responded. "Have you talked to Bobby?"

Peggy looked concerned. "Not in the last couple of days. Why?"

"Well, he came by my office last week and saw Bob's Bible sitting on my desk. He got very upset and said that it was his father's Bible, and he wanted it." Ben paused. "So, I let him take it." Peggy's face turned pale. "At the Sunrise service he had the Bible," Ben continued. "I forgot about the family tree." Ben's face looked pained and his words came in the way of an apology. "I think he saw it, because he was looking at the Bible and then looked at me and stormed off."

They were both silent, neither sure what to say. Peggy reached up and placed her hand on Ben's arm, "There is a purpose for every season," she said.

Peggy was the wisest person he knew. Her perspective was always so clear. He wanted to respond by saying, *yes, and hell just froze over!* He had so much to learn from Peggy.

"How would you like to handle this?" she asked calmly.

"I have no idea." He shook his head pathetically.

Peggy looked thoughtful before she spoke. "I suggest we just wait. Let's see what Bobby does."

Is that fair to Bobby, Ben wondered? "I defer to you, Peggy."

"You better move along to your meeting," she said as if he were a kindergartner about to miss recess. And, Ben obeyed. Peggy drew in a deep breath. Through the window and across the field, the tiny parsonage caught her eye. She was suddenly consumed with memories of when she and Buck had shared the tiny home. She did not miss it. And, what she had come to realize over the last months was that she did not miss Buck as much as she thought she would either. Her life with him had been privately lonely and full of personal grief. Being the pastor's wife, she had no one to go to. She had been living a lie as much as he had all those years, because she never let him know that she knew all of his deep dark secrets. Mostly, she knew that at some point in time he had turned away from God and his ministry truly was in vain –yet she played along. She was without a doubt as guilty as he. But, she was still alive, and she believed that when you asked for forgiveness that it also meant repentance. She intended to do what was right and she knew that presence of the Holy Spirit was her strength.

* * *

AT THE END of their Bible study, Miss Mary placed her Bible back into her tote bag and collected her cane to stand. Leon, who had been sitting next to her, steadied his own footing and then offered her his hand. She graciously accepted. Each time their hands touch it sent a charge through her body, to which she was unaccustomed –it landed in the pit of her stomach and made her heart beat more rapidly. She smiled.

"May I persuade you to join me for lunch today?" Leon asked.

Unintentionally, Miss Mary batted her eyes. "Well, I'll have to check my calendar," she replied in a jovial tone. She pretended to look at the palm of her hand. "Ah, it appears I've had a cancellation."

Leon chuckled, "It's my lucky day."

"You certainly are sure of yourself!" Miss Mary replied and then from sheer embarrassment, a blush broke across her face. She could not believe she just said that. *That's not what I meant,* she wanted to yell. She looked away from Leon's face not wanting to meet his eyes at this particular moment.

"What I am certain of," she heard Leon say, "is that I am blessed to be with you."

Her heart pounded harder. *For goodness sakes,* she thought to herself, *I am an eighty year old woman. This is ridiculous!* She had never felt so wonderful in her life.

* * *

THEY SAT AT a table for two in the small restaurant down the street from First Covenant Chapel. Sandler's was the only place to sit down and eat within miles. The atmosphere was quaint and the food was simple, but very good. The conversation was even better. They laughed and chatted. Miss Mary talked about her childhood and growing up in Wakefield. Leon particularly loved hearing her talk about being a little girl and growing up in First Covenant Chapel. As he thought of his own little Alex, he envisioned Miss Mary running through the fields with her pigtails bobbing in the wind.

"I was on a destroyer in the Atlantic," he said. Miss Mary listened intently as she remembered her days working for the Red Cross during World War II. "I'll never forget the day that we heard a huge crash. A couple of the first mates ran below to the torpedo room. They opened the door and rushed in." He paused. "That was a mistake." His face told her that the story was not totally grim. "A couple torpedoes had somehow come loose. They were rolling freely with the motion of the ship." He smiled as if to laugh, but stopped short. "It truly isn't funny." His face shifted to serious. "Do you know how much a torpedo weighs? If you could have seen those men dancing around trying to dodge those rolling missiles! One of the men did get hit and it snapped his leg right in two." Miss Mary squinted her eyes with a grimace. "He was in a cast up to his hip for almost four months. Each month he was in that cast, the story got better about how he was hit by a torpedo and lived to tell about it!" Leon let out a deep laugh. "He milked it for everything it was worth. We didn't have any women on the ship, but the minute we got back to the States, he took all the sympathy he could get from the nurses."

Mary watched Leon has he shared his stories. She liked how he was such a gentleman and so kind, but he was also a man of strength and character. The lines across his face were handsome and distinguished. Although his shoulders were slightly rounded, their broadness was still evident and their strength still obvious.

They lingered over lunch for more than two hours. Leon paid the bill and drove Miss Mary home. Helping her from the car, he walked her to her front door. There was a long uncomfortable moment as they stood there. This was the first time since his wife's death that he had felt this way. Leon wanted to kiss Miss Mary –he wanted to hold her. She fumbled in her purse for the key to her front door.

"Here they are," she said and she held them up. She put the key in the lock and opened the door. "Thank you for a lovely afternoon."

"Mary," he said nervously. "This Friday there is a dance at the American Legion. Will you do me the honor of being my date?"

"A dance?" she inquired thinking about her cane.

"Yes," he affirmed. "Will you go with me?"

"I would love to," she responded. Then with great confidence asked, "What time will you pick me up?"

"Seven o'clock?"

For as long as she could remember she was getting ready for bed by seven in the evening. "Perfect!" She stepped inside the door to give herself space and time to absorb all that was happening. The screen door now separated them. "I'll see you Friday."

Leon's heart was full and the smile on his face relayed it. "I'll see you then." He turned and walked toward his car, smiling all the way.

* * *

THE STAFF MEETING was short and efficient. Ashley having successfully completed the Sunrise service, had little on his agenda. Bobby had not shown, which was a telltale sign to Ben that there was going to be a showdown when the two brothers finally did see each other again.

Chapter Twenty-six

BEN SAT IN his study working on sermon notes. It was past ten o'clock at night and all seemed quiet with the world. He looked out the window. The night sky was illuminated with a nearly full moon. The sky was motionless. Thoughts of Sylvia kept creeping into his mind. She was everything he desired in a woman. More and more, it was becoming obvious to him how much he desired her. It was also becoming obvious to him that he was going to have to do something about it because the desire was becoming stronger than that which he could ignore. He stood up and paced the room. He walked back and forth as thoughts of her raced through his mind. He lifted his hands to his face and rubbed them back and forth across his temples. He quickly turned and headed down the stairs. Grabbing his tennis shoes, he ran out the front door. He had too much energy right now and what he needed was a good three or four mile run. He did not make it more than the far side of the church when a light caught his eye. *Why is the light on in the church offices,* he thought to himself? He slowed his run to a walk and turned toward the church.

Cautiously, he entered the building. The reception area, where Margaret's desk sat, was empty. Ben passed through to the hall and looked in both directions. The direction to the right was silently dark, but to the left revealed a light which was coming from Ben's office. Ben quietly moved down the hall, praying that the old floorboards would not tell on him. As he approached his door he could hear noises affirming someone's presence. Ben pressed his back up against the wall in the hallway and took a deep breath. Suddenly his attention was drawn across the hallway to the portraits of the previous senior pastors who had served First Covenant Chapel. The glass on the portraits created a reflection that allowed Ben to see inside his office. "Bobby!" Ben whispered. Now he was mad. What little fear Ben had, now was outright anger. Ben quickly whipped around and made his presence known in the doorway.

Bobby, who was sitting at Ben's desk and looking through the bottom right hand drawer, looked up. He did not look the least bit intimidated by Ben. Hatred pierced through his eyes.

"May I help you?" Ben offered in a non-congenial voice.

Bobby pushed away from the desk and stood up. His fists were clenched by his side. "What do you want?" Bobby snapped with a fuming tone.

"What do *I* want?" Ben echoed rhetorically as he walked further into the room. "You're the one rifling through my desk."

Bobby moved from behind the desk and the two men stood facing each other divided by no more than fifteen feet. "This is my father's desk!" Bobby's voice was strong and loud.

Ben could no longer mince words. "Your father is dead, Bobby."

"My father's spirit is alive and well and it is what is guiding this church." A vein on Bobby's neck was pulsing visibly as he spoke.

"The only spirit which guides this church, is the Holy Spirit." Ben's shoulders stiffened with pain.

"You wanted my father out of this church since the day you arrived," Bobby accused.

"You have no idea what you are talking about, Bobby."

"Don't I?" Bobby responded with full sarcasm. "I know your mother was a whore," he paused, "and you are a bastard!"

Ben used every bit of strength he had to hold back his anger. His jaw tightened. "Is that what is bothering you, Bobby? The question of my legitimacy? Or, can you just really not stand the fact that I am your brother?"

Bobby stepped closer. Ben's judgment told him to step back, but his ego refused to let him budge. "You are not my brother," Bobby said slowly. Then suddenly a wave sliced through the air as Bobby's knuckles broke across Ben's cheek. "And, I will not sit by and watch you destroy my father's legacy."

Ben brought his left hand to his face and felt his right hand clenched into a fist as he began to step forward. Moving toward Bobby his immediate reaction was prayer –a cry for help. Silently it screamed through his head. He now stood inches away from Bobby. His fist remained clenched. *I will not hit him, I will not hit him,* he thought to himself in rapid repetition. "Get out of my office," he hissed.

"With pleasure," Bobby turned and left.

Ben watched Bobby walk out the doorway. He stood for a moment in a daze and then dropped into one of the chairs in front of his desk, his body slumped into exhaustion. He sat motionless for a long while; his mind was blank. Lifting his hand to his cheek, he rubbed it gently. In a moment, he stood and stretched his neck from side to side releasing tension. Slowly, he walked out of his office and headed toward the sanctuary. The sanctuary was dark with the only glow being from the emergency exit sign that hung over the door. The faint outline of the cross was visible in the shadows. He breathed in deeply and released it with satisfaction. There is a Presence in this place –not a perfection, but a Presence. It was real and it was powerful.

Chapter Twenty-seven

MISS MARY LOOKED into the mirror of her antique dressing table. The oval mirror in the mahogany frame spoke to her in mixed messages. The wrinkles across her aged face told her she was foolish for thinking that someone could be falling in love with her, but the sparkle in her eyes was youthful and revealed the fullness of her own heart. She smiled at herself and tucked a stray piece of white hair behind her ear. She lifted the bottle of Chanel No. 5, which she reserved for very special occasions, and dabbed some behind her ears and on her collarbone. She took a deep breath and realized that she was more alive at this moment than she had been in years. Grasping the mother of pearl handle on her cane, she stood. Her legs were shaking more than ever. How was she ever going to dance? It was a ridiculous thought; she should have never accepted this date. She sighed. But oh, how she wanted to go.

The doorbell rang and she could feel her pulse quicken. She was an eighty year old woman with the nerves of an eighteen year old girl. She opened the door and there stood Leon looking very debonair in a dark pinstriped suit. His face reflected his nervousness in wondering if Miss Mary would be pleased. Softly, he confessed, "My grandson took me shopping. Do you approve?"

Miss Mary could not help but grin, her own face exposing her shyness. "You look very handsome. I will be the luckiest lady at the ball!"

He grinned back. The ice was broken. He offered her his arm. "Shall we?"

* * *

THE ARMORY STYLE room was elegantly dressed. Small round tables with white tablecloths bordered the room. Each table hosted a small

134

flickering votive candle that offered a romantic glow in the dimly lighted room. A five piece band played music from the 1940's, only slightly off key. Leon proudly introduced Miss Mary to the friends he had made in his short time in Wakefield. The room was filling rapidly and the chatter made the room buzz. Although everyone in the room could clearly remember FDR's Fireside Chats, the room could not have been more exuberant if it had been filled with teenagers. It was clear tonight that this was where life begins.

Miss Mary and Leon fixed a plate of hors d'oeuvres, poured beverages and moved to a table. They ate in a polite silence as they watched other couples move to the dance floor. For a moment, they both appeared as wall flowers, but the chemistry between them radiated across the table; they both were afraid to look at the other. Couples were swaying across the floor, light and carefree, as Cole Porter kept their rhythm. One couple proved that wheelchairs can dance as gracefully as ballet slippers.

Leon broke out in a slight sweat and his heart was racing rapidly. If it were not for the fact that the thought of holding Miss Mary in his arms made other parts of his body react as well, he would have dialed 911 by now, certain he was having a heart attack. Finally, he stood with confidence and faced Miss Mary. Extending his hand he said, "May I have this dance?"

Miss Mary smiled as she placed her hand in his. "I'd be delighted." She rose to her feet and with her free hand grasped her cane.

Leon paused and then placed his hand over hers on the cane. He placed his other hand under Miss Mary's chin and lifted her face until her eyes met his. "Mary," his voice was soft and strong, "you do not need your cane. I will hold you, and I promise I will never let you fall."

Miss Mary bit her bottom lip and at the same time she offered a smile that told Leon she trusted him. They carefully moved to the dance floor as Miss Mary's cane remained in the shadows by the table. Leon placed his hand at Miss Mary's waist and she placed hers on his shoulder. Slowly they began to move around the dance floor to the rhythm of the music lost in the moment and the warmth of their touching hands. At the end of the song, Leon stepped back slightly to look at Miss Mary. "Would you like to sit down," he asked.

Her response was simple, "Only if you do."

He pulled her back to him, this time a little closer, as the band started to play again. He leaned toward Miss Mary's ear, "You are quite the ballroom dancer," he said.

"You make it easy," she replied.

He chuckled and moved his hand tighter around her waist drawing her into him. In a few more measures of the music, he placed his cheek against hers. There was nothing more natural than the way their bodies fit together on the dance floor.

* * *

THE CANDLES HAD burned down and the band was packing up. It seemed to both Miss Mary and Leon that they had only just arrived. Miss Mary collected her cane and they began to make their way to Leon's car. As they walked into the coolness of the night Leon gently reached down and took Miss Mary's hand. Holding hands they walked slowly, not wanting this evening to end.

Chapter Twenty-eight

BEN STARED OUT of his office window into the darkness. All was quiet around him. Earlier the worship band had been practicing, which caused the walls to vibrate, making it very difficult to concentrate. How someone could worship to that noise was beyond him. But, he also accepted that many people, especially those his own age, drew closer to God through the rattle. He had respect for the new contemporary Christian music. Still, it was not where he found reverence. He thought a bit more and wondered if this is what Jesus meant when he talked about the rocks will begin to shout –that you cannot hold back worship in any form. He smiled realizing that he needed to be more opened minded.

He stood and walked over to the window. The moon was a sliver in the sky surrounded by a sea of stars, residing in the darkness. He took a deep breath as thoughts of Sylvia penetrated his mind. She had attended church several more times. To see her in the congregation gave him incredible joy, and energy. Richard Davies had also been attending with her. Ben was conflicted over Davies. He was certainly glad that Davies was attending church, but he was also certain that he was only coming with Sylvia, for Sylvia. Honestly, that made him angry. *Sylvia is my girl,* he thought to himself. *Well, sort of.* "She just doesn't know it," he said out loud, unaware that he was speaking. He looked around embarrassed. He had become so lost in his thoughts that he had forgotten where he was. Realizing he was alone, he turned back to the window. In a few moments he glanced at his watch. It was almost nine-thirty p.m. Why was he still at his office anyway? He needed to go home, or go somewhere. He needed to go tell Sylvia how he felt about her. She was on call at the hospital until eleven p.m. Hopefully it was a slow night in the ER, because he needed to tell her how he felt –now. He turned out the lights in his office and headed to his car.

He arrived at Salem Regional Medical Center after what seemed like an eternity. Walking through the automatic sliding glass door, he walked over to the registration window where Charlene sat chomping gum and looking bored as usual. He would never forget when he first met Charlene, shortly after he had been appointed to First Covenant Chapel. They had not hit it off real well at first, but Ben had become such a regular at the hospital that he now considered her a friend.

He stuck his head in the window. Charlene looked up and smiled, "Hey, Reverend Montague. You're here mighty late."

"Hi, Charlene," he replied.

"It's been a slow night, what did they call you down here for?" she asked.

Good, a slow night, he thought. "Actually, I was trying to catch Dr. DiLeo. Have you seen her around?"

"She's around somewhere. Check the cafeteria or the doctors' lounge. I saw her heading down the hall a little while ago."

"Thanks, take care." He patted the sill of the window as he turned to make his way down the hall.

Richard Davies relaxed in a reclining chair in the doctors' lounge. Sylvia was resting in the one next to him. The room was divided into two parts. The backside was a makeshift kitchen area. A counter held a microwave oven and a coffee machine. There was a small table surrounded by four chairs hovered by a fluorescent light. On the other side were a sofa and several reclining lounge chairs arranged with side tables. A flat screen plasma television hung on the wall. The lighting was soft and low. This room was home away from home for the many doctors who devoted uncounted hours to the profession of caring for others. Richard Davies and Sylvia were the only two in the room.

It had been a somewhat slow night. Sylvia was tired and more than ready for her shift to end so she could go home. "You know, Dr. Davies," she began, "I could just use a pager and be called in when there's an emergency requiring an orthopedist."

Davies had implemented a new policy, when he came on as chief of staff, requiring the on call specialist to be "in house" during their shifts. She was not the only one who did not like the new policy.

"My aim is to be a five star hospital," he responded proudly. "That means we pull out all the stops." It also allowed him to control when he could be with Sylvia. He made sure that he scheduled himself when she was scheduled. And, he tried to arrange the late night shifts when possible. Fewer people where around and there was often more "down" time. "Don't you like being here with me?" Davies fawned hurt.

She smiled back and coyly said, "I could think of other things I'd rather be doing."

"Like being with Reverend Montague?" he chided.

She looked at him with a slanted eye of disapproval, "Like sleeping." She leaned her head back and closed her eyes.

"Sleeping is no fun. We could play a game." He sat up from his reclining position and turned to face her. "How about poker?"

She turned her head and opened her eyes, "Poker?" she echoed.

"Right. You want fun," he said to mock her, "strip poker then?" The tone of his voice said much more than his words.

Closing her eyes again she said, "You seem to be confusing me with those nurses who think that humoring you will equal a promotion."

He dramatically clutched his chest. "I'm wounded," he cried.

She sat up and swung her legs down to the floor. Now she faced him. "You are misled," she responded curtly. She rose to a standing position. "I think I'll go to the emergency room and see if I can find someone with a need about which I actually care."

He rose to face her. "Seriously, Sylvia, why do you keep turning me away?"

"Because, I am not interested in you that way?" She posed it as a question, but both knew it was rhetorical.

"What does Reverend Dogooder have over me?" His tone was challenging.

"Ben," she said forcefully, "is a gentleman. And, what on earth makes you think you're competing with him anyway?"

"Because I've seen the way you look at him," he responded curtly.

They were standing uncomfortably close.

"That is none of your business. Besides, you and I have a professional relationship," she retorted.

Davies could see she was getting agitated –and he thought it was cute. "Isn't your relationship with the Reverend Dogooder professional?"

Her voice was rising in pitch, "Why are you so worried about my relationship with Reverend Montague?"

"Because, he is getting in my way with you." His statement was point blank.

She had no response; his frankness took her off guard. "I want you Sylvia." He paused. "And, I believe you want me too."

Davies' eye was caught by a movement at the door. Through the glass paned window he saw a person approaching. He recognized him as Ben Montague. *Watch this Reverend Dogooder,* Davies thought to himself. Just as Ben placed his hand on the doorknob and pushed the door open, Davies pulled Sylvia into his arms and placed his mouth over hers in a passionate kiss. When she finally succeeded in pushing him away, Ben was already in the room. Sylvia turned to see Ben, who had witnessed the charade. Her mouth dropped open when she saw Ben standing there. With a look of shock on her face she tried to speak, "Ben?"

Ben felt a pain run through his chest as if Davies had just dragged a dull scalpel across it. He clenched his teeth and with painful politeness said, "Forgive me for interrupting. I didn't realize…" He turned to walk away.

"Ben!" Sylvia said again, this time with a pleaded tone. But, it was too late; Ben was already out the door.

Sylvia started after him when Davies grabbed her arm and pulled her back to him. "Stay here with me," he said softly.

She shook her arm free. "Stay away from me!" she shouted and she ran toward the door.

Davies sat back down in the reclining chair, crossed his arms over his chest, and smiled –very satisfied.

In the hall, Sylvia looked both ways. There was no sign of Ben. "Ahhh," she let out a heartfelt sigh. Why had she not seen this coming? She looked at her watch. There was still over an hour left on her shift. Her head dropped and she began making her way down the corridor with no real destination in mind.

* * *

HE SLAMMED HIS car door and sat lifelessly for a moment. "God!" he whispered under his breath —it was a curse, it was a prayer, it was a cry for comfort. "You're testing me, aren't You?" He reflected for a moment and then continued, "Well, I hope you have confidence in me because right now I'm having a few doubts myself." A blinking caught his attention from the corner of his eye. He looked down to see that his cell phone was flashing, indicating it had a message. Grabbing it quickly, he hoped that he would hear Sylvia's voice. He pushed a few buttons and placed it to his ear. "Hi, Ben. This is Suzie." Her voice was shaky. "I am sorry to call you so late, but I really need to talk to you. I am so upset and," she stumbled around her words for a moment, "and...and I need to pray and need your spiritual guidance. Please call me back."

Great, he thought to himself. He took a deep breath and blew it out. He lifted his phone and pushed recall.

* * *

SUZIE WAS SITTING on the front steps of the church when he arrived. It was pitch dark and the only light came from a lantern on Porter's old country store across the street. Ben put his key in the lock and opened the door. "Let's go inside where we can have some light," Ben said. He closed the door behind them and flipped on the overhead light switch brightly illuminating the room.

Suzie covered her face, protecting her eyes from the brightness. "Please, could we just turn on the little table lamp?" She reached beneath the shade and turned it on. Ben nodded and turned off the overhead lights again.

He sat down in one of the armchairs in the narthex. "Tell me what's going on." He hoped his voice did not sound as impatient as he felt.

Suzie lowered herself to the edge of the sofa, but remained silent.

"Are you okay, Suzie?" His voice had compassion.

She could feel the heat rise in her body. She desired him more than she had ever desired another man. He was perfect in her eyes – sweet, gentle. In her mind, she knew that God had appointed him at First Covenant Chapel and she did not believe God would do that unless Ben was perfect. "I don't know where to start, Ben." She paused. "I am so empty and lost."

He waited for her to offer more, but when only silence came he asked, "What are you lost about?"

Why is he asking questions? She thought. They were alone in the darkness of the night. He is a very attractive man and she is a very attractive woman. "Can we go to the altar and pray?" she asked.

Confused about the purpose of her need, he replied, "Sure." They both stood and walked through the doors that led up the center aisle of the church to the altar. Ben paused giving Suzie the opportunity to kneel, but she just stood there apparently fixated on the Cross which hung on the wall behind the pulpit. Giving her room for her own reflection with God, Ben lowered his knees to the kneeling pads and bowed his head. *I could really use prayer myself right now,* he thought.

Within a moment Ben felt the warmth of Suzie's body brush up against his as she lowered herself to the kneeling pad. Her touch momentarily made him uncomfortable as he became very aware of her as a woman. "Suzie," he began to speak in a whispered tone.

"Shhh," she cut him off. "Let's just pray for a moment."

But, he could not pray right now. He was too preoccupied with his own body as it was reacting to hers. He lowered his head again and tried to focus on God, but visions of Sylvia in Davies' arms and the sensations his body was absorbing from the touch of Suzie were more than he could handle.

In a few long moments, Suzie turned to a sitting position on the kneeling pad. She let her back rest up against the altar rail. Ben remained as he was. "Do you believe in destiny?" she asked as she looked off in the distance.

He wondered what her question really was. "Destiny? Well, I believe that nothing comes to us without having first gone through God."

She reached over and placed her hand on top of his. "Do you believe that God punishes us?" she asked in a low sultry voice.

He did not, but the way things were going tonight, he certainly felt like he was being punished. He turned to look at her. "No, I don't Suzie, but is that really what is troubling you?" He was beginning to see a clearer picture.

She began to lightly caress his hand with hers. "We have been seeing each other for months now. I think you can feel it as strongly as I do."

Feel what, he thought? *Seeing each other? She comes to church with three hundred other people every Sunday.* "Suzie?" he said slowly, giving himself time to think.

"Shhh," she placed a finger to his mouth.

He was overcome with feelings and emotion. Anger was the strongest –at Sylvia. He would like nothing more than to do the same thing to Sylvia that she had just done to him. And, he was overcome with need himself. He needed comfort. He desired the touch of another human being –a woman. His head was swimming, his heart was hurting and his body was aching. Slowly and gently he placed his hand over hers –the one she held to his lips. His hand was large and it melted around the delicacy of hers. He slowly moved their joined hands to the altar and then released her hand and stood. He looked at her tenderly. Gesturing to the altar he said, "Here is where you will find your comfort, not in me." He turned to walk down the aisle. Pausing, he said, "Please lock the door when you leave."

When Ben reached the night air and the door to the church was safely closed behind him, he took a deep breath. He looked at the parsonage to his left and then turned right to start his jog, which was what he had set out to do in the first place, much earlier that evening. With every stride, tension left his body. He breathed deeply and purposefully. He had learned many lessons today. The one he now understood most, he had first learned in an ethics class while still in seminary. Now he truly understood the warning —never allow yourself to be placed in a situation which will find you totally alone with a member of the opposite sex. He thought about Sylvia, Davies, and Suzie —how well he understood.

Chapter Twenty-nine

TWO DAYS HAD passed and Sylvia had not heard a word from Ben. Her heart hurt. She really believed that they had begun a relationship. More than that, she really believed that she was in love with Ben. Obviously, that must not be mutual. She was lost in her thoughts while sitting at the nurses' station. She was attempting to make notes, for which she was meticulous, in a patient's chart.

"Penny for your thoughts." She looked up to see Richard Davies standing over her.

"Hello," she said coldly.

"I'm sorry, will you forgive me?" he said in a pitiful voice.

She glared at him with no response.

"Look, I had no idea that Ben would walk in," he lied in a whisper so that no one else around could hear the content of the conversation.

"Ben or not, what made you think you could just do something like that?" she whispered back.

"Sylvia," his voice became passionate, "I can't help myself around you." He looked at her sweetly. "I really care about you." How many times had he had to use that line in the last month –and with how many women?

She gave him a little half smile. "Let's just forget about it, okay?" she replied. "I've got to check on a patient," she said as she got up and walked away.

He watched her walk away paying close attention to her backside. He smiled. "Back in her good graces," Davies said under his breath, feeling quite proud.

* * *

SYLVIA ENTERED THE elevator and pushed the button for the first floor. She moved to the back of the elevator and lowered her head glad that she was alone on the ride down. At the second floor the doors opened but she did not look up; she did not feel like making contact with anyone right now. The doors closed again.

"How are you?" came a cold voice which she recognized.

She immediately lifted her head and tried to change her whole demeanor to one less pathetic. "Hello," she replied. "I'm very well, thank you. And, you?"

"Just fine, thank you."

The tension froze, suspended in the air, which was chilled. Sylvia softened her face. "I am sorry about the other evening," she began, but he cut her short.

"No apology necessary. You don't owe me an explanation." Ben's voice was frank, to the point, and downright cold.

"I want to explain," she said. But, the doors opened before she could say anything more.

"Have a good day," Ben said as he stepped out and went on his way. What he really wanted to do was turn around, grab her, and kiss her just the way he had seen Davies do. He kept walking.

The doors to the elevator closed again. She never got out and rode the elevator right back to where she started. On the way back up her hurt began to turn to anger. Now, she was fuming. *Who does Ben think he is,* she thought to herself? The doors to the elevator opened again and she stepped out —right into Davies who was still on the third floor.

"That was a quick trip," Davies said.

"Yeh, well my plans changed," she snapped. She sat down on a rolling stool and looked at the counter top of the nurses' station for a few moments and then got up and walked back over to the elevator and pushed the button to head down again. Davies watched, curious and amused.

* * *

SYLVIA FOUND A table in the back corner of the cafeteria and set down her bowl of vegetable soup. She chose the chair that faced the back so no one could see her face. She did not feel like being sociable or even being seen at all. She was fed up with Ben Montague, and with

Richard Davies. Davies, obviously, wanted one thing and Ben, obviously, had no idea what he wanted at all! She sat staring at her soup, not really hungry.

"May I join you?" Sylvia looked up to see Ben smiling through his own fear.

"Sure," she replied softly, careful not to show any emotion.

Ben sat, and silence echoed between them for what seemed like an eternity. Neither one of them knew where to start.

"Your friendship is very important to me," Ben finally said.

Sylvia looked at him with a blank face. *Friendship?* She wanted to shout. "Thank you," she replied nonchalantly and took a sip of her soup.

"It hurt me to see Davies kissing you. I'd be lying if I said that it didn't. But, I had no right to get upset." His voice was sincere.

"Ben," Sylvia started, "it wasn't what you think."

"It's none of my business," he cut her off.

"It could be…" she began to say when the public announcement system interrupted.

"Dr. Sylvia DiLeo, please dial extension two-four-six. Dr. Sylvia DiLeo, two-four-six." The voice came over the loud speaker of Salem Regional Hospital.

"Oh no," she said with dismay. "That's never good news. Excuse me just a minute." Sylvia set down her napkin and pushed her chair away from the table. She walked to the phone which hung on the wall in the hospital cafeteria and pushed the buttons. Ben watched her from the distance. She did not speak, but simply nodded her head. As she walked back toward the table Ben could tell it was something bad.

"It seems there has been a bad accident on the freeway coming in from the South side. Life flight is bringing in someone. I've got to get over to the ER and be prepared."

Ben bit his lip and shook his head. There is never just one victim in a situation like this. Even if it was a one person accident –the family and friends of that person become victims as well. He pushed his chair way from the table and stood. "Come on. Let's go. I'll hang out in the waiting room. There is sure to be family arriving." They walked out of the cafeteria together and headed toward the emergency department.

"Please pray," Sylvia said to Ben before she turned and walked into the emergency room through the doors which flapped back and forth, leaving Ben alone in the waiting area. He knew this room well. CNN was on the television, playing with no sound, as usual. The rows of connected chairs covered in royal blue plastic still remained, looking more worn than the last time he had waited here. A murmur came from overhead that gradually became louder. Ben finally recognized the rumble as the life flight helicopter approaching the landing pad. He lowered himself into one of the blue chairs and bowed his head. He prayed for healing, and comfort. He prayed for wisdom for the physicians. But, most of all he prayed for those who loved this injured person. Ben well knew the fear and pain that a person feels when someone they love is in a critical condition – whatever that condition might be.

Sylvia and the rest of the medical team stood prepared as a man was rushed in on a stretcher. Three people ran in unison, one holding a bag of fluids high in the air over the man. "We can't get him stable!" yelled a young man. "Move him into three!" "Where's Davies?" People were shouting from left and right in a professional frantic. The room spun in a dizzied frenzy. The man on the stretcher was in his mid-thirties. The well defined features of his face were covered in blood. His head and neck were immobilized with supports. He was unconscious. The pale blue dress shirt which he was wearing was torn exposing his chest which was visibly swollen; around his neck hung a silver Cross that was resting on his bare shoulder. Sylvia stood to the side prepared for whatever was needed. The silver Cross caught her eye and slowly became her only focus. The Cross which once held a twisted and tortured body now rests silently comforting a twisted and tortured body. For the first time, Sylvia was flooded with an understanding that the only true hope this person has is his faith. She turned and ran out of the room. Exiting through the doors which flapped back and forth, she searched the room for Ben. He sat in the corner, hands folded, blindly staring at a silent CNN. "Ben!" she called.

He turned. When he saw her, he stood up and immediately moved toward her. "What is it?"

"You've got to come!" she reached for his hand and pulled him behind her.

They quietly moved into the room where commotion still continued in effort to stabilize the victim. They slipped behind the door where they were out of the way. "We have to pray," she whispered. "I've seen this before, Ben. It doesn't look good." She paused. "Look," she nodded toward the man, "he's wearing a Cross around his neck. He would want us to pray."

Ben nodded. He leaned over and whispered back, "Even if he wasn't wearing a Cross, I'd still pray."

"We found a card in his wallet with a number to call in case of an emergency," a nurse said from across the room. "We reached somebody, they are heading here now."

Ben's prayers turned toward the person who would be coming to witness this scene. He felt weak and sick at his stomach. He could only imagine how the people who love this man will feel. The room was spinning.

Twenty more minutes passed and the medical team was still unable to stabilize the man. "Has the family arrived?" somebody shouted.

"Yes, one person is in the waiting room!"

"Somebody go get 'em and bring 'em back here!"

"No!" shouted another. "We've got to get this man stable first."

"We're losing him! Bring the family in!"

"You can't bring family in to see this!"

A pause came over the room as if waiting for a final judgment. A deep voice of authority spoke. "Let the family come say goodbye," Richard Davies said calmly and with finality.

"Yes, sir," answered a nurse who quickly turned and left the room.

Within moments she returned. A single person followed her. Dr. Davies approached; he did not offer his hand or waste anytime with small talk. "I'm sorry, he's not going to make it. You may say goodbye." With that, Davies walked passed, exiting the room.

The person trembled, walking slowly toward the stretcher. "Oh my God!" came a weak voice wrought with pain.

Hearing the voice, Ben and Sylvia both lifted their heads. "Oh my God!" Ben said under his breath.

The person leaned against the side of the stretcher and feebly placed a hand on the arm of the man. "Guy, please don't go," came tearful whispers. "Please, stay with me just a little longer."

Ben folded his hands under his chin and began to shake.

Sylvia leaned toward him and whispered, "Is that Ashley?"

Ben simply nodded. He closed his eyes. *God I need more strength now than I have ever needed. He prayed silently. Be my mouth, my heart, my hands. I cannot do this alone. I completely submit myself to you as your servant alone.* His thoughts were begging. He opened his eyes just in time to see the line on the beeping heart monitor machine go flat and the alarm begin to sound.

A man in a white doctor's coat pushed a button that stopped the screams of the alarm. "Time of death, one twenty-two p.m." he said, and then walked away. The room fell silent as the medical staff calmly left the room one by one, including Sylvia.

Ashley, bent over Guy's lifeless body, shuttered. "No!" he whimpered. Sensing a presence in the room, Ashley lifted his head to see Ben standing there, only barely visible behind the door. Their eyes met for a moment and then Ashley quickly lifted himself and ran from the room. Ben took a deep breath and let it out. He stepped out of the room to see which way Ashley had gone. There was no sign of him.

Ashley was in no shape to drive and Ben knew that he was not foolish enough to try. His senses told him that Ashley would have sought solace in the hospital chapel. Ben left the emergency room and walked the long corridor which led to the hospital lobby. The tiny chapel was through a single door identified by only a plaque which had CHAPEL spelled out in capital letters. Inside, the room was small but contained two rows of seats, each row holding six chairs, three on each side of the narrow aisle. The chairs faced a small wooden altar with a kneeling pad which faced a large piece of stained glass with a descending dove holding an olive branch in its beak. Ben quietly opened the outer door and peered inside. Ashley sat in the furthest chair to the front on the right hand side. He was bent over with his arms on his knees and his face buried in his hands. Ben carefully entered and let the door slowly close behind him. He saw Ashley's shoulders tighten as to indicate that he knew someone had entered the room. Ben slowly moved toward the front and sat in the chair next to Ashley. Ben leaned slightly forward and rested his forearms on his thighs. Keeping his focus straight ahead, he remained silent.

For a long time neither spoke. Then, Ashley broke the silence. Through a crushed voice he said, "So, now you know."

Ben thought for a moment on how to respond. "So, now I know what?" It was a rhetorical question, so he continued without giving pause. "I know that a man has died and someone who cared deeply for him is grieving and in need of comfort."

"You'll mock me like the others," Ashley said sharply.

"I see nothing to mock," Ben said with sincerity.

Ashley sniffed hard, and then raised his head and reached for a tissue from the box that sat on the floor in front of him.

"What do you want me to say?" Ashley snapped. "Do you want my resignation?"

"Ashley," Ben's voice was pastoral, "why are you talking about work right now? You have just lost someone very important to you. This doesn't involve your job."

Ashley turned and looked at Ben. "God must hate me," his voice was weak and shaky. "I have tried so hard to gain God's approval, but I was never able to change who I am."

Ben remained silent trying to figure out the bits of information that Ashley was revealing.

Ashley continued, "I have given my whole life to God. I have tried so hard to please Him with my music. I am trying so hard to build a music program that He will be proud of."

It was all making sense to Ben now. The louder, busier, and flashier that Ashley could be, then maybe God would not see who he truly was. Ashley seemed to think that the more he did for God, then the more God would love him, and in turn forgive what Ashley thought was a terrible sin. "Ashley," Ben's voice was distraught with pain brought on by a world under misapprehension, "God does not love you because of who you are. He loves you because of who He is."

Chapter Thirty

PEGGY RESTED HER head on the back of the rocking chair and let the warm spring sun soak into her face. She had grown fond of the front porch at Amy's home. Living with her daughter and her family was peaceful and pleasant. It worked out well. Peggy enjoyed her grandchildren and Amy appreciated the extra help. Rocking back and forth, she closed her eyes and let her thoughts drift. Her hands ached with arthritis; she stretched her right leg in front of her and rotated her foot in circles trying to relieve the pain from her sacroiliac. She pictured herself as the young woman she once was, before her face became etched with lines which told the story of her life. The story really was not a pleasant one, as she scanned the scenes of her memory. Although, she did not really remember her life being as bad as her memories –there was a strange continuity of unhappiness. She could have been miserable all those years if she wanted –all the elements were there. But, that is not what she chose. Instead, she chose to be happy because of all the many blessings in her life. A slight smile broke across her face as she continued to rock –her eyes remained closed.

The steps to the porch creaked. Peggy opened her eyes as Bobby was taking the final step to the porch. "Hi, Mom." His voice was sullen.

"Bobby." Her voice was welcoming. "What a pleasure. How are you, Honey?"

Bobby smiled and walked to the vacant rocking chair next to his mother and took a seat. He rocked slowly and silently. Moments passed and neither said a word.

"What's on your mind?" Peggy finally asked, her gaze remained straight forward; she already knew what was troubling him.

Bobby took a deep breath and let it out, blowing forcefully. "It was your handwriting. I recognized it." Bobby's words were shallow and pained.

Peggy thought for a moment before speaking. It would be easy to say, *what are you talking about?* because he had provided so little information –but, she knew exactly to what he was referring. "Yes," she replied simply.

They both continued to rock; the silence supported itself.

"Is it true?" he asked, his focus still forward.

"Yes." Her tone expressed no emotion.

"The bastard!" Bobby said with anger.

Peggy rocked steadily, she contemplated Bobby's statement, unsure of to whom he was referring. "Do you mean Ben or your father?" she asked frankly.

Bobby turned and looked sharply at his mother. "Ben!" He paused. "This isn't funny!"

"Nor, do I think it is," Peggy's voice showed no inflection.

"Who does he think he is coming here like this? I could kill that son of a…"

Peggy turned sharply and glared at Bobby, "Watch your mouth, young man." Her words were stern and evenly separated.

"Are you defending him, Mom?" Bobby's voice showed betrayal.

"Come on Bobby, you're a grown man." She did not mean to sound condescending. "Do you not understand conception?" He looked at her with a look that clearly said, *what is that supposed to mean?* She continued without giving him a chance to respond. "Do you think that your father and Katrina asked Ben if he wanted to be brought into this world? Ben was never given the choice. He was just another child who was made to pay the consequences of something for which he was never given a choice." She turned her gaze back to the distance and calmed her tone. "Ben only just found out himself. The day that both his mother and father died was also the day he learned that Bob Buck was also his real dad." Silence filled the air. They continued to rock. Moments passed without either of them offering a word.

"Your father's love for you was never in question, Bobby." She took a deep breath and let out a sigh. "But, have you stopped to think about me? When your father decided to sleep with another woman, don't you think that placed his love for me in serious question?" She was venting –for the first time. "Your father adored you Bobby. Nothing could ever change that. When you were born it didn't change his love for David, Amy, or Elaine. Ben's existence doesn't change his love for you either." She became silent and contemplative; Bobby was still.

Peggy let out a small sigh. "Truth is, your father didn't even know that Ben was his son until the day of his death. I'm the guilty one."

Bobby looked at his mother. "What do you mean, you're the guilty one?" His voice was confused.

She slowly nodded her head as she began to speak again, "I have known since Ben was a baby that he was your father's child. I am the one who kept the secret."

"How did you know, and why didn't you ever say anything?" Bobby understood less and less as the conversation went on.

"Ben's mother, Katrina, was your father's secretary at his first appointment in the church. Her husband was Stuart Montague. Soon after Katrina became pregnant, Stuart divorced her and moved out of town. It was a shock to everyone, and no one really understood why he would leave his pregnant wife. Several months later I received a letter from Stuart. The letter told me all about Katrina and your father's affair and that the child she was carrying was your father's. Stuart said in the letter that he was never going to speak another word of it, but he wanted to let me know so that I could handle it in the way I saw fit. I burned the letter and that was the end of it until several months ago."

Bobby sat silently, begging the rocking chair to soothe him. Moments passed again and neither said a word.

"Do David, Amy, and Elaine know?" Bobby finally asked, breaking the silence.

"No, not yet."

"Good. We've got to get Ben out of here before they find out. They don't have to go through this too." Bobby was definitive in his tone.

Peggy stopped rocking and scooted to the edge of her chair. Turning to look at Bobby, she said, "Bobby, I don't think you understand." He returned the glance. "I have no intention of getting rid of Ben. He is family."

Her words sliced through him. "You've got to be kidding me," Bobby replied with disgust.

"No," her answer was frank. "Bobby," her tone became sympathetic, "your father had many faults. He did some wrong things. And, although he did not always practice them, he did believe in the teachings of Jesus and when he preached on those he was sincere." She sighed painfully. "Jesus taught love and acceptance. This is how we will treat Ben." She did not form her words as a question, but fact.

Chapter Thirty-one

TOM SORTED THROUGH the papers on his desk. He was glad to finally have a day where he could catch up, file, sort, throw out, and generally organize. The last six months, since becoming aware of his wife's affair, had been hard and very time intensive. Never in his life had he been so negligent in staying on top of things. He began to make piles of what needed to be accomplished immediately and those which could be finished next week. Everything else went into the trash can. A ton of junk mail had piled up; he did not even bother to look at it before he dumped it into the circular receptacle at his side. He picked up several receipts from Lisa's visits to her obstetrician which needed to be filed with the insurance company. Tom held them firmly in both hands and stared at them. *Could he really love this child if it turned out not to be his?* He tossed the papers aside. He and Lisa were not on the same page with this pregnancy. As much as Tom was glad that Lisa seemed to be totally finished with whomever the other man was – Tom was not finished. They had agreed never to talk about her affair again, but that was before they learned she was pregnant. As far as Tom was concerned, that changed all the rules. He pushed away from his desk and stood up. He wanted to know who the other man was and he was going home to ask Lisa.

* * *

WHEN HE PULLED up to their house, Tom left his car in the driveway rather than pulling it into the garage. He sat there for a moment collecting his thoughts and what he would say to Lisa. Looking upward he said, "God, will you help me?" And then, he opened the door and got out.

When he entered the kitchen Lisa was sitting at the table with a cup of tea and the newspaper. "Hey!" she said with a startle in her voice. "What are you doing home?" She moved her feet, which she had propped in another chair, to the floor and sat up straight.

"Just wanted to see you." He walked over to her, leaned down and kissed her on the lips. He pulled out the chair next to her and sat down. "How are you feeling?"

"Fine. Just a little tired which is par for the course this time of day," she responded. "How are you feeling?" The question came across curious. Tom's coming home midday was unusual.

"Fine," he said with reservation.

"What's up, Tom?" she asked, point blank.

"I want to talk."

"Okay," she said nervously. "About what?"

He folded his hands together and leaned with his forearms on the table. It was obvious that something was troubling him. Lisa leaned forward and rested her arms on the table as well.

He moved his mouth as if to speak, but nothing came out. As he tried again to speak, he began to feel anger welling up in him, which was not what he intended. Sitting there thinking about the man who violated his sacred relationship with his wife infuriated him. The words finally spilled out, "I want to know who he is!" It did not come out the way that he had planned.

Lisa looked at him and scrunched her eyes. "Who, who is?" she replied, although she was fairly sure about "whom" he was talking.

"You know who," he said firmly. "The man…the man…" He wanted to say all kinds of crude statements, but he refrained himself – which was difficult, "…the other man –whose child this might be."

"Please, Tom. We agreed not to talk about it," she pleaded with tears welling up in her eyes.

He took a deep breath. "I know what we agreed, but that was before I knew you were pregnant."

"What does it matter who he was?" Lisa said in a defensive tone. "He's gone!"

"It matters a lot! A man has the right to know if he has a child. And, more than that," he paused and slowed his speech, "a child has the right to know who is father is."

"Tom, don't you trust me," she asked.

Considering the fact that she had had an affair and they were discussing the possibility that she might be pregnant with someone else's baby, he did not think it would be out of line to answer that question with a simple, *"No,"* but he refrained. "Don't you trust me?" he asked in return.

Lisa stood up from her chair and moved close to Tom. She made her way in between his legs and sat on his lap. She put her arms around his neck and kissed him on the cheek. "Of course I trust you. I trust you more than anything. I trust you so much that I am having this child with you." She lifted his hand and placed it on her swollen belly. "This is our child, Tom." She moved his hand in a circular motion across her tummy.

Tom could feel his heart sink. It felt good to hold her on his lap and touch her. In spite of everything he deeply loved Lisa and he desperately wanted this to be his child. "I need to know, Lisa. I need to know that I can love this child without the fear that someone will come and take my love away one day."

Lisa brushed her hand across his cheek and kissed his lips softly. "I promise you that will never happen."

"How can you promise me that, Lisa?" Tom voice was showing agitation again.

She pulled away from him and directed her gaze out the window. "Trust me, Tom."

"Work with me, Lisa. You are asking me to trust you, but you are not giving me anything to go on!" Tom was showing anger again.

She stood up from his lap, grabbed her tea cup and walked to the kitchen sink. Setting the cup into the sink she said, "He's dead, Tom. Okay? He's dead. Does that help you?"

Tom was silent with shock. He did not know how to respond. Was he supposed to say he was sorry that her lover was dead –because he was not? And, it now begged the question, did she come back to him because she loved him or because her lover was dead? He needed to get out of there –and think. Tom stood up and walked to Lisa. He put his arms around her and kissed her on top of the head. "That is fine. I love you."

"I love you," she said softly.

"I've got to go back to work," he said and turned to head toward the door.

"Tom," she said just as he was exiting. He turned to look at her. "I'm sorry," her voice was sincere and Tom knew she meant it.

Chapter Thirty-two

THE DOOR TO the church offices flung open and Julia entered carrying several large shopping bags. Margaret watched curiously as Julia clumsily made her way to the sofa which sat on the opposite side of the room and released the bags onto it.

"What on earth?" Margaret questioned.

Julia turned and began sarcastically, "Hello, my name is Julia and I am a recovering boob idiot."

Margaret lowered her eyes and peered at Julia questioningly through half mast lids.

Julia crossed the room and sat in the chair in front of Margaret's desk. "I have a theory!"

"Okay," Margaret said slowly. "What is it?"

"Do you know the definition of the word 'boob'?" Julia asked.

"Uhhh...," Margaret muttered.

Julia cut her off, "An idiot! Also known as a 'booby'! That's where we get 'booby trap'! A trap that catches an idiot!" Julia was speaking fast and excitedly. "And, there's the 'boob tube', rightfully called such. Have you ever seen someone staring at a television set with their mouth hanging open like a codfish?" Julia looked intently at Margaret. "You know what I mean?"

Margaret lifted her hands from her desk to gesture her confusion.

Julia continued, "That's why I figure women's breasts are called boobs! They are booby traps! They catch a man's attention and suck all the intelligent life out of him and these things," she pointed to her chest with both index fingers, "can make him act like an idiot!" Julia paused to reflect for a moment.

Margaret raised her brow and blinked her eyes attempting to sort through the drama. She shook her head to clear it. "So what's in the bags?" She turned her head to look at the sofa.

"Ahh!" Julia said as she stood and walked back toward the sofa. "This is my new wardrobe." She opened one of the bags, took out a shirt, and held it in front of her. "What do you think?"

"Very nice," Margaret offered cautiously.

"Do you know that I am two sizes smaller now?" Julia questioned. "And, I feel fabulous! Getting rid of those boobs is the best thing I ever did!"

A noise at the hallway drew the attention of both Julia and Margaret.

"Reverend Montague!" Margaret exclaimed, embarrassed even though she was not the one who had been talking.

Ben entered the room and walked toward Margaret's desk. He held up his hand in a stop position. "Please, don't tell me more than I want to know," his voice begged.

Julia blushed.

"I just wanted to know if you have heard from Ashley?" Ben asked Margaret.

"Yes, he'll be in at one," she replied.

"Thanks," Ben turned to head back down the hallway to his office. As he walked he angled his head to look at Julia. "Very nice blouse."

Julia smiled.

As soon as Ben had cleared their presence, Julia whispered to Margaret, "You think he has ever been caught in a 'booby trap'?"

Margaret shook her head and sighed. "Hey, my husband and I are going with some friends to this new little music venue over in Salem on Saturday night. Do you want to join us?"

"What is it?"

"It's called Harry's on the Square. They bring in local musicians. They have tables set up and you can take your own bottle of wine and some food if you want. It's really fun. Come on —you can wear your new blouse."

"I'd be the lone single, wouldn't I?" Julia asked.

"So what! I thought you said you weren't going to worry about men anymore."

Julia looked at Margaret with offense. "I never said any such thing! What I said was that I wasn't going to use my boobs as bait anymore!"

"Whatever!" Margaret replied. "Are you going to go or not?"

"Fine. What time?"

"Meet us there at eight on Friday night."

Chapter Thirty-three

BEN ENTERED THE familiar elevator of Salem Regional Hospital and thoughtlessly pushed the button illuminating the number three. The vision of Sylvia in Richard Davies arms intruded his thoughts. He tensed at the vision and shook his head trying to clear it from his presence. Somehow, though, the thought took over and he found himself fantasizing about how he would deal with Davies if they lived in ancient Rome. He was dressed in armor, wielding a sword, ready to defend the honor of his lady. He could hear the whisper of her voice echo, "My Lord!" As that thought passed, he was led right into a scene at the Colosseum. It was packed with people yelling and cheering. He stood on the main level and looked across to the center of the arena where he saw Richard Davies cowering. Ben looked up to the gates as they opened and a lion appeared from a chamber below.

"Get real, Montague!" Ben said out loud. Startling himself by his outburst, he looked around thankful that he was in the elevator by himself. The doors opened and he exited onto the third floor of Salem Regional Hospital. He only had two parishioners to visit today. Spring was always a welcome relief, there seemed to be fewer illness requiring hospitalization. He walked down the familiar corridor. The sounds of his steps echoed down the hall and then were met with a responding echo approaching from the opposite direction. Ben looked up to see Richard Davies approaching him. Blood rushed up Ben's spine and he could feel the heat in his face.

Richard Davies was cool and collected as he approached. Upon seeing Ben, he slowed his pace and smiled insincerely. Ben collected himself and slowed to acknowledge Davies.

"Hello, Reverend Do...," Davies began and then caught himself abruptly about to say Reverend Dogooder. "Montague."

"Dr. Davies," Ben replied emotionless.

The two men shook hands with a grip that was unusually firm from both sides.

"Out visiting?" Davies asked with an air of arrogance.

"Yes," was Ben's simple reply.

"Listen," Davies began, "I've been meaning to tell you how much I am enjoying your church."

Davies' words twisted like a knife in Ben's gut.

"I hope you feel at home there," Ben's voice was monotone.

"I do." Davies paused to calculate. "I'm just glad Sylvia is coming too. Church has always been a big part of my life," he lied, "but, Sylvia stepped away from the church." Davies smiled pensively, as if soaking in his own precious thought. "You know if she and I are going to keep seeing each other, we must be equally yoked," his words were intentionally manipulative. "Don't you agree?"

"Seeing each other?" Ben asked in a confused manner.

"She is one incredible woman," Davies returned. "You know what I mean?"

Ben nodded slowly, "Yes," he paused, "I think I do. Well, if you will excuse me Dr. Davies, I have some parishioners to visit."

"Certainly," replied Davies.

They each turned and continued on in their original direction. Ben was fuming as he walked along. He had hoped to see Sylvia today, but after his encounter with Richard Davies he had changed his mind.

* * *

THE TIME IT took to visit his parishioners was good. He needed it to cool off. He had a hard time believing that Davies and Sylvia had developed a relationship and were seeing each other. He reflected for a moment and then decided that he did want to see Sylvia, after all. Walking to the nursing station, he prayed along the way that Davies would not be there.

"Thank you, God," he whispered when he reached the station.

"Hi, Reverend Montague," a young woman greeted him.

"Hi Anna," he replied. "Is Dr. DiLeo around?"

"She was here a minute ago. Let me see if I can find her." The young woman picked up the phone and pushed several buttons. In a moment she hung up the phone. "She's down on two. I told her you were looking for her. She asked if you could meet her in the lobby."

The lobby? That is odd, Ben thought to himself. "Thanks!" he replied and headed for the elevator.

He arrived in the lobby of the hospital and looked around for Sylvia. He did not see her. The area was crowded and full of noticeable tension. It was nearly always the same, you rarely see anyone laughing and having a good time in a hospital waiting area. He sat down in one of the royal blue plastic chairs and waited. Sitting across from him was a heavyset black woman in her late thirties, maybe early forties. She was dressed in black pants and a white shirt, both of which appeared uncomfortably tight. She was wearing black work shoes and a baseball style cap with the MTA logo across it. Behind the cap peeked a black do-rag. She looked at Ben. Ben smiled. She nodded her head toward him in recognition.

"MTA?" Ben asked.

The woman smiled. Her teeth were beautifully straight and white, much in contrast to the rest of her appearance. "Metropolitan Transit Authority," she said with a sweet voice.

Ben was overcome by the contrast between her harsh appearance and her sweet voice. "Ah! Do you work for them?" he asked.

"Yup. Bus driver. Fifteen years." she replied proudly and quickly.

"Well, that's a fine job," Ben returned, trying to make pleasant conversation.

"Used to be."

"Used to be? What do you mean?" Ben asked curiously.

"Used to be people was pleasant and happy to be goin to work. They'd get on the bus and I say, 'morn!' and they'd answer me back the same. Nowadays with the economy being likes it is, peoples gettin on the bus, you can see it in their eyes. There just ain't no hope no more. Most them out lookin for work now."

Ben's heart went out to this lady and the people she serves. "You care about those people, don't you?" Ben asked.

"Sure do! And if that ain't bad enough, it ain't always safe to be ridin the bus no more. I mean, thems good peoples, but some of thems are startin to steal. Not cause they want to or that was the way they was raised. It's just the only way they can live."

"Do you mind if I ask why you're here at the hospital?"

"Naw, 'at's fine. Don't mind me a bit. My Maw's here. She's a diabetic." The lady paused and shook her head with disbelief. "She done run out of her insulin and don't have no money to get more. I done told her a hundred times to call me and I'd take care of her. Now look, she gone and got herself laid up here."

From a distance Ben could see Sylvia walking down the corridor. He looked back at the lady. "May I ask your name?"

"Thelma."

Ben stood up and walked over to her. He extended his hand. "Thelma, I'm Reverend Ben Montague." They shook hands. He handed her one of his cards and then said, "It has been an honor to meet you today. Please let me know if my church or I can ever help you. God Bless." She smiled at him. Ben smiled back and then headed toward Sylvia.

Sylvia waved as she approached Ben. They paused in the hallway.

"Hey there!" she said cheerfully.

"Hey," he replied with a tone of reservation in his voice. "So what's with the clandestine meeting in the lobby?"

She giggled, "Clandestine? You're not becoming like one of those T.V. preachers are you?"

He loved her sense of humor. "That will be the day!" he responded.

"Nothing suspicious. It's just I'm finished for the day and I thought I could coax you into letting me treat you to an early dinner. Are you free?"

Ben was pleasantly surprised, especially in light of his recent conversation with Richard Davies. "Well, sure, I'm free," he hesitated, "but, what would Dr. Davies say?"

Sylvia tilted her head and looked at him with confusion. "You have a strange fascination with that man."

"I wouldn't want to hurt his feelings."

"Believe me, that's not possible, the man doesn't have any feelings," she said as they exited the hospital.

"I don't believe that is true," Ben replied. "He certainly has feelings for you."

"Why Reverend Montague," she looked up at him as they continued to walk toward the parking lot. "If I didn't know better, I would say you are jealous!"

Ben was becoming uncomfortable. "Because I'm concerned for a fellow human's feelings, you think I'm jealous?"

"I forget, you're a man of the cloth. No feelings there!"

"Believe me," he said with emphasis, in order to mimic her, "we have feelings just like the rest of mankind."

"So?" she said inquisitively. "You and Dr. Davies have more in common than meets the eye. Is that what you are saying?"

"We're both men if that's what you mean. But, we are significantly different."

"How so?" she taunted him.

"I like to think I've got character."

They had reached Ben's car.

"Are we riding together or should I take my own car?" Sylvia asked curtly.

He reached to the passenger door and opened it. Giving her a flirtatious smile he firmly said, "Get in."

This was a new level of conversing for Ben and Sylvia. It was defensive and jovial at the same time, yet there was a tone of anger in both of their voices. However, what was most obvious was the ardent passion that was so prevalent in the air between them.

After Sylvia was settled in her seat, Ben closed the door and walked around to the driver's seat. He started the car and began to backup.

"So are you?" she asked sternly.

He glanced toward her. "Am I what?"

"Jealous!"

"What is there for me to be jealous of?" he returned in a cool voice.

A look of hurt came across her face. "Gee, thanks."

He looked remorseful for his careless statement. "You know what I mean."

"Frankly, I don't."

167

"We are friends. If you want more of a relationship with Dr. Davies, who am I to stand in the way?" His voice sounded sincere.

"Point well taken."

They rode in silence for several moments. They each were trying to assess the meaning of their conversation. Sylvia was frustrated and did not understand Ben and what motivated him. She had an overwhelming desire to slap him across the face and say, "Wake up! Can't you see how I feel about you?!" Ben was frustrated by Sylvia. All he could think of at the moment was how desperately he wanted to take her in his arms and kiss her.

They pulled into the parking lot of Leo's. Sylvia looked out the car window at the restaurant. "So, is this where I am taking you for dinner?"

Ben suddenly realized that they had never talked about where they would go. He just drove here. "I'm sorry. I was so caught up in our banter I didn't even ask you where you wanted to go. Is this okay?"

She smiled sweetly at him. "Hum, that's just like a man."

He smiled back realizing her sarcasm. "Truce?" he said, and offered her his hand.

"Truce." She placed her hand in his. The magnetism was strong. They sat, intent on each other, lost in the seductiveness of their touch. Ben gently moved his thumb back and forth to caress her hand. Sylvia felt butterflies rise in her stomach. Their eyes locked for a moment. Ben felt heat spread through his body. A drawing power grasped him, pulling him toward Sylvia. He parted his lips.

"Davies?" Sylvia said, interrupting the moment.

Ben turned to look over his shoulder. Through the car window he saw Richard Davies' face. Ben quickly let go of Sylvia's hand. He opened his car door, got out and stood tall.

Richard Davies offered his hand to Ben. "Well, hello again, my good man," Davies said through sarcasm.

Ben met his hand with a firm shake. "Hello."

Sylvia got out of the car and walked around to join them.

"What are you doing here?" she said with obvious surprise.

"Not just me." Davies turned and pointed to a crowd of her collegues walking toward Leo's from the parking lot. "Didn't you get the memo?"

"Memo?"

"I'm just kidding," Davies placed his hand on her shoulder and began to massage it gently, "there was no memo. A bunch of us just decided it would be fun to have dinner. Come join us." He turned toward Ben. "You too, Reverend. I'll even treat."

"You don't need to do that," Ben said offendedly.

"Nonsense!" Davies replied. "You do good work, Padre. And, the pay can't be too good."

With every once of strength Ben could muster, he held his tongue. This was a game more than anything else and he would not lower himself to Davies' level.

Davies began to walk toward the restaurant, his hand still on Sylvia's shoulder, helping her along. Ben followed.

Inside, the group was settling around a large table. Two empty seats were next to each other, another empty seat remained at the other end of the table. Davies took one of the two seats which were together, purposefully making conversation with others to avoid the situation which intentionally separated Ben and Sylvia, leaving their seating arrangements to their own accord. Ben looked at Sylvia, smiled, and pulled out the chair next to Davies in order that she could sit. Reluctantly, she accepted. Ben walked to the remaining empty seat at the other end.

Ben introduced himself to two nurses he had not yet met while doing his visitations. The conversation was lively and vibrant. A waitress came to the table to take the drink order.

"A bottle of Chianti here," Davies said as he gestured to the table in front of him. "And, the gentleman at the end of the table is on my tab too." He pointed toward Ben.

"What'll you have, Reverend? Coke? Iced tea?" Davies called down the table. The insult was obvious.

Ben's blood was boiling. "I'll have a beer, thank you," Ben spoke loudly in order to be heard over the chatter.

Pamela Jackson

"Well, Reverend!" Davies said obnoxiously, "You're not as good as I thought."

"Beer is not a mortal sin," he replied cooly.

Davies turned to interject into a conversation in the other direction. Ben listened in on the conversation around him. It all seemed rather like a blur. The waitress came and went, orders were taken, dinners were served and dishes cleared. Ben watched as Davies poured another glass of Chianti into Sylvia's glass. The chatter became a hum which began to dull Ben's senses. He watched Sylvia. She was talking with a woman on the far side of her. Ben could only see Sylvia's profile. Her long brown hair fell softly over her shoulder. Her mannerisms were elegant and graceful. Richard Davies had his arm around the back of her chair, comfortably relaxed, he was speaking with a gentleman at the very end of the table —the exact opposite from where Ben was sitting. Sylvia appeared to be totally unaware that she was cradled in Davies' arm. Or maybe she just did not care?

Ben took a final sip of his beer leaving the glass half full. He pushed his chair back. "It was very nice to meet you both," he said to the ladies with whom he had been sitting. "I really must be going. I've got an early day tomorrow."

Ben pushed in his chair and walked around to behind Sylvia. He leaned over Richard Davies' arm, which was still on the back of Sylvia's chair, and spoke into her ear. "I need to be going."

Sylvia jumped. "Ben!" She turned to look at him and giggled. "You startled me!"

"I have an early staff meeting tomorrow," he replied almost sternly.

She giggled again and her head swayed slightly.

Davies interrupted. "Ah, she's having a good time. I can drive her home, Reverend. Don't worry about it, it's not a problem."

"I'm sure it's not," Ben said point blank.

"My car's at the hospital," Sylvia said with a slur.

"Not a problem," said Davies. "I'll drive you there."

"Sylvia," Ben said firmly, "I will drive you home." He turned toward Davies. "Thank you for your offer, but she should not be

170

driving tonight." Ben placed his hand under Sylvia's arm to help her up. "Thank you for dinner, Dr. Davies."

Sylvia and Ben walked to the exit. Ben kept his hand on Sylvia's arm to help her stay steady. Not a word was exchanged between them as they got in Ben's car. This first few minutes of the ride were quiet.

Sylvia stretched her legs in front of her. "My goodness, I didn't realize what a lightweight I am. That glass of wine really got me."

"Glass of wine?" Ben retorted.

She sat up straight. "I only had one glass!"

"You had three glasses," Ben stated. "Davies took the liberty to keep refilling your glass."

She giggled. "He's a funny man." She turned in her seat like a little girl. "Did you have a good time tonight?"

"It was all right. I met some very nice people." He paused.

"But?" she interrupted.

"But???" He sarcastically.

"But???" She giggled in reply.

Another moment passed in silence.

She yawned noticeably. "I guess I still owe you dinner."

"You don't owe me anything."

She was not so lightheaded to know that she was tired of Ben's standoffishness. She was collecting her thoughts, afraid of saying the wrong thing —but she needed to say something.

Pulling into the parking lot at the Sheridan Towers, Ben said, "We're here," before she could speak her thought.

She looked out the car window, disappointed.

He got out of the car and walked around to the passenger side. He opened the door and waited for her to put her shoes back on her feet, which she had slid off during the ride home. He offered her his hand and helped her out of the car. She toppled into him. Her body felt good next to his and he savored the moment. She looked up and giggled.

"I'm sorry," she said gleefully.

Their faces were inches from each other. He could taste her breath. She smiled at him with that crooked smile which made him melt with desire for her. He looked deeply into her eyes and at her beautiful face. In all of the awkwardness of moment it was never more obvious how much he loved her. And, in spite of her state, he had never wanted her as badly as he did at this moment. There was something so sweet and genuine about her, even as she was right now. His arms pulled more tightly around her in effort to help her stand. It would be so easy to kiss her now. His own head was spinning, his blood was pulsing.

"Not here, not now, not like this," he said in a whisper.

"What?" Sylvia said with confusion.

He smiled at her. "Let's get you inside." He chortled.

They walked into the lobby of the Sheridan Towers.

"You're a fine man, Ben," she said with sincerity which penetrated all else.

He looked deeply at her. "It means the world to me that you think that."

He pushed the elevator button. When it arrived in the lobby, he entered it with her. It was the first time he had ever been inside the elevators in the Sheridan Tower —for all the many times he had been there.

They walked down the hallway. "This is my door," she proclaimed.

She reached in her purse for her key and unlocked her door. "Are you going to come in?" she said as her head swayed again.

He wanted to desperately. But, he was honestly afraid of what he might allow himself at this particular moment. "Not tonight," he said.

Chapter Thirty-four

BEN WALKED THROUGH the door to the church offices. Inside, people mingled everywhere. The small room to the right hosted a committee meeting for Vacation Bible School; although still months away, it was just around the corner. Doug Miles and two others created a makeshift cubicle with straight back chairs in the front corner of the reception area. They were planning the first mission trip which First Covenant Chapel would take in the fall. Leafing through information on various programs, they were trying to decide which was most fitting for the tiny country church. The elderly members of the Celebration class filed through on their way to the Sunday School room where they met for their weekly Bible study. As Miss Mary and Leon passed through, the entire room took pause, except for Margaret who typed away at her computer. The fragrance of the remaining Easter Lilies still filled the air. Ben, with a soulful feeling of satisfaction, surveyed the scene. It was surreal. First Covenant Chapel was alive. The daily events of the church were a celebration –where everyone was invited.

Today would be the first staff meeting Ashley would attend since Guy died three weeks prior. It would also be the first staff meeting which Bobby would be at since before Easter. Ben was not looking forward it. He smiled as he passed through the brightly lighted reception area on his way to his office. When he approached the wall which held the portraits of the previous senior pastors who had served First Covenant, he paused. Looking deep into the eyes of each man, he pensively bowed his head. Ben felt unworthy to be in their presence. He wondered what it had been like in their day. And, how he wished he could sit down and talk with each of them –Ben knew he still had so much to learn.

The agenda for today's staff meeting was sitting on Ben's desk. It was a long agenda –indicative of the vibrant church life he had just witnessed in the front office. Ben scribbled notes in the margin as he looked over it. He glanced at the clock on the corner of his desk – twenty minutes until meeting time. He rolled his eyes and let out a deep sigh –he hated staff meetings. Swiveling in his old wooden desk chair, he turned to face the back wall. Ben folded his hands together and raised them to his chin. He allowed stillness to become his companion, and the rest of the world was gone. The chatter which could be heard through his office walls slowly began to dissipate. The sunlight which shone through the window to his left rested on his closed eyelids and blinded him of any previous vision he might have held before he entered this place of solitude. He took a deep breath and slowly began to smile. This was communion with God. Everything else was gone. Here, there was no tiny white clapboard country church, no Bobby Buck or Ashley March, no building committees or finance committees, no sickness, no illness, no suffering, no Sylvia and no Richard Davies. He basked in God's glory and his own breaths began to keep rhythm with the music that slowly filled his being –as real as if angels had formed a chorus before him. With each breath his music became more vivid until his own mouth joined the chorus and he breathed the words, only barely audible...

> *Sweet hour of prayer! Sweet hour of prayer!*
> *That calls me from a world of care,*
> *And bids me at my Father's throne*
> *Make all my wants and wishes known.*
> *In seasons of distress and grief,*
> *My soul has often found relief,*
> *And oft escaped the tempter's snare*
> *By thy return, sweet hour of prayer!*

With a loud creaking, he swiveled his chair back around to its original position. He was ready –ready to face the day, ready to face the meeting, ready to face Bobby, ready to face.... "Ashley!" Ben said with a startled voice.

"Good morning, Ben." Ashley voice was calm and gentle.

Ben stood up from his desk. Ashley walked toward him.

"How are you?" Ben inquired still taken off guard.

Ashley crossed his arms across his chest and smoothed his sleeves with his hands. He lifted one hand in a fist to his mouth and cleared his throat. "I, um," he cleared his throat again. "I am well. Very well. Thank you."

Ben nodded his head slowly. "Good."

"Look," Ashley began, his eyes shifted to the floor, "I wanted to thank you."

Ben cocked his head to the right. His faced revealed that he did not understand for what Ashley was thanking him.

Reading Ben's nonverbal communication, Ashley clarified. "For telling me that God doesn't love me because of who I am, but because of who He is." He paused. "I needed to hear that."

Ben smiled slightly with affirmation and nodded his head.

"I'll see you in the staff meeting," Ashley said, and then turned and walked out the door.

Ben sat in silence for a moment, collecting his thoughts. It always amazed him how God brings things together for good.

He picked up the phone and dialed Sylvia's home number. There was no answer. He tried again on her cellphone. She answered on the third ring.

"Hello?"

"Hello," his voice was soft and gentle to her ear. "Well, how are you this morning?"

"Embarrassed?" she asked jovially.

"Not at all."

"Let's just say that I am so glad I don't have any surgeries planned for today."

Ben laughed. "I bet not as glad as your patients."

"You're right about that!"

"Do you need any help retrieving your car today?" Ben asked.

"Thank you," she said sweetly. "Actually, Dr. Davies drove me to work early this morning."

"Oh." That was all Ben knew to say. The very mention of Davies' name stabbed him. "Well, I need to get to my staff meeting."

"I still owe you dinner. Don't forget." she said.

"Sure. Bye now." Ben set down the phone and leaned back in his chair.

* * *

ROY MACY CALLED the room to order. The members of the Celebration class were certainly social. "Order!" Roy called. "We need to be about the Lord's work –so, you chatterboxes in the corner need to pipe it down!" Roy had a harsh way of speaking, but everyone knew that he was nothing more than a big teddy bear. Even through his rough exterior, Christ was evident in him and it shone for the world around him to witness. He was the self appointed leader of the Celebration Class, although each week they rotated who would lead the lesson.

The folks shuffled around, refreshing their coffee, and getting settled in their seats. Canes and bifocals were customary accessories as was the collective shift to get them all settled. Leon made himself comfortable next to Miss Mary.

"I'll jot down the prayer requests," a lady offered, pen and paper in hand.

"Where's Peggy?" Miss Mary questioned.

Heads rotated around the room verifying that Peggy was not present.

"Anyone heard from Peggy Buck?" Roy barreled in a deep voice.

A collective answer of heads shaking and a few verbal, "Nopes," were offered.

"Better put Peggy on the prayer list," Roy suggested. "We aren't spring chickens around here. Everyday that passes is an opportunity that one of us is going to be, as they say, pushing up the daisies in the old bone yard!"

Just then, Peggy Buck appeared in the doorway.

"Peggy! You're all right!" One of the ladies called out.

Peggy surveyed the room with a ruminative look. "Yes," she said slowly and definitively.

"We were beginning to worry about you," Roy said as Peggy made her way over to an empty seat.

Peggy smiled, "Well, thank you for the concern, but I was trying to fulfill my assignment before coming to class." Peggy looked at Miss Mary and took particular notice of how youthful and happy she looked. She noted as well that Leon Jefferson, who was sitting remarkably close to Miss Mary, looked the same.

"What assignment?" asked one of the ladies. "Was I supposed to do an assignment?"

Peggy took a chair and sat down. "On Heifer."

"Heifer? You mean like the cow?" a newcomer to the class asked. "That's it!"

"What in Sam Hill's name are you talking about, Peggy?" Roy barked.

She smiled. Roy was such a gentleman, regardless of his demeanor.

"I told y'all I would find out why Spring Rock Church was selling animals. Remember?" Peggy posed the question to Roy.

"Oh yeah," Roy responded. "It's such a ludicrous thing; I tried to put it out of my mind." He paused. "I guess this falls under old business –so what did you find out?"

Peggy looked at the group and smiled as if embarrassed. "Nothing," she responded.

She had not had an opportunity to talk with Bobby about anything, least of all about Heifer. Bobby had been withdrawn and aloof since the conversation they had had about Ben. She hoped that she would see him this morning since he would be coming to the church for the staff meeting. That is why Peggy was late to class. She had waited in her car in the church parking lot for him. But, he never showed. However, her time alone in the parking lot was not in vain. It was cathartic as she allowed scenes from the past, both distance and recent, race through her mind. Sometimes she worried about herself –about her sanity. Although her thoughts stayed within reality, recently a fantasy kept making its presence known in that reality. Peggy would be remembering a place or a time from her past, Buck was present in these thoughts, but it was always painful. Buck would be in a hurry to leave Peggy –to get onto what was "more important", or he was critical of her, his way of keeping her in "her place". In these thoughts, as Buck would walk away, she could see another man in the distance —watching. She could see his face clearly. It was softly aged and neatly framed with silver hair. His eyes were pensive and of the palest blue. He gave her comfort, but she did not know why. He beckoned her. She had never seen him until after Buck's death and now he was omnipresent. She even dreamed of him —and her sleep was peaceful.

"I haven't had a chance to catch up with Bobby," she confessed. "He's been dealing with a lot recently." She paused to reflect. "Could we add him to the prayer list?"

"By all means; write him down," Roy said directing his statement to the lady jotting notes.

* * *

BEN ENTERED THE Sunday School room which was the usual stage for the staff meeting. Margaret was serving coffee from the cocktail tray which was now present at every church event. Tom sat at the far end of the table next to Ashley. What caught Ben's attention was the interaction. Ashley and Tom were conversing in an almost meditative state. Tom's compassion was evident, even from the distance, and Ashley appeared almost demure. To the left Sandy, the pianist, was doctoring her coffee in a way which more appeared as if she was adding a little coffee to her cream. Most evident to Ben, was that Bobby was not in the room.

"Good morning," Ben offered.

A collective, "Good morning," was returned.

"Did you save a little coffee for me?" he asked.

Margaret handed him a cup and then placed the tray in the middle of the table.

Ben sat down and thoughtfully arranged his notes in front of him. He looked up. "First, I would like to say to Ashley, that we are all glad you are back. You have been sorely missed."

Ashley nodded with recognition, but made no verbal comment.

"I would like to begin this meeting," Ben started, "by reading to you the prayer of Saint Francis." He opened the well-used little book which sat in front of him to the marked page and began to read.

Lord, make me an instrument of thy peace;
Where there is hatred, let me sow love;
Where there is injury, pardon;
Where there is doubt, faith;
Where there is despair, hope;
Where there is darkness, light;
And where there is sadness, joy.

O Divine Master,
Grant that I may not so much seek
To be consoled as to console;
To be understood, as to understand;
To be loved, as to love;
For it is in giving that we receive,
It is in pardoning that we are pardoned,
And it is in dying that we are born to eternal life.

He closed the book and looked up. It was noticeable that Ashley was moved –his trembling lips were clenched tightly as if to hold something in and a tear was evident in the corner of his eye. For the first time, Ben did not feel that Ashley's emotions were staged. "We have a lot to cover this morning," Ben said.

Reports were offered, suggestions made, prayer requests asked...Ben mentally took note at how smoothly and peacefully the meeting was progressing. There was no animosity and no pretense –a definite caprice was evident. He momentarily smiled, appreciating the change, which ended abruptly as Bobby entered the room. Even before Bobby spoke the whole demeanor of the room shifted, as did Ben's own mood.

Bobby moved through the room and took the empty seat next to Ashley. He patted Ashley on the shoulder and whispered just loud enough for everyone to hear, "How are you doing, brother?"

Ashley nodded in recognition and almost appeared embarrassed that he had become the center of the interruption of the meeting.

"Sorry, I'm late," Bobby offered. "I was with Ken Arnold."

Ben narrowed his eyes. *Why would he be with Ken Arnold,* he thought to himself?

Ken Arnold was a friend of Bob Buck's, and the architect who had been working on the plans for the new sanctuary building which was the catalyst of Buck's ministry at First Covenant Chapel.

"Not a problem," Ben said attempting to refocus the meeting.

"Victor Elliott was with us as well," Bobby interrupted.

Now, Ben was worried. Bobby having a meeting with both Ken Arnold and Victor Elliott, the bank president who was crazy enough to offer the $8.5 million loan to Buck, could only mean one thing —a hidden agenda.

"Do you have something you would like to share with us?" Ben asked with obvious irritation.

"Sure! Thank you," Bobby said with returned sarcasm. "I was going to wait until the end of the meeting, but…since you asked."

Did I have a choice? Ben thought to himself as he smiled.

"Ken Arnold has agreed to make finishing up the plans for the new sanctuary a priority," Bobby said with complete pride. "And, Victor Elliott has informed me that the offer for the loan is still ours for the taking."

Tom looked at Ben. Both of the faces revealed the same thought. "Uh, Bobby," Ben started, trying to collect his thoughts at the same time he spoken. "What are you talking about?"

"What am I talking about?" Bobby echoed rhetorically. "The new sanctuary building that *my father* was working on before his untimely death."

The emphasis which Bobby placed on "my father" did not go unnoticed by Ben. Nor, did it go unnoticed by Margaret who raised an eyebrow at Bobby's possessive intent.

Margaret raised her fingertips to her temple and applied pressure – *another weekly staff meeting,* she thought.

"Bobby," Ben spoke firmly, "this is not something you can arbitrarily decide on your own."

"I haven't decided anything on my own," Bobby defended himself. "We had a church meeting and we voted." He turned, looked at Tom and snidely said, "Remember, the one in which the district superintendent threw *you* out?"

That dreadful meeting flooded back into Ben's memory. It was certainly one for the history books –more proof that not all Christian gatherings are that of peace. It should have been a simple meeting to vote on approving the $8.5 million loan to build the new sanctuary for which Buck had been campaigning. The problem was the church could not afford it. Tom brought this to the attention of the congregation, which Bobby was prompt to retaliate against.

"Tom was not thrown out," Ben defended, "he chose to leave."

Tom appreciated Ben's words but could handle this alone. He had no intention of getting into a shouting match with Bobby Buck. "Look Bobby, with all due respect to what your father started, the finance committee has met and feels a loan of this magnitude would destroy this church. We simply can't afford it. The monthly payment would kill us."

Bobby looked at Tom and smiled. Calmly he said, "Ahh, that's where you are misinformed, as usual, Brother Tom." He did not miss the opportunity for the slight. "In talking with Victor, the bank is offering us an interest only loan. And," he said with added emphasis, "the first payment will not be due until eighteen months after the completion of construction! That would give us more than enough time to fill the pews with even more giving units!"

Ben never liked the term "giving units"; it did not reflect how he felt about his parishioners.

"We can't do something like that!" Tom protested.

"It's an awesome deal!" Bobby replied. "Of course we can do it!"

Ben moved to the edge of his chair. "Gentlemen," he said trying to calm the tone. Directing his gaze toward Bobby he said, "Bobby, there are Biblical ways in which to borrow money. An interest only loan does not fall into the Biblical means."

"Interest only loans were not part of the banking industry when the Bible was written," Bobby retorted. "They are the way of the world now!" He was becoming stronger and more definitive in his tone.

Ben was quick to retort, "So are sex, drugs, and rock n roll, but you don't see me offering them as programs in the church!"

The demeanor in the room had totally changed since Bobby had arrived. Tension was not in short supply.

Bobby directed a piercing gaze toward Ben, "This isn't about Biblical financial responsibility. We both know that —don't we, Ben?" Bobby's words came across as a threat.

The others in the room exchanged quizzical glances.

In a very controlled manner Ben replied, "It has everything to do with Biblical responsibility." He paused. "And, nothing else."

Bobby stood up, forcefully pushing his chair with the back of his legs. "I'll take this to the finance committee." He walked to the door, stopping short he turned and looked directly at Ben. "This church *will* build my father's dream." He stormed out of the room.

Peggy Buck was walking to her car when her son, Bobby, stormed out of the church. She took a deep breath. Bobby was hurting, she knew that. But, she did not know how to stop his hurt. Life comes at us fast –and with no warning signs.

"Bobby!" she called after him.

Bobby looked up to see his mother. He stopped and a small smile came to his lips. The sight of her was comforting to him. "Hi, Mom," he said in a voice which almost sounded defeated.

"How about lunch?" Peggy asked.

Slowly, he nodded his head in acceptance.

* * *

BOBBY SIPPED HIS cola through a straw from the glass which remained on the table, as if he were a six year old little boy. Peggy watched him in silence, feeling his pain. How she wished she could make things different. Bobby had changed since his father's death. His face was bitter, his shoulders rounded; he had become cold and unpredictable.

"It's a lovely day out, isn't it?" she said to her son.

"Sure."

"How's work going?" she continued.

"Same as usual."

Peggy looked off in the distance. She had a sudden urge to cradle Bobby and rock him back and forth, like a baby. She wanted to stroke his head and say, *everything will be all right, my love. Mama's here, you do not need to be afraid.* She glanced back at her son and reality returned. He was a full grown man with lines of aging across his own forehead.

"You know, Bobby," she began, "our happiness in the world is based on what we do, what we give, and what we get in return."

Bobby looked up at his mother, but had no response. His stare was full of anger.

Peggy stared back at her son. "Why do you think you are so entitled?" his mother questioned. She was becoming angry herself.

"What do you want from me, Mom?" He shook his head slowly in disillusionment. "Do you want me to stand up and shout 'hooray! I've got another brother!' Maybe Ben could come move in with me and we'll share a room and catch up on years lost."

Peggy took a deep breath and let it out. She did not have the answer. "I just want you to let things settle before you do anything."

"Settle? What's to settle? Do you think something is going to change when it settles?"

"Yes. I do," his mother said emphatically.

"What?"

Peggy looked at him pensively and her face softened. In a hopeful voice she said, "Your attitude."

Bobby lifted his hand to his face and rubbed it as if to clear away a fog. When he lowered his hands, he smiled at his mother. "Could we change the subject, please?"

"Okay. In fact, I do have something else I have been wanting to ask you about."

"What's that?" Bobby replied.

"Well, some of the folks in my Bible study class have said that Spring Rock Community Church is selling animals as a fundraiser — in order to send mission dollars to impoverished areas. Do you know anything about this?"

"Yeh! It's a wonderful program. I'd love for First Covenant to get involved," he said with enthusiasm. "But, they're not sending dollars. They send the animals."

"Ah," Peggy responded, as if it were beginning to make sense.

"It's through an organization called Heifer International. They are really making a difference in this world."

Peggy tilted her head to listen more intently. "How?"

"In a nutshell, through donations, Heifer sets up projects in certain areas all over the world and teaches the people how to care for and breed the animals. The animals in return provide milk, eggs, wool, and other vital necessities for the community. The key here is passing on the gift. Each community that has received animals from Heifer must pass their first born animals onto another community in need."

"What a great thing," Peggy replied. "I want to learn more."

"I could introduce you to Gerry Jonah, if you like. He's the one over at Spring Rock that heads up the missions program there."

"I think I would like that," his mother replied. She paused for a moment and then asked, "Is he any relation to Uriah Jonah?"

"He's Uriah's father."

Peggy was excited to learn more about this mission. She needed something more to do with her time, and she wanted to do something that would make a difference to somebody in this world.

Chapter Thirty-five

TOM LEANED BACK in his chair and stared out his office window. The afternoon sun shone across the lake and the beauty was magnificent and tranquil. He thought about the events of the morning staff meeting. He shook his head in disbelief of the continued fiscal irresponsibility of Bobby Buck, and the fact that he wanted to drag an entire congregation into the abyss with him.

Tom thought back to his weekly meetings with Bob Buck at the Dixie Diner, where they went over the finances of the church. Tom never felt comfortable with Buck's careless way of handling the church's money, but he had always deferred to Buck, thinking that Buck was older and wiser. At the time, Tom did not have much experience in dealing with church finances. He rather assumed that accounting for a church was different than other businesses. But, what he knew now was that a church is a business just like any other and handling the finances was no different.

Tom thought about Bobby's suggestion of an interest only loan and suddenly he remembered a similar conversation he had had with Buck. Buck had the entire scheme planned out —an interest only loan with no payments due for eighteen months after the completion of $8.5 million structure. Just before completion, he would take out a second mortgage for $250,000 for furnishing. "The congregation wouldn't even have to know about the second mortgage," Tom remembered Buck saying to him. When Tom had questioned Buck about that, Buck said, "Brother Tom, that's what the church administration is for. You can't involve the membership in everything. Too many hands stirring the pot makes for a godawful mess."

"Where is that file?" Tom said out loud, remembering he still had all the notes from his meetings with Buck. He swiveled his chair around and opened the file drawer on his desk. He thumbed through the files. Not there. He looked around his office trying to remember where he had stored the notes from all those meetings. He went to the credenza on the opposite side of his office and opened the drawer forcefully, causing the framed picture atop to shake and nearly topple over, but he caught it before it spilled to the ground. He glanced at the picture resting safely in his hand. It was of Lisa and their two sons while on vacation at the beach several years ago. He gently placed it back on the credenza and began to thumb through the files there. Not there. He stood up straight and brought his fist to his mouth. Deep in thought he scanned the room. "What did I do with those files?" Everything was so orderly in his office. His eye caught the gold handle of the closet in the back corner of his office and he recalled several cardboard boxes of stuff which he had stored in there. Determined, he walked to the closet, opened the door and lifted out one of the boxes. He carried the box to his desk, set it in the middle, and opened the overlapped flaps. He began to sort through the papers and files which had been stacked into the box with no sort of concern. A report about new tax laws, he tossed it in the trash can. An application to a gym, which he had intended to join, followed the tax law into the trash. A Valentine's Day card from Lisa, which he opened and read again with fond memories. He set the card up in a display fashion on his desk. Minutes from a PTA meeting at his sons' school. He glanced through them to jog his memory as to why he might have saved them in the first place; he tossed them in the trash. He peered back down into the box to the next piece of paper which more than caught his attention. He stared hard at it; it nearly stopped his heart.

"Oh, my God!" he said in disbelief.

Frozen, he stared into the box. He took a deep breath and his chest shuttered as he breathed out. Slowly, he reached his hand into the box and lifted several legal size pages which were stapled together in the upper left hand corner. Holding the papers in his hand he mindlessly walked backwards until he felt his chair at the back of his legs and he sat down, his eyes fixed on the pages he held in his hands. Tom's mind raced, his stomach turned, his heart ached, and his fists became clenched and wrinkled the edges of the papers which they held.

Quickly, Tom stood with such force that his chair hit the wall behind him. He snatched his keys off the corner of his desk and stormed out his door. As he passed his secretary in the front office he spoke curtly, "I'll be back later!"

The drive from Salem to Wakefield was tedious, especially for the second time in one day. Tom was agitated and his driving was aggressive, which was unusual for Tom. He pulled into the parking lot and unintentionally slammed his car door when he got out. Realizing his anger, he took a deep breath and tried to compose himself before walking into the church. He slowed his pace and walked in a controlled manner.

Margaret looked up from her desk. "You're back?"

Tom smiled painfully. "Is Ben back there?"

"I think so. Let me check." She picked up her phone and began to press buttons.

Not giving her the opportunity, Tom said, "That's okay." He headed down the hall to Ben's office.

The door was opened and Ben was sitting at his desk. Tom walked over and tossed the papers down in front of Ben, and then turned and started pacing back and forth in front of Ben's desk. Ben watched Tom for a moment noting his agitation and then picked up the papers which had been tossed before him. He looked at the papers, flipping to the following pages and then looked up at Tom. Ben's expression was of confusion.

"What's this?" Ben asked.

"House comps," Tom replied sharply.

"I can see that," Ben returned, even more confused.

"Lisa and I refinanced our house about a year and a half ago."

Ben shook his head still not able to make sense out of the situation. He looked at the papers again. "Did something go wrong with the loan?" Ben questioned not really knowing what to ask.

"The loan is fine," Tom snapped.

Although Ben had no clue what, obviously something was upsetting Tom terribly. He stood up from his desk and walked around to the front. He gestured to one of the two chairs and said, "Why don't you sit down?"

Tom sat on the front edge of one of the chairs and Ben sat comfortably in the other. "Look at it!" Tom repeated in a forceful voice.

Ben glanced at the stack of papers again and then back at Tom. "I'm sorry Tom. You're going to have to help me out here. I'm just not understanding what is wrong."

"Look at the bottom house."

Ben looked down.

"That's my house," Tom's voice commanded ownership.

Ben nodded, but still needed more direction.

"Look to the right. Do you see the breezeway that connects the house to the garage?"

Ben did see it. And, now understood why Tom was so upset. Ben closed his eyes in disbelief for a moment and then opened them to see the picture again. It was faint, but clear enough to see that standing in the breezeway of Tom's house was Lisa. And, she was kissing a man who was clearly not Tom and clearly his own father, Bob Buck.

"I see," Ben said.

Tom slumped back into the chair and stared off into the distance. There was silence in the room. "It all makes sense now." Tom paused. "Just the other day Lisa told me I didn't need to worry about the other man, because he was dead." He spoke as if he was in a trance. "Bob Buck is dead. Bob Buck was the other man. Bob Buck may be the father of the baby inside Lisa."

"Tom," Ben said, not knowing what else to say.

"Bob Buck has stripped me, this land, this church, and this community of every bit of human decency." Tom's voice still remained tranced.

Ben thought about his own situation and what would happen to what was left of this community when they found out that he, too, was actually Bob Buck's son. It's true, Ben thought to himself, children do suffer the sins of their parents.

Chapter Thirty-six

"HEY, GIRL!" BEN said with enthusiasm. He kneeled down to re-tie one of his tennis shoes and waited for Angel to reach him. He put both hands on her head and petted vigorously. "How are you today?" She licked him across the face. *If only others would greet me with this enthusiasm,* he thought to himself. Specifically, he was thinking about Sylvia. They had not seen each other in over a week and had barely talked. And, that left him feeling empty. He could no longer deny it. He was in love with Dr. Sylvia DiLeo. He just was not certain if she felt the same. Dr. Richard Davies somehow seemed to be omnipresent and Ben was beginning to wonder if maybe he was the one who was interfering with Sylvia and Davies' relationship. He patted Angel one more time. "I'll be back girl," he said, and headed out for a run.

Running was Ben's best therapy. It cleared his mind and helped him focus his path. And, today he knew exactly what he was going to do. He was going to the hospital, find Sylvia and tell her they needed to talk. And then, he was finally going to tell her how he felt about her.

After two miles, he made it back to the house and ran up the stairs with exuberant energy. He showered, dressed quickly and headed out —before he lost his nerve. On the drive to the hospital he played the scene over and over again —none was the same. "I love you, Sylvia," he said out loud. "Sylvia, I have wanted to tell you for a long time how I feel about you. Sylvia, I think I am falling in love with you." He laughed out loud. *I don't think I'm falling in love. I know I am in love,* he thought to himself.

He pulled into the parking lot at Salem Regional Medical Center and it into the space marked for "Chaplains Only". He felt better than he had felt in a long time. He glanced in the review mirror and nodded with approval, and then bowed his head to asked for God's blessing. Closing the car door behind him he reached over his shoulder with the clicker to lock the door, and then, hurriedly made his way toward the entrance.

"Reverend Montague!" he heard from the side. Ben slowed. Turning, he saw Richard Davies approaching.

No God. Not now, Ben thought to in a tone he feared audible.

Richard Davies approached him. "How are you today, Reverend Montague?"

Neither man offered a hand to shake.

"I'm fine. And, you?"

"Better than fine!" Davies said with a hidden agenda. He paused. "I have been wanting to thank you for taking Sylvia home the other evening. I had intended to, but since I was the informal host of the dinner party, I couldn't rightly just get up and leave."

His words burned Ben. "No thanks necessary, Dr. Davies," Ben replied. "I didn't do it for you."

There was silence for a moment. Davies smiled slightly. "Well, I went by her place later to check on her and she had definitely gotten home," Davies paused to add emphasis to his hidden meaning, "safely." He paused again. Ben made no response. "Always good to have a man of God around —you can trust them."

"At least she could count on somebody to take care of her. I suspect left to you, you would have stuck her in her car and let her drive home after you intentionally got her drunk." Ben's voice showed his anger.

"Think what you will. But, you are sadly mistaken. I took very good care of her. I stayed with her all night to make sure she had extraordinary care. I even took her to work the next morning." Davies' words were manipulative.

Ben clearly understood what Davies was implying. The thought of Sylvia with another man hurt him deeply. His stomach sank. He could not believe it was true. He did not want to believe it was true. *Could it be true?*

"Exactly what are you trying to say, Dr. Davies?"

"I'm not saying anything," he replied nonchalantly.

Ben's blood was boiling and it was taking every ounce of strength he had not to haul off and punch Davies. He wanted to know the truth. "Did you sleep with Sylvia?" Ben asked, point blank.

Davies smiled lightly. "Reverend Montague, may I remind you, you are not a priest and I am not Catholic. I am not confessing anything."

The two men stared at each other. Silence.

In a moment, Ben interrupted, "If you'll excuse me, I have someplace I need to be." And, he turned and walked back toward his parked car.

"Have a nice day," Davies called after him.

Ben opened the car door and got back in his car. He slammed the door behind him and started the engine. Closing his eyes he repeated softly, "The Lord is my shepherd, I shall not want. The Lord is my shepherd, I shall not want." In a few moments he opened his eyes and put the gear shift in reverse. Before backing, he paused and took a deep breath. Blowing the air out of his lungs hard, he pushed the gear shift back into park, turned off the engine again, and got out of the car. He closed the door and then lifted the clicker over his shoulder to lock the door and with a determined stride, he headed toward the hospital entrance, as originally planned.

* * *

HE RODE THE elevator to the third floor, the most likely place to find Sylvia. Before stepping out of the elevator and onto the floor, he took a deep breath. He looked around. The all-to-familiar halls seemed narrow and tight. The hospital smells disturbed him and fluorescent lights were blinding. He slowly walked over to the nurses station and stood there as if void of thought. He moved his head from left to right. Sylvia was not in sight. He took another deep breath. Just as he filled his lungs he felt a jab in both of his sides which forced the air out of his lungs in a gasp. He made a muffled sound and quickly turned.

"Hey there, stranger. You look lost," Sylvia said with a smile on her face.

"You startled me," he said quickly.

"I'm sorry. I just couldn't resist doing that." She lifted her shoulders in a shrug. "The little girl in me."

Ben could not help but smile warmly at her.

"Looking for someone?" She asked after a brief moment of silence.

"No. I mean, yes."

Sylvia looked at him confused. "Well, which is it?"

"I just was wondering if you had time for a break," Ben asked nervously.

She looked at her watch. "I would welcome one," she said enthusiastically.

"Come on," he gestured toward the elevator. She followed.

When the elevator doors closed, Ben stood there silently. He smiled at her when he noticed she was staring at him oddly.

She squinted her eyes and looked at him seriously. "Are you okay?"

"Yeh. Sure. Why do you ask?"

"You look like something's bothering you?"

"No."

"Okay," she replied with a tone of disbelief, not wanting to pry further.

When the door opened on the bottom floor, they exited.

"Would you like to get something to drink?" Ben asked.

Sylvia looked at him again inquisitively, "Sure."

They walked into the cafeteria. Each got a large cup of iced tea, simultaneously applied a plastic lid and stuck a straw through the hole in the top.

"Well done, Watson," she said jokingly. "What's next?"

Ben allowed a slight laugh. "Why don't we go out in the courtyard? It's nice out today."

"Sure." She walked through the door as he held it open for her.

Outside, they found a table with an umbrella and sat down. Nearby was a group of doctors in scrubs. Ben fiddled with his cup. Sylvia watched him. He looked at her and smiled tenderly. He wanted to say something, he tried, but nothing came out.

"What's wrong? Did somebody steal your new toy?"

He looked up at her and made a slight noise in agreement. If she only knew that was exactly how he felt. Dr. Richard Davies had stolen something very important to him. "No!" he said adamantly. "It's just been a rough day. You know, we preachers have off days every once in awhile too." He paused. "The day started off okay, but, it's kind of faded here in the middle."

"I'm sorry," she responded sweetly. "Is there anything I can do to help?"

Ben gathered his thoughts. He looked at her face; she was beautiful, and sweet, and caring —the very woman of which he had always dreamed. In a few moments, he finally spoke. "I enjoy your company very much."

Sylvia understood very little about this disjointed conversation, "And, I enjoy yours," she returned in a monotone, confused voice.

He looked into her eyes with serious emotion. "Listen, I do not want to stand in the way of you and Dr. Davies."

Sylvia straightened her back, tilted her head to the right, and a baffled look came across her face. "You don't?" she asked curiously.

"No," he responded firmly.

That was not exactly the response she wanted to hear. She stared at him for a moment. "First off, why would you think that you are coming between Dr. Davies and me, and secondly, why wouldn't you want to?" She was becoming defensive.

"Look, we are good friends and I don't want that to change." His voice was soft and sad.

"Yes, I know. We are *good* friends," she said with sarcasm. "And, it has been quite obvious for some time now that you *don't* want that to change."

Now, Ben was feeling a little defensive. "Look, when I saw you in his arms, kissing him that night, I should have gotten the message."

She interrupted him abruptly, "Look! Look! Look! Will you stop saying look! And, you look! I thought you ministers weren't supposed to be judgmental! You never let me explain that night! I was not kissing him! He was kissing me and I was trying to get away from him!" She lowered her voice into a whisper to keep from drawing attention from others.

193

"Maybe so, but there is more between the two of you, and you know that," he said accusatorially.

"I don't know any such thing, but you seem to. Why don't you tell me, since you seem to know so much!"

"Look." He paused, "I'm sorry I didn't mean to say that again." He paused again. "I didn't come here to argue with you. If you only knew, that is the last thing I wanted to do with you."

She looked at him. Her eyes widened and she smiled sweetly, "You're jealous."

He stiffened his neck and pushed his shoulders back. "I am not!" But, he was mad now and could not hold his tongue. "You spent the night with him, Sylvia!" He quickly stood and started to walk away. After a few steps he stopped and turned back toward her. "You're right, Dr. DiLeo. I am jealous." And then, he turned back around and continued to leave.

Sylvia was a little taken back and her first instinct was to let him go. But, she knew she could not do that; she had to act quickly. She stood up, as if her legs had a mind of their own, and went after him. "Ben!" she quietly called. Catching up to him and grabbing his right elbow with her hand, she gently, but firmly, turned him toward her. "You can't just make an accusation like that and then walk away."

He stopped and turned to look at her. Her face showed deep hurt, and the mere fact that she came after him spoke more than words.

"I have no idea what you are talking about," she continued.

Ben looked at her firmly. "Did you sleep with Dr. Davies?"

Sylvia's eyes widened with surprise. "I have never spent the night with Dr. Davies or slept with him at anytime, and what's more, I have never even had the desire."

Ben's face remained like stone. He made no reply. That was all he needed to hear. He turned away from her again and went back into the hospital from the courtyard. He walked firmly down the long corridor focused only on his destination. The sound of his dress shoes against the terrazzo echoed through the hallway. When he reached the end he made a sharp right onto the hallway which housed the administrative offices of the hospital. When he reached the door marked Dr. Richard Davies, Chief of Staff, he opened the door without pause.

Inside a pretty young woman exposing ample bosom sat at a desk. *How apropos,* Ben thought to himself. "I would like to see Dr. Davies, please," he said sternly.

"May I tell him your name, please?" the young lady asked.

"Reverend Benjamin Montague."

The young woman picked up the telephone. Ben waited. In a brief moment she said, "He said to please send you in." She gestured at a door to her right.

Ben walked to the door, took a deep breath and then put his hand on the knob, opened the door and walked in.

Dr. Davies sat behind a large mahogany desk covered with a disarray of stacks of papers and medical journals. Behind him was an oversized credenza which was home to what appeared to be an assortment of distracting computers. Two burnished-brown leather chairs sat in front of his desk. One was littered with an overcoat, doctor's jacket, and a few other miscellaneous articles of clothing.

Davies looked at Ben, but did not stand from his seated position behind his desk, nor did he offer Ben a seat. "Well, Reverend Benjamin Montague," he said with rising sarcasm. "To what do I owe this second visit in one day from the good man?"

Ben stood firmly with his feet planted squarely in one place. He spoke very slowly. "I do not care what you do with your personal life. I do not care if you hit on half the nurses in the hospital, I do not care if you sleep with each of them as a one night stand, I do not care if you carve each of their names into your headboard and call it art." Ben paused for a moment and crossed the very large room so that Davies had to rotate his chair to the left to be able to see Ben. The two men faced each other, Ben still standing firmly. He continued, "I do not even care if you come to my church and make a mockery of worship. That is between you and God." He paused again and took one slow step forward. "But, I do care about Sylvia DiLeo and I do care if you slander her reputation and her integrity."

Davies smiled coyly. "What did she tell you? Did she say she didn't sleep with me? You know as well as I do, Man, she was drunk that night."

Ben took another slow step forward. He leaned his face lower to be level with Davies. "You leave Sylvia alone. Is that clear?" He did not give Davies a chance to respond. "If you want to attack somebody, you go after me." Then he straightened up. "You are nothing but a coward who feeds his ego off of shallow relationships and hiding behind his own fear of the truth." And then, he turned back toward the door. "If you want to go after me, go ahead." He started walking slowly toward to door. "I'll make it easy for you. Here's my back." When he reached the door, he stopped for a moment. Then he swung it open and left.

Chapter Thirty-seven

FINALLY HOME FROM a too long and emotionally draining day, Sylvia poured herself a glass of Chardonnay and leaned back on the oversized off-white sofa in her living room. She rubbed her hand across her forehead to ease the pain of the stress. Why had Ben just walked away from her when she told him she had not slept with Richard Davies? And, why on earth was Ben so blind to the way she felt about him? She lifted her free hand into a fist and slammed it into the sofa. "Ahhhhhh!" she screamed. She could not deal with this anymore. How dense could a man possibly be? "What more do I have to do for him to see that I love him," she said out loud. "How much clearer do I need to make it?" She took a deep breath and blew it out. Quickly downing half her glass of wine, she got up and began to pace around the room. "I am over this! I am over this!" She yelled to no one in particular. She walked to the wall switch, flipped off the lights and then headed toward her bedroom to go to bed. "Alone!"

Chapter Thirty-eight

JULIA SAT ON a bench outside of Harry's on the Square. It was a quarter to eight; she had arrived early. The night air was crisp and pleasant, but just around the corner was the promise of the sweltering summer nights that would soon be upon them. She breathed in the freshness and smiled. Julia was happy – finally content with who she was and what she had to offer the world.

The square in Salem was a busy place on Friday evenings. Leaning back on the bench she surveyed the scene. Across the street, Leo's was already bursting at the seams. Under a street lamp a young couple was kissing. A smile broke across her face. What a gift to be able to love and show affection. She was envious.

Walking toward her, a man wearing blue jeans, a plaid short-sleeved dress shirt, and a black derby hat caught her attention. As he moved closer, what she noticed most were his eyes, which were fixed on her. In particular, she noticed that his eyelids bobbed up and down as if they were attached by rubber bands. She smiled. He returned the gesture, then tipped his hat and added, "Evening ma'am," as he walked past her and into Harry's.

"That was odd," she said out loud, speaking only to herself.

"Have you been waiting long?" she heard called from the other side. Julia turned her head to see Margaret and her husband John.

"Hey!" Julia responded joyfully as she stood up. She reached her arms around John's neck and gave him a hug. "Good to see you! No, not too long. Besides, this is a great place for the fine art of people watching."

Another couple walked up. "This is Eileen and Jim Etrows," Margaret said, and then gestured toward Julia. "This is Julia Matthews."

Hands were extended and jovial conversation passed around.

"I brought a bottle of wine," Julia said as she held it up for approval.

"So did I," responded Margaret displaying hers.

Inside, Harry's was much larger than it appeared from the outside. The old buildings of Salem were full of charm and character. The slightly uneven floorboards had been refinished and the diffused glow of the light reflected from their shine. The windows across the front were draped in rich brown velvet. Small café tables and bentwood chairs of cherry wood were dotted across the room. Each table was a pedestal for a crimson votive candle. The interior walls displayed the same brick as the exterior. The room was crowded and people were still trying to settle in their seats amid conversations which were too enjoyable to end.

"This is darling!" Julia said as they made their way into the venue.

"Doesn't it make you think you've just stepped off the Champs Elysees?" Margaret replied. "Let's take that table over there." She pointed toward the front, near the small stage area.

"That's a great table. Let's get it before someone else nabs it!" Eileen grabbed her husband's hand and pulled him along quickly. Margaret, John, and Julia followed. Margaret pulled a small square tablecloth from the straw bag she was carrying and draped it over the little round table. Eileen placed wineglasses atop and Julia set her wine bottle dead center.

"To the side please," Margaret said in a jovial command as she held a small vase of richly colored zinnias which had been carefully nestled for transportation in the straw bag.

Julia smiled and complied by sliding the wine bottle to the left so Margaret could place the vase of flowers in the center. She glanced around viewing the other tables being individually decorated by their guests. This was an art form in-and-of-itself. A larger table displayed an elaborate arrangement of sunflowers bursting with yellow petals, breadsticks stood in ceramic pots at either end of the table, and paisley cloth napkins were folded at each place –the very vision of what she imaged Tuscany to be.

To the left another table sported a motif that was clearly from South of the border.

"This is a charming place!" Julia said. "What a clever idea."

"We love it," replied Margaret. "It's just a music hall...they provide the place and the entertainment, you provide your food and drink. You can tell the regulars, they're the ones with the really decked out tables!"

"How fun!" Julia smiled.

"All the musicians are local, and most of them are really good. You won't believe the talent!"

Julia glanced to the stage. Two or three people were tuning guitars, one a mandolin. Small stools were arranged with music stands in front of them. To the side sat a straight back wooden chair. In the chair sat a man holding an acoustic guitar in his lap. He was tapping his foot and bouncing his fingers on the front of the guitar. Keeping rhythm with his foot and fingers were his eyelids –all keeping time to the silence of whatever his private thoughts were. Julia recognized him as the man who greeted her on the street.

They settled themselves at the table and Margaret pulled a wooden cheese board from the straw basket, placing it on the table. She added cheese, crackers, and fruit which the others immediately began to enjoy. John uncorked a bottle of red wine and filled the glasses. Other tables were doing similarly. Julia lifted her glass to her lips and took a sip. "Fabulous!" she said gesturing to her glass of wine. She set it back on the table and surveyed the room. It was elegant, artsy, and fun. She was glad she had decided to come with Margaret and John. As she took in the surroundings she felt a presences of someone. She turned her head slightly to the left, toward the stage, and her eyes, once again, met with the eyes of the gentleman who passed her on the street. Peering from beneath his black derby hat their eyes locked momentarily. He offered a small wink and then went back to tuning his guitar. Julia smiled slightly —he was so odd, but so intriguing. She took another sip of her wine and tried to shake his image from her mind.

"See that young man at the right of the stage?" Margaret asked, "he's really good. He's a high school senior, but writes all his own music. Wait until you hear him!"

Julia glanced toward the young man and then peered from the corner of her eye toward the gentleman in the derby hat, observing again how his eye lids kept rhythm with the beat of tuning guitars. "How many people are performing tonight?" Julia asked.

"There are usually about five or six," John replied. "They go in rounds. It's pretty neat. You get a variety of styles. Kind of like putting your stereo on shuffle."

"Have you heard all of them before?" Julia inquired.

John glanced around the stage. "All but the one in the very back." He nodded his head in the direction of a middle aged woman tuning a mandolin.

"She's earthy looking," Julia commented.

John smiled.

"And, the guy in the derby hat, who is he?" Julia tried hard to sound nonchalant.

"His name is Arnold. He's a regular here. He's pretty good. Really what he is, is a poet. Be sure to listen to his words!"

Arnold? Julia thought to herself. *What kind of name is Arnold?* She was expecting something more like David or Charles —but, Arnold! "He sounds like a nerd," Julia said in jest.

"Could be," John returned, "but he sure does have talent." John paused and smiled obviously having more to add which Julia would find humorous.

Noticing his smirk, Julia was curious. "Pray tell."

"You want to know his last name?" John offered through his own amusement.

Julia nodded.

"Pigeon."

"Pigeon?" Julia repeated.

John nodded with a mischievous look.

"You're kidding me?" she asked. "His name is Arnold Pigeon?"

John continued to nod.

Julia glanced back toward the stage to look at Arnold Pigeon again. She shook her head in disbelief. *Arnold Pigeon,* she thought to herself.

The lights dimmed and Harry, the owner of the venue, welcomed the crowd and introduced the talent. Candlelight glowed throughout and the chattering of the people died out as the first musician was introduced and began to play. Somehow, in this setting, the wine, cheese, and fruit tasted just a little better.

Julia settled back into her chair and took in the moment. She felt fine. She was more at peace than ever before in her life. The woman with the mandolin took the center stool on the stage and began to play and sing. The melody was beautifully sad and she sang about broken hearts and lost love. Julia could well relate. She took a deep breath and smiled. Leaning toward Margaret she whispered, "Thanks for inviting me tonight." Her words were solemn and sincere.

As the woman with the mandolin closed, Arnold Pigeon stood and prepared to move to the center stool. Julia watched him carefully. As he sat on the stool, he plugged in and adjusted the cord to his electric acoustic guitar. Julia listened intently as he thanked the crowd for being there while at the same time giving his instrument some last minute tuning. Arnold Pigeon's voice was soft, but deep; it resonated in the room and Julia thought it oddly sexy in comparison to his overall appearance. His skin was very fair and somewhat pale. His eyelids were troublesome, the way they bobbed, giving an appearance of someone who was only "home" about half the time. He strummed a few cords on his guitar. Julia noticed his hands which were large, strong, and downright gorgeous. He put his right hand flat across the strings to silence their vibration and then said, "This one is for the pretty lady at the front table." He nodded his head toward Julia as his hand took off across the strings with a thunderous melody.

Julia blushed and then looked around to see if Arnold Pigeon was perhaps referring to someone else. Margaret elbowed Julia acknowledging that it was indeed Julia that Arnold had intended. Julia felt a butterfly in her stomach as she listened to Arnold Pigeon sing about the possibilities of love and love to come. His words were beautiful and poetic and the message was in definite contrast to the woman with the mandolin. At the end of his song he stood from the stool, lifted his black derby hat from his head and tipped it toward Julia. She blushed again.

"Looks like you have yourself an admirer," Margaret whispered.

Julia chortled, "Just what I need, some flower child reject!"

"He's a great musician!" Margaret offered in return.

"Yeh, but, have you seen his eyelids? The way they bounce? I don't think he's got much else in there."

The audience began to applaud as the young man in high school took the center stool. "Listen to this guy," John leaned over and said to the two women. "Now, he's a real philosopher!"

The crowd roared as they listened to the young man poke fun at the government and the public school system through his music. At the end, the entire room stood in applause.

"That was fabulous!" Julia said as the lights in room brightened signaling the end of the evening.

Julia was helping to clean up the table and pack the contents back into the straw bag in which Margaret had brought them when she felt a slight tap on her shoulder. She turned. Arnold Pigeon was standing beside her with his guitar case in his hand and his derby hat on his head.

"Hi," Julia said a little startled.

He extended his hand. "I'm Arnold."

She reached her hand to his. "Julia," she said in a dazed fashion.

"I just wanted to thank you for so kindly being the object of my affection this evening." Arnold's voice was mesmerizing as he stared into her eyes.

"My pleasure," she returned, now a little confused. Was she merely a stage prop?

"Would you like to join me for some dessert down at the Pastry Shoppe?" he asked.

Julia turned and looked at Margaret as a child asking permission from a parent. Margaret smiled but offered no comment.

"Huh...," Julia was lost for words.

"It's just two doors down. They have the best chocolate eclairs!" He offered.

She hesitated a moment more and then said, "Sure, why not?"

"Great!" he said and then turned and looked at the others picking up around the table. "Thank you all for coming this evening. I hope you enjoyed it."

"Oh!" Julia said with embarrassment. "These are my friends," she pointed to them, "Margaret, John, Jim, and Eileen."

Pamela Jackson

"Pleasure," he said as a half statement as he extended his hand to each of them.

John gripped his hand. "Enjoyed it throughly," he said. "We've seen you several times before and each time is more pleasurable."

"Thank you for kindness, my friend," Arnold returned. "Hope you all will keep coming back." Then he turned to Julia and offered her his elbow along with, "My lady."

Julia placed her hand in the crook of his elbow. As they headed toward the door she turned back and looked at Margaret with an expression which clearly relayed *this is really odd!*

They walked silently down the sidewalk but, from the corner of her eye she could see Arnold's eyelids bobbing up and down. Panic ran through her. *What am I doing?!* She stiffened her back and shoulders. *I am not going to be able to have any sort of intelligent conversation with this man!*

They reached the Pastry Shoppe. Arnold Pigeon opened the door for her with one hand and bid her entrance with the other as if she were royalty.

"Thank you," she said, feeling quite out of her element. Julia always had the upper hand; she was naturally poised with confidence and words never eluded her —for some reason, tonight was an exception.

They settled at a small table covered with a simple white tablecloth. The bentwood chairs were reminiscent of a 1930's free public library. The shoppe was crowded with a mixture of young and older people. A group of teenagers sat at a table in a back corner being a little louder than they should, but nobody really seemed to mind.

"Have you ever been here?" Arnold asked as he helped her with her chair.

"No, this is my first time. When did they open?"

"About a month ago," he replied. "Can you believe how they have changed this downtown Salem area? It's becoming the real night spot!"

"I live over in Wakefield, so I don't come this way that often, but, it's really charming."

"Wakefield! That's only ten minutes away," he said with surprise.

"Twenty, if you have any respect for the speed limits," she came back, feeling a little bit more like herself.

"Ah, details," he shook his head.

The waitress approached the table, "How are you all this evening?" She turned and looked at Arnold. "Good to see you, Dr. Pigeon. Did you all have a big crowd tonight?"

"We did. This is Julia. She's from out of town, way over in Wakefield. First night out on the town so we must impress her."

The waitress turned toward Julia, "Welcome!"

Arnold continued, "Julia, this is Rose. She is the owner of this fine establishment. So, she is the best waitress in the joint!" He smiled and his eyelids bobbled.

"Thank you," Julia replied as she observed the woman standing there. Rose was an older woman and very robust —obviously a victim of her own pastry shoppe. Her face was sweet and her eyes friendly. People probably stopped by just to say hello to her.

"What can I get for you all this evening?" Rose asked.

"Two chocolate eclairs and pot of herbal tea. Two cups of course!" Arnold offered without consulting Julia.

"Coming up!" Rose turned and headed back toward the pastry counter.

"You like herbal tea, don't you?" Arnold asked.

"Sure," she said meekly, feeling a little off balance again. She watched him thoughtfully unfold his napkin and place it in his lap. *A simple task,* she thought, requiring just a little too much effort on his part. "Did she call you Dr. Pigeon?"

"Ahhh, sweet old lady! She has a great sense of humor too! She is the reason this little shoppe will be so successful. She knows how to woo a customer!"

Julia looked at Arnold pensively for a moment. He was still wearing the black derby hat. The Julia she knew would come right out and say, "Gentleman don't wear hats inside a building!" But, she was not the usual Julia right now.

"So, Julia," he interrupted her thought, "what did you think about this evening?" He was abrupt in his manner.

She cocked her head slightly to the right. "I think gentlemen don't wear hats inside a building."

He smiled, slowly raised his right hand to his head, lifted the hat and set it on the edge of the table. In a slow and steady voice he said, "That's what I like, a woman who speaks her mind."

Julia blushed and cringed, slightly startled by her own abruptness. "I'm sorry," she offered. "I shouldn't have said that."

"And, why not?" he asked.

Rose returned to the table breaking the train of conversation. She set a white ceramic teapot in the center of the table and a matching teacup and saucer in front of each of them.

"Thank you," Arnold said.

The demeanor at the table changed. Arnold lifted the pot and first poured tea into Julia's cup and then his own. Before he had finished, Rose had returned to the table with a chocolate eclair for each of them.

"This will surely be the best eclair you have ever had," Arnold said rather monotoned.

They each took a bite. "Umm," Julia murmured. She looked at Arnold whose eyes were rolling back with ecstasy.

"What did I tell you?" he asked, opening his eyes to look at her. He set his fork on his plate. He rested his elbows on the table, placed his chin on his hands and set his focus on Julia. "I hope that you enjoyed the music this evening."

Finishing her bite, Julia smiled. "I did. I really did."

Arnold began to tell her about how Harry's began and how the local talent had flocked to the place. Julia listened. It was interesting and she was enjoying his company. Their conversation was easy and they mutually enjoyed a similar sense of humor. They enjoyed their eclairs, tea, and the company of each other.

"So, I'd love to know a little more about you Julia," Arnold asked.

"Me? I'm not so interesting," Julia said shyly.

"What do you do for a living?"

Julia had enjoyed the evening, but she did not really care to tell him much about herself. She already knew that they were quite opposite and although it had been a fun evening, she was not really interested in striking up a relationship with a man whose greatest endeavor was being a minstrel. "Nothing as interesting as being a talented poet and musician," she finally offered.

"Well, then you probably have a job that pays the bills better!" His comment was joking, but enlightened her all the same.

He must be looking for a woman to support him, she thought to herself.

"I do all right," she said.

"Well, tell me about it," he said.

She was not going to see him again, so why did it matter if she told him or not. "I'm a mortgage broker. I deal with numbers all day. Pretty boring stuff."

"Not at all! With the economy like it is now, being a mortgage broker has got to be a creative outlet."

She smiled, "Not too creative. The Feds frown on it!"

"Ahhh, details," he offered again.

"What about you?" she asked. "Do you do anything else besides picking out tunes?"

"Yeh, I got a day job too. It's pretty boring stuff."

"Tell me about it?" she mimicked.

"If I told you about it, I'd have to kill you," he whisper in a jovial tone.

"Ah, I see," she responded, playing into his joking manner. "High security stuff. Are you a spy?"

"Nothing so adventurous. For the most part I just clean up other people's messes."

"Ah, like a janitor?" she quipped.

He laughed. "That's one way of looking at it, but I like to think of it more like being a rocket scientist. It's kind of like the chem lab, when the young scientists, who think they are so smart, tip over the test tube and they spill the contents all over the floor. I'm the one they call to sop up the mess and get it back in the tube. It's dirty work, but someone got to do it."

Great! a janitor with an inflated ego, Julia thought to herself with a sigh. "I hope you enjoy it," she said with an emotionless tone.

"Yeh, I do." He paused and then said, "And, it pays the bills."

"So where are you a 'rocket scientist'," she asked in a joking manner. "I didn't know that we had such places in Salem."

"That's because you're from Wakefield and wouldn't know," he came back with a smile.

"Hey, we've got plenty of janitors in Wakefield!" she retorted with a gleam in her eyes.

"Touché!"

They smiled at each other. The moment became quiet and slightly uncomfortable. Julia had enjoyed the evening and found Arnold to be delightful, but it was time to say goodnight and move on.

"Would it be all right if I called you sometime and we could have dinner?" he suddenly asked.

Julia did not want to hurt his feelings. They did get along well, but how can she tell him that she is not interested in a man who works as a janitor for a living?

"I've really enjoyed this evening, Arnold," and then she paused. She hoped he would say something. "And, you were right. It was the best chocolate eclair I've ever had." Maybe she could change the subject. "Why don't we head outside. It's getting late." She put her napkin on the table and stood up.

"Sure," he replied quietly and followed. "I'll walk you to your car."

They exited the Pastry Shoppe into the night air. It was a lovely evening with only a slight chill in the air.

"It's beautiful out!" Julia said nervously. "I love this time of year. Before we know it, it will be sweltering at midnight. That's one of the hazards of living in the South!"

"Yeh, but I wouldn't live anywhere else," Arnold commented. "Have you been to Rosemary?"

"That's that little restaurant on the other side of the square, isn't it?"

"It's really good. Would you like to go there one evening?" he asked hopefully.

They continued to walk down the sidewalk which was still busy in spite of the late hour. How she wished he would stop asking her out.

She had no choice but to just be straight with him. "Arnold," she began.

"Dr. Pigeon! Dr. Pigeon!" came a voice from behind him.

Arnold stopped and turned around. Julia turned with him.

A young man in his early twenties approached them. "Dr. Pigeon, I am so glad to see you," he said.

"Hello, Joseph. Fancy meeting you here," Arnold replied.

Julia looked on with confusion as the two men conversed. This was the second person to address him as Dr. Pigeon.

"I just wanted to thank you," the young man started. "Your letter of recommendation got me accepted into the program at Harvard."

"Fabulous!" Arnold replied and extend his hand to shake the younger gentleman's. He then turned to Julia. "Julia, this is Joseph. He has been working with me for sometime. Now, it looks like I'm going to lose a fine employee. And, to add insult to injury, to Harvard of all places!"

Julia was totally confused. "Very nice to meet you," she offered cautiously.

The young man shook her hand and then turned to Arnold and said, "Well, I'll see you at the lab on Monday morning."

Julia and Arnold turned back and continued to head toward her car.

"That's the second person who has called you Dr. Pigeon," she said.

"Well, that's my name."

"What kind of doctor are you? I thought you said you were a janitor."

Arnold laughter, "When did I tell you I was a janitor?"

"At the Pastry Shoppe."

"I told you I was a scientist," he replied.

"You said, 'a rocket scientist' and I thought you were joking," Julia defended herself.

"It was no joke. I really am a rocket scientist." He paused, "Okay, the truth is I am a senior research scientist."

Julia smiled. "And here I thought you were just an aging musician."

They both laughed and then walked silently until they reached her car.

"Thank you for walking me to my car, and for a lovely evening." She reached into her purse for her car keys and took out one of her business cards as well. "I've heard Rosemary is delicious. Call me."

Chapter Thirty-nine

MISS MARY STOOD in front of the full length mirror which was positioned in the corner of her bedroom, next to the window. The morning sun shone brightly and reflected off the mirror onto Miss Mary highlighting her youthful spirit, even if the mirror itself told a different story. She took a deep breath and sighed pleasantly as she thought about Leon. Pulling in her stomach, she pushed her shoulders back and turned sideways to look at herself one more time. She was pleased with herself in spite of her aged appearance. She stepped closer to the mirror and peered at her own face. Smiling she lifted her hand to loosen a strand of hair in front of each ear. The silver locks fell softly around her face. She nodded with approval, collected her cane, and began to head toward the kitchen. As she approached the bedroom door, she stopped short and turned toward her dresser which was covered with a white crocheted dresser scarf that had been made by her grandmother. She touched the corner of the scarf as fond memories played through her mind. Then, she lifted the bottle of Arpége perfume and dabbed some on each wrist and behind her ears.

Miss Mary and Leon Jefferson had become quite close recently. He had taken over Julia Matthews' job of being her chauffeur, they had lunch together two or three times a week, and he called her nearly everyday. And, everyday she waited anxiously for the phone to ring. Today, Leon was coming to Miss Mary's house for lunch. It would be the first time they would be truly alone. She was nervous.

In the kitchen, she opened the oven door and peeked in at the chicken casserole she had made. Smiling with approval she closed the door again. She picked up the silverware and cloth napkins she had set out on the counter and took them to the table. Just as she was finishing setting the table, her doorbell rang. Miss Mary stood frozen, unable to move. Why was she acting like such a school girl? Her stomach was full of butterflies. Surely, she was not going to be able to eat a thing for lunch. The doorbell rang again. Miss Mary collected herself and walked to the front door. She opened it and there on the other side of the screen door, which still stood between them, was Leon Jefferson. Leon stood there smiling, holding a bunch of bright yellow tulips.

"Hello!" Leon offered.

Miss Mary was speechless. She thought he was such an attractive man, and so kind and thoughtful.

"Hello?" he said again.

"Hello," she finally responded with embarrassment. "How are you today?"

"Well, I am looking at the most beautiful woman in the world, so I am just fine!"

Miss Mary blushed. "What beautiful tulips," she responded.

"I'm glad you like them." With a sheepish grin he added, "I just picked them from your neighbors yard."

She chuckled and then silence stood between them for a moment, as well as the screen door.

Leon smiled sweetly. "If you invited me in, I could give them to you."

"Oh my!" She opened the screen door and welcomed him in. "I am so sorry. I didn't mean to leave you standing outside."

As Leon walked passed her, he caught the scent of her perfume and it aroused his senses. "Well, it is a beautiful day out today."

"Yes," she replied nervously. "And, I think I'll leave the door open to let some fresh air in." When the screen door closed again, she latched the hook on it and then turned and headed toward the kitchen. "Please, come this way."

Leon followed Miss Mary down the hallway. The floor creaked with age as they passed through to the kitchen. Along the way, he took in Miss Mary's home, he had never been further than the front door before. In the kitchen, Miss Mary opened the cupboard for a vase. She filled it with water, trimmed the end of the tulips and gently arranged them. Admiring them she said, "These are so lovely."

"They don't do you justice!" he replied.

Miss Mary blushed again. "I made us a chicken casserole. I hope you'll like it."

"I'm sure I'll love it! You know what they say? The way to a man's heart is through his stomach!"

Miss Mary lifted the casserole from the oven and set it on the stove. For a moment she was lost in her own thought. She was remembering the evening when they went to the armory for the dance and Leon held her in his arms on the dance floor. That was where she wanted to be right now —in Leon Jefferson's arms.

"May I help you?" he said again standing close to her. She obviously had not heard the first time he asked. "A penny for your thoughts."

Startled, Miss Mary quickly recovered. "Oh, no, thank you. I was just trying to figure out the best way to serve this."

"Why don't I take it to the table," he replied.

"Perfect!" She handed him the potholders. "I'll get a trivet."

Leon followed Miss Mary, casserole in hand.

They lunched for over an hour, which was not unusual for them. They were never at a loss for topics of conversation. When they were together, the rest of the world was very far away.

"Would you like some more tea?" Miss Mary asked Leon.

"No, thank you. It was terrific. Everything. And, that was the best chicken casserole I've ever had. It got me right here!" He took his hand and tapped it against his heart."

Miss Mary smiled. "Thank you. I'm glad you liked it."

A serious look came across Leon's face and he was silent for a moment. Miss Mary noticed him with concern.

"Are you all right?" she asked.

He smiled. "Very all right." He paused. "Mary, I really enjoy being with you." He paused again. "I just want you to know that."

Miss Mary looked downward shyly. "I enjoy you too, Leon."

Moments of silence passed and then Leon offered, "Well then, why don't I help you clean up this mess?"

"That would be delightful," she responded.

They both pushed their chairs away from the table and stood, each taking a moment to gather their balance before they moved further.

Leon lifted the casserole dish from the middle of the table and carried it to the sink. Miss Mary lifted a plate with one hand and gathered her cane with the other. She slowly made her way to the sink as Leon passed her heading back to the table to clear the rest of the dishes.

They made small talk about church, the community, and upcoming presidential election. For the most part, they were of similar mind, differing only on minor issues of the bigger topics.

Miss Mary brushed the plates before placing them in the dishwasher and Leon took charge of cleaning the table.

"This is a job much better accomplished with two," Miss Mary commented referring to doing the dishes.

"I couldn't agree more," Leon returned. Taking one final wipe of the table with the dishcloth, he tossed it in the air and caught it again with a swoop. "There!" he proclaimed and then returned to the sink and set the cloth on the counter. Miss Mary had finished her chores at the sink and was drying her hands on a dishtowel. Leon was now standing very close to Miss Mary —he liked the feeling of being next to her. He breathed in deeply. Her sweet smell intoxicated him. Miss Mary was nervously aware of his presence next to her. She did not want him to move away, but she was as equally afraid to turn around and face him. She continued to dry her already dry hands.

Leon remained still beside her. For a brief moment his thoughts moved to his late wife, Nancy, who had passed away over fourteen years ago. He had loved her deeply and never dreamed that he could possibly ever desire another woman. For an instant, he was conflicted. He looked blankly into the vastness, not really knowing for what he was seeking —perhaps permission to love another woman.

Miss Mary fell frozen. She had deeply loved a man once before, but had never been so fortunate to share her life with him. That was a long, long time ago. She had forgotten these feelings which were quite different from the feelings she had for friends, family, and even her love for God, which had been her constant companion over the many years.

Feeling a sense of comfort, Leon focused on Miss Mary, who was still nervously drying her hands. He place his hand on her shoulder and turned her to face him. The warmth of his hand was strong on her shoulder. Still holding the dishtowel, she shyly looked up and their eyes met. Everything around them faded away. Leon smiled gently. She returned the gesture. Not removing his one hand from her shoulder, he took his other hand and slowly reached for the dishtowel in Miss Mary's hand. Without breaking their eye contact, he reached to the side and placed the dishtowel on the counter. He then placed that hand on Miss Mary's other shoulder and pulled her close to him. Leon lifted a hand to Miss Mary's face and gently brushed the lock of silver hair which softly framed her face. In response, she tilted her head toward his hand. Slowly, Leon moved his face closer allowing his lips to gently touch hers. Miss Mary's body went limp and leaned closer into Leon's, accepting his invitation as if this was the kiss she had been waiting for all of her life. Leon kissed her again and then pulled away for a slight moment to look into her eyes.

"I love you, Miss Mary Fletcher." He paused. "With all my heart, my soul, and my mind —I love you, Mary." And, he returned his lips to hers.

Chapter Forty

BOBBY AND HIS mother pulled into the Spring Rock Community Church. The sprawling parking lot made way to a large modern building which resembled an office complex. Peggy took in the view. They drove past rows and rows of empty parking spaces.

"They need all these parking spaces?" she asked her son.

"And more!" he responded. "On Sundays they park in that grass field over there too." He pointed to her right.

Peggy observed the space and its distance to the building. "That sure is a hike! I guess I'm glad we are here on a Thursday."

Bobby pulled into a space close to the building and parked his car. Peggy stared out the windshield and then turned to Bobby. "Where's the front door?"

"It's right there," he said, pointing to a large set of double glass doors which looked more like the entrance to a shopping mall than to the vestibule of a church.

"I see," Peggy said. She got out of the car.

When they reached the doors, Bobby pulled one side open and held it for his mother. She entered slowly, overcome by the size of the foyer. Above her, the sky opened to a cathedral of glass void of anything but bright sunlight. It was a glorious sight, but she shuddered to think what the room must be like during a thunderstorm; anything but comforting, she was certain.

"This way," Bobby said, as he began to walk the expanse of the room.

Peggy followed.

The walls were stark and of a neutral palette. They approached a contemporary style table neatly organized with pamphlets, flyers, and other literature. Peggy glanced at it as they walked by. Shortly past the table was a corridor to the right, which Bobby entered and Peggy followed. The hall was cold and their footsteps echoed as they walked along. Peggy thought it curious that they had not seen another person since they had entered the building.

"Where is everyone?" Peggy asked.

"They're here," responded Bobby. "Probably in their offices."

"What about the people?"

"What people?" Bobby returned.

"The people who go to church here —the fellowship."

"Most of them are at work, I imagine."

Peggy crossed her arms across her chest and rubbed them to warm herself. Her only thought was how lifeless the building felt.

They came to a set of glass doors which were etched with the word "Reception". Again, Bobby opened the door and held it for his mother. Peggy entered. Directly in front of them was a custom-made, rosewood reception desk of a style similar to the table which they had passed in the foyer. On either side of the glass doors were six black leather chairs, symmetrically arranged along the barren walls. A professional-looking woman sat behind the desk. Her hair smoothly swept up in a French knot and her clothing was as immaculate as her greeting. "Welcome to Spring Rock Community Church. How may I help you today?"

"We're here to see Gerry Jonah. He's expecting us," Bobby answered.

"If you would like to have a seat, I'll let him know you are here." She gestured to the symmetrical black leather chairs. "May I please have your names," she asked with a robotic voice.

"Peggy and Bobby Buck."

"Thank you. May I offer you a beverage while you wait?" she asked.

Silently, Peggy shook her head. This was all too surreal. She lowered herself into one of the chairs.

"Isn't this a fabulous church?" Bobby interrupted her thought as he sat down next to her.

"How can you tell it's a church?" his mother said slowly.

"What do you mean?" Bobby looked at his mother inquisitively.

"Where are the people? Where are Sunday School rooms with crayons, glue, and construction paper?" she asked in a monotone voice. She looked up at the young woman sitting behind the reception desk and then rubbed her hand across the fine leather of the chair in which she was sitting. "Where are the friendly faces and the upholstered chairs, well worn from hours of fellowship?"

Before Bobby could respond, Gerry Jonah appeared from the hallway through the glass doors. Bobby stood up.

"Mr. Jonah." He extended his hand.

With a gentle smile, Gerry Jonah returned an extended hand. "A pleasure to see you again, Bobby."

Bobby turned. "This is my mother, Peggy."

Peggy stood and extended her hand to Mr. Jonah. "Very nice to meet you. Thank you for taking the time to see us."

Gerry Jonah's face was gentle, softly worn, and in great contrast to the room which served as its backdrop. He was wearing faded blue jeans held up by a pair of red clip-on suspenders. Peggy noted that the blue oxford-cloth shirt beneath the suspenders was neatly starched and pressed and was the only thing about this gentleman that seemed to be consistent with his surroundings.

"My pleasure, Mrs. Buck. If it weren't for missions, where would the church be?" He smiled at Peggy.

Bobby leaned toward Gerry Jonah as if to whisper. "Mom is in a little state of shock. It's the first time she's ever been here."

"Please forgive me, Mr. Jonah," Peggy said with some embarrassment.

"Nothing to forgive," he replied in a deep southern accent. "And, my friends just call me Jonah." He paused. "Will you be my friend?"

Peggy returned the smile. "It would be an honor."

Jonah turned and pulled the glass door open. He leaned toward Bobby and Peggy to whisper. "Let's bust this joint. They're a bit stuffy in here."

They headed down the hallway, this time turning in another direction that took them down a different hallway which was equally as barren as the others.

"I sure hope you know where you are going," Peggy said jovially. "Because I'm lost."

Pamela Jackson

"Nothing short of a labyrinth in here; but, you get use to it," he replied.

They continued to walk. Peggy absorbed the atmosphere. "And, so clean," her words were slow.

They turned the corner and approached a wooden door. "Please excuse the mess in my office." He opened the door. Peggy followed him in and Bobby entered behind her.

The room was a breath of fresh air. Peggy scanned the room with a sense of comfort. A simple wooden table, which showed its age, was against the far wall; it was surrounded by colorful plastic chairs. To her left was a beautiful large wooden desk reminiscent of the 1940's.

Jonah noticed Peggy looking at the desk. "It was my father's. He was a newspaper man." There was a moment of silence as they both stared at the desk. "He didn't believe in church. Never went." Jonah smiled quietly. "His desk has more religion now than he ever did."

"But, you're a church man," Peggy replied; they both still stared at the desk.

"Can't say I always was."

Peggy turned to look at him. "So what brought you?"

"Ah...that's a long story. I'll tell you someday." He turned to meet her gaze. In a moment, he gestured toward the wooden table and plastic chairs. "Let's sit over here." He picked up a stack of papers from the old wooden desk and carry them to the table. Bobby pulled out a royal blue chair and sat down. Jonah gave him a quick glance of disapproval for not have helped his mother with a chair and then pulled out an orange plastic chair and offered it to Peggy. She smiled and graciously nodded as she sat in the chair. Jonah sat in an avocado colored chair. He spread the stack of papers out on the table in front of them; there were brochures, pamphlets, flyers, and more. He picked up one and handed it to Peggy. "This will tell you all about Heifer International."

Peggy looked at it. On the front cover was a circular picture of two children and a goat. Encircling the picture were the words, "Ending World Hunger, Saving the Earth." The background was a divided scene of brown barren land on the left and lush green farmlands on the right. A picture speaks a thousand words.

218

"Heifer is all about ending world hunger," Jonah began. His deep voice jarred Peggy from her fixed stare on the brochure. She turned to look at him. "They provide livestock, training, and lots of resources for these communities, to help them become self-sufficient. When they become self-sufficient, Heifer requires that they in turn help another family which is struggling by 'passing on the gift'. That is, they give another family the offspring from their livestock and train the next family in the skills necessary to become successful in raising the animals and farming their land. And, so on and so on."

Peggy smiled. It warmed her heart as she flipped through the brochure and saw the pictures of prospering families and their healthy animals. "Is it just cattle they send?"

"Heifers, you mean?" Jonah's voice was tender, "No, look here." He reached across her and turned her brochure to the back. Pointing he said, "They send llamas, goats, honey bees, chickens; they even supply trees!"

"I like this!" Peggy said with excitement. "So, how can I get my little church involved?"

"Little church!" Bobby said with exasperation. "Mom, we're not a little church anymore. We have almost 500 members now." That was the first thing Bobby had said since they had been sitting there. His pride was evident.

Peggy looked at him scornfully. "Attendees are not counted as members," she said in rebuke.

"There are many ways churches can get involved," Jonah interjected. He looked at Bobby, "Whatever the size."

Peggy, looking at some of the other literature, smiled to herself.

"Alternative gift giving is one of the easiest things you can do." Jonah handed her another pamphlet. "This explains it. Instead of giving gifts at Christmas, birthdays, or whenever, you can give a heifer, goat, or bee colony in honor of that person. They have beautiful cards to send."

Peggy continued to look at the brochures. "This is fabulous," she said softly. Peggy was excited about this opportunity. She wanted to do something that made a difference. For forty years she had done nothing but live in Buck's shadow, been his puppet, and acted blindly to his ambition. Without thinking she turned to Jonah and spontaneously said, "Will you help me?"

Jonah smiled sweetly at her. The lines around his eyes were reassuring.

Embarrassed by her impulsiveness she quickly added, "Does your wife work with you on missions? I would love to meet her."

"My wife taught me everything I know about missions. She's the reason I do this."

"How wonderful," Peggy offered.

"But, she passed away five years ago. I'm a widower."

Peggy's face was full of compassion and understanding. "I'm sorry," she said gently.

"Don't be sorry," he replied, "They were the best forty years of my life. I'm just waiting to see how God's going to top it."

Peggy wished she could feel the way he did. Her forty year marriage to Buck had been the hardest, most painful years of her life. Her constant prayer now is for God to offer her happiness in what is left of her life. "My husband died nearly a year ago," Peggy said sadly.

"I'm sorry," Jonah said.

A smile broke across Peggy's face as she thought about the irony. "Don't be," she replied.

* * *

GERRY JONAH WALKED Peggy and Bobby back through the labyrinth of Spring Rock Church. "I will call you next week to see how I can help. Thank you for taking an interest in this mission."

"Thank you for giving me the opportunity," Peggy replied.

On the drive back home Peggy talked the whole way about Heifer International and her ideas for building the missions program at First Covenant Chapel. Bobby listened intently; he could not remember his mother ever seeming this excited about anything.

Chapter Forty-one

HE WAS SITTING on the bench where he had first seen her. That is where they were to meet. Arnold was early, as was his usual habit. Dressed in his finest freshly pressed khaki pants, short sleeve plaid button down shirt, and polished cordovan loafers, he anxiously waited for Julia to arrive. While he waited, he surveyed the busyness of downtown Salem and nervously lifted his Derby hat, replacing it on his head again each time.

"Hello."

Arnold jumped and turned around. "Well, hello there! You startled me. Somehow I had calculated that you would be arriving from the other side."

"Now, how can you calculate such a thing?" Julia asked with a smile that made Arnold take notice.

He took a moment to visually absorb her. *She is lovely,* he thought. Julia was wearing simple black slacks and a lacy white blouse.

Julia felt uncomfortable for a moment as she noticed his eyelids bobbing. She recalled that was the first thing which she had noticed about him. That, and the fact that his fashion sense was slightly off. She was nervous. This was only their second meeting, although they had talked on the telephone several times since the evening they had shared eclairs and hot tea.

Arnold stood and offered her his arm. "My lady," he said in a Shakespearean manner.

She smiled and accepted his offer.

They began to walk down the brick sidewalks of Salem. "Wait until you taste the food at Rosemary. It is a gastronomical treat!"

"You seem to know where all the best food is," Julia responded.

"Well, you know what they say," he returned.

"No. What do they say?"

He turned to look at her as they walked along. He smiled gently and then turned his eyes back in the direction which they were walking. "A way to a man's heart is through his stomach."

Rosemary was packed when Julia and Arnold entered. People were sitting on benches and standing wherever they could find a spot.

"Goodness," Julia said. "This must be a really popular place. We're going to have a wait."

"Excuse me. Coming through," he said to the crowd. He pushed his way through the crowd to the podium. Julia close behind him.

"Good evening, Dr. Pigeon!" the young woman offered.

He lifted his Derby hat and slightly bowed his head. "Good evening, Miss Carmichael."

He began to replace his hat when he suddenly recalled the comment which Julia had made about gentlemen and hats at the Pastry Shoppe. He looked at Julia, cleared his throat, and lowered his hat to his side.

She smiled.

Turning back to the young lady he said, "Looks like a pretty long wait."

"At least an hour," she replied.

"Ah, well, whatever you can do will be fine," he answered. "We'll be at the bar."

He stepped back to allow Julia to pass in front of him.

When they reached the bar, he spotted one empty stool and pulled it out for Julia. "Hey, Charlie," he called to the bartender.

"Dr. Pigeon!" The man came over to them.

He extended his hand across the bar and the two gentlemen shook.

"This is my friend Julia," Arnold turned toward Julia and smiled. "What would you like to drink?"

"A glass of Chardonnay would be great," she replied shyly. She glanced at Arnold. *How did he know everybody?* She studied him as he was giving Charlie their order. Again, what caught her attention most was how his eyes gave the appearance that there was nothing behind them but great vastness.

Arnold turned back toward Julia. "Don't you just love this place?"

"It's great!" She said with little thought. "But, an hour wait? Is it worth it?"

"Worth every bit the wait! But," he hesitated and then leaned closer to her to whisper, "we'll be seated in five minutes."

"Five minutes?"

"The young lady is an employee of mine. She is doing her internship. She's got a brilliant mind."

Julia smiled and nodded. "I see."

"It's not what you know…it's who you know!" he continued.

They had gotten their drinks and in less than five minutes, just as Arnold predicted, the young lady came to tell them, very discreetly, that there was a table ready for them. She took them to a perfectly situated table for two.

"Ah, my favorite table," he exclaimed as he helped Julia with her chair again.

Curious, she asked, "So, what's so special about this table?"

"People watching. This is the perfect table for people watching!"

Julia looked around. "I see." Yet again, she was at a loss for words.

The waitress approached their table. Noticing they had drinks, she told them about the evening specials and then left.

"Why don't they ever tell you how much the specials cost?" Julia commented with irritation.

"She did. Didn't you hear her?" Arnold replied with a smile. "She said it was market price."

She returned the smile, enjoying his sarcasm. "Oh, I see. It's like when you ask somebody what time they will arrive and they say, 'Early'." Julia looked at her watch and began pointing to it forcefully for dramatic emphasis. "I usually respond by saying, 'My watch has numbers on it! Could you please be clearer about what early is?!'"

Arnold nodded in agreement as the waitress returned.

"Are you all ready to order?" she asked.

Arnold grinned roguishly. "Well, could you please be a little clearer on what 'market price' is?" He glanced toward Julia who was grinning too.

They both ordered the special, at market price, and then Julia and Arnold immediately got lost in their conversation. Arnold was as bold as Julia, which somehow made her seem almost demure. But, the more they talked, the more comfortable she became, and the more she held her own against him.

They watched people mill about. Julia was surprised at how busy the place was, and delighted at how this tiny spot was situated to offer a periscopic view.

"Look at that man! What's the thing through his eyebrow?" Arnold said, referring to the odd piercing. He paused for a moment. "I don't get it. Why would someone do that to himself?"

Julia stared at the man, her own eyebrows crinkled, but she did not offer a reply.

"Is that attractive?" he asked with disbelief. "I mean, to women. Do they like that sort of thing?"

"You've got to be kidding me!" Julia exclaimed and then retorted, "Do men find the women who wear the low-cut pants with the short-cut shirt exposing a roll of blubber with a belly-button ring attractive?"

Arnold laughed hard. "Yeah, I especially like it when they have tattoos!" His sarcasm was evident.

"You mean 'tramp stamps'?" she returned.

Arnold looked at Julia with a mischievous grin. "They are called that for a reason, you know."

They were both laughing hard now.

The waitress brought their salads and placed them in front of them, but they were talking so intently, they barely noticed. However, at the same moment they both noticed the woman who walked through the front door of Rosemary.

"Oh my!" They both exclaimed in unison and then turned to look at each other, startled they both used the same expression at the same time.

The woman who had come through the door was in her mid-forties, the same as Julia. She wore tight black leather pants and a gold sleeveless top, which scooped extraordinarily low, allowing her abnormally huge breasts to appear to almost spill out the top.

"Now, that is a work of art," Arnold said with delight.

"Are you going to tell me, you don't approve," Julia said curiously.

"Well," he said with a contemplative pause. "It does create the 'awe factor'. But, her plastic surgeon is really no different from Michelangelo."

Julia laughed.

Arnold continued, "You tend to look at something like that the same way you look at the sculpture of *David*."

"Pray tell," Julia asked, not quite understanding his parallel.

"It is a fearsome sight to behold, but nothing human is really that big!"

"Oh, come on!" Julia said. "That is every man's dream."

"The woman, or *David*?" he asked sarcastically.

"My point exactly!"

His glance to her was serious, suggesting that she might be wrong in her thought, which caused her to briefly think about her own situation. And, at this moment she was pleased with her own body, now the size which God originally gave her.

"I mean, just look at her!" Arnold exclaimed. "She looks like she's got her knees stuffed up in her shirt."

Julia smiled, completely content with herself.

Chapter Forty-two

WEDNESDAY MORNINGS HAD become a pointless time to attempt to work for Margaret. Her desk was situated right at the entry to the offices of First Covenant Chapel and on Wednesday mornings it was the door which everyone used to enter the building. All she could do on Wednesday mornings was meet and greet, and she finally had given up trying to accomplish anything else.

"Good morning, Margaret," was said in unison by two of the members of the Celebration class as they strolled passed, heading toward the classroom which hosted their Wednesday morning Bible Study.

"Morning," she replied in a monotone voice and gave a slight wave.

Julia Matthews opened the door and breezed in joyfully. "Good morning, all!"

Margaret looked up, glanced around the room confirming that, indeed, there was no one else in the room. "Who are you talking to?" she asked curiously.

"Well, at least to you," Julia snapped.

"Why are you so happy?"

"Better question," Julia replied, "why are you so glum?"

"I'm not glum. I just get alarmed by the unusual."

"You may call me unusual if you like. Won't bother me a bit." Julia said as she crossed the room and sat down in the chair in front of Margaret's desk.

Margaret smiled at her inquisitively. "So, how is Dr. Pigeon?"

Julia pretended to blush shyly. "I am here to stuff and stamp newsletters, not gossip."

"That's unusual too! You're always here to gossip!" Margaret proclaimed.

"Not when it's about me!"

"So, there is something to tell!" Margaret exclaimed gleefully.

The door to the church offices opened again. Miss Mary and Leon Jefferson walked in. They both appeared unusually youthful.

"Well, good morning you two," Julia said in an inquisitive manner.

"Top of the day!" Leon replied.

Julia and Margaret looked at each other.

Miss Mary turned to Leon, "I'll catch up with you in a moment, if that is all right."

He nodded at her with a tender smile. "Absolutely," he said gently.

Miss Mary walked closer to Julia and Margaret. She held her hand out toward Julia. "Good morning, Angel. How are you?" Julia took her hand and squeezed.

"I'm well," Julia replied.

Miss Mary turned and looked at Margaret. "And, how are you today, Margaret?"

"Just fine, Miss Mary. Thank you. And, you look exceptionally well, if I might say so."

Miss Mary smiled with a blush.

Julia narrowed her eyes as she surveyed Miss Mary. Still holding her hand Julia blurted, "So what gives?"

"So what gives, Dear?" Miss Mary echoed.

"What gives?" Julia repeated.

Now, Miss Mary beamed. "I have some wonderful news," she said very softly.

"What?" Julia demanded.

"Well, Angel, I'm getting married."

Julia dropped her hand and stood rapidly.

"What!" Julia practically shouted.

"That is fabulous!" Margaret interjected.

Julia's eyes were large and her face beamed. She grabbed Miss Mary and hugged her small frame tightly. "This is wonderful!" She pulled back and looked in Miss Mary's face. "I presume it's Leon, isn't it?"

"No, I've had several other men on the side," she replied sarcastically, out of character for Miss Mary. "Of course it's Leon!"

"Oh, Miss Mary, I am so happy for you! When's the big day?"

"We are going to talk with Reverend Montague after our Bible Study class today. We would like to have it in the next two weeks."

"Two weeks!" Margaret said startled. "That's so soon. Why the rush?"

Miss Mary giggled and looked at Margaret. "Honey, I'm over eighty years old. Every minute counts!"

"This is just so wonderful," Julia repeated over and over.

Miss Mary took both of Julia's hands in hers and looked her in the eyes. "Angel, I would like for you to be my maid of honor."

Julia's face lighted up for a moment and then sank. "The story of my life. Always a bridesmaid, never a bride."

"Dr. Pigeon..." Margaret said in a teasing manner.

Julia turned and looked curtly at Margaret.

"How is Dr. Pigeon?" Miss Mary asked.

Julia pursed her lips and raised her eyebrows. "I enjoy his company very much, thank you."

"I enjoy his company very much," Margaret mimicked in a childlike tone.

Julia ignored her and turned her focus back to Miss Mary. "I would be honored to be your maid of honor."

"Thank you, Angel," Miss Mary replied with apparent gratitude. "Well, I must head on to class. Leon will be worried."

Margaret and Julia watched Miss Mary walk down the hall.

"That is so sweet," Margaret said.

Julia sat back down and began to stuff newsletters in envelopes. "Well, it gives me hope for the future. Maybe by the time I'm eighty I'll get married too."

"Dr. Pigeon..." Margaret said again in a teasing manner.

"Hush up!" Julia barked.

The door opened again and in walked Bobby. Recently, his demeanor had noticeably changed, in Julia's opinion. He had gone from being arrogant and self-absorbed to being generally unpleasant and downright rude.

"Good morning, Bobby," Margaret said.

He nodded in recognition and offered a simple, "Hey."

Julia pushed her shoulders back with irritation and managed a smile, "How are you today, Bobby?"

"Good."

His incivility cut through Julia. With arrogance in her own manner she replied, "Actually, I was not inquiring into either your morals or how you might taste. I was simply inquiring into how you felt today."

Bobby turned and glared at her. "I'm well, thank you." And, he walk passed them.

"He certainly has been sour recently," Margaret noted as she turned back to her stack of newsletters and envelopes.

Julia stared aimlessly in deep thought. "Something's up."

* * *

Spinning a pencil on his desk, he aimlessly looked out the window. Ben picked up the telephone, held it in his hand a moment and then put it back down. He stood from his chair and walked to the window. It had been nearly a week since he had confronted Sylvia, and confronted Davies. Ben had called and left numerous messages for her, but she had returned none. When he was visiting at the hospital, he had looked for her, but she was nowhere to be found. Had he blown everything with Sylvia?

He looked at his watch. Fifteen minutes until staff meeting, he thought to himself. He was not in the mood for another draining staff meeting. He shuffled through his notes for the meeting, totally uninterested in what he was looking at.

Ben picked up the phone and dialed Sylvia's number again. "She has to answer eventually," he said out loud.

The phone rang one time and Sylvia picked up.

"Hello," she said in a tone which indicated she knew who was calling.

"Don't sound so disappointed," Ben replied, not meaning to sound curt.

"Oh, Ben. I didn't realize it was you."

"Who else would it be when your Caller Id says, 'First Covenant Chapel'?" he retorted.

"Well, I could think of at least a half a dozen people," she replied with a giggle in her voice.

Her jovial tone comforted him.

"How are you?" he asked.

"I'm fine. And, you?"

"Fine." He paused, knowing he needed to get to the point. "Could we talk?"

"I thought we were?" she replied sarcastically.

"I mean really talk."

There was silence on the other end of the phone. Sylvia was tired of this relationship which seemed to be going nowhere.

"Sylvia?"

"Sure." Her response was cold. "Come by this evening about seven. I've got to stop at the grocery after work and then I'll be home."

"I'll be there."

He gently set down the phone. Folding his hands together, he lifted them to his face. "Oh, Lord," he said out loud. "Please be my words when I talk to Sylvia this evening." He sighed and then stood, prepared to face his next great battle —staff meeting.

Chapter Forty-three

JONAH CALLED, JUST as he had promised. "I got a whole box of brochures on Heifer International for you, so you can give them to everyone in your congregation."

"Well, thank you," Peggy answered shyly. She had not expected him to go to all that effort. "I hope I haven't troubled you."

"Trouble!" he said firmly. "What kind of trouble is it to serve other people?"

Peggy smiled. Her heart was touched. Gerry Jonah was a genuine man of God. *A rarity in the church,* she thought. Although, she was aware that her view was tainted —not all men are like Buck.

"I'll come by the church and pick them up this afternoon. Would that be all right?" she asked.

"Actually, I'm heading out to lunch in a few moments. Would you care to join me? I could give them to you then."

Peggy placed her hand on her stomach in response to the sudden butterflies which had appeared. "I'd be delighted."

* * *

PEGGY AND JONAH sat at a small table in the deli on the corner of a side street in Salem.

"This is my favorite deli," Jonah said. "Have you been her before?"

"No, I haven't."

"It's as close as they come to the ones up in New York City. Be sure to try the potato salad," he said with enthusiasm.

Peggy smiled, "I will."

A thirty-something year old man came to the table. His dark hair was slicked back and he wore a dirty white apron around his waist. Pulling a notepad from the apron pocket he said, "What'll you have?"

Jonah looked at Peggy. She grimaced not quite sure what to order. "What do you suggest?" she asked Jonah.

"They have a killer Rueben," he responded.

"Then, that is what I'll have." She set the menu back down on the table.

Jonah looked at the waiter. "We'll have two Ruebens with a side of potato salad."

"What to drink?" asked the waiter, as if a demand.

"I'll have iced tea, please. Unsweetened," Peggy added.

"And, I'll have sweet tea," said Jonah.

The waiter made a "tsk" sound and said, "Southerners," under his breath before he turned and shouted, "Ruebens on the two top, side of potato!"

"Very authentic," Peggy said with wide eyes.

"Wait till you taste it!"

Peggy had not really enjoyed a meal since Buck had passed away. She had lost a lot of weight and become quite thin.

"I'm looking forward to it," she responded.

Jonah smiled at Peggy. "I kind of suspected you needed a good meal."

Peggy looked at him curiously, not understanding his statement.

"What I mean is," Jonah said, "I know the loneliness of losing your spouse. Fellowship becomes very important."

Peggy was touch by his generosity and caring. She looked at him deeply for a moment. His pale blue eyes caught her attention. She somehow felt she had seem them before, but she could not place where.

"Order up!" the waiter interrupted. He set diner-style plates in front of each of them and walked away quickly.

Jonah folded his hands at the edge of the table, tilted his head to the left and glanced toward the ceiling. Softly he said, "Thanks, God."

Peggy nodded in agreement.

"So, tell me how you came to be so involved in missions," Peggy said.

"Well, it was a long road, but, here I am."

Peggy looked at him expectantly.

"By profession, I was an attorney. Man of the law. Professional liar, some would call it." He chuckled. "Just like politics," he glanced at her seriously. "But, we won't go there. I did a lot of domestic stuff. It's the most hateful thing you can image. It was commonplace for me to see families ripped at the seams and gutted like a poacher with a wild animal. Except, I was the poacher." He looked ashamed. "My wife, Ava, was a very beautiful woman, and a very strong Christian. She grew up in the mission field. Her parents were missionaries. She lived all over the place. And, she was poor herself. I mean, they had what they needed, but nothing extra. When she graduated from college, she came to work as a legal secretary for the firm where I worked. We fell in love, got married. You know the story." Jonah paused and took a bite of his sandwich.

Peggy was intent on every word he was saying.

Jonah continued. "We were very happy. But, we didn't always see eye to eye. Not that we really differed. It was just that I didn't see the importance in church. I believed in God, but more just like a creator. I didn't really see Him in the day to day workings of the world. Ava did, however. I didn't mind going to church every now and then, but when the boys were born, it became real important to Ava that I go to church with her every Sunday. That caused some conflict."

Peggy watched his expressions as he spoke. He was so straightforward, so honest. His eyes were sincere and gentle; again, their blueness caught her attention and there was something familiar in them.

"The thing for me was, it was hard to spend my Monday through Friday destroying people's lives and then decompress by Sunday to hear about forgiveness and redemption. Those just didn't exist in my world. Ava and I started growing distant." He sighed. "Let's just say, I didn't handle things to well." He suddenly lifted his head and looked

Peggy straight in the eyes. "But, I was never unfaithful to my wife. I may have been many things as a man, but I was never unfaithful."

Peggy nodded her head softly. How she wished that she could have said the same thing about her husband.

"We went on like that for a long time. Don't get me wrong. We were all right happy. I mean, I loved her dearly. She was the best woman and wife a man could dream of." He reflected contemplatively for a moment. "Anyway, when the boys were in their early teens, Ava planned a trip to see her parents who were still in the mission fields; this time in Africa. I didn't want to go, but I sure wasn't sending my wife and two sons without me to protect them. I tried to talk her out of going, but she wouldn't budge. So, I went. I really went full of resentment."

He looked at his plate for a moment, and then picked up his fork and moved the potato salad around on his plate. Peggy could tell there was something very emotional behind his sudden silence.

"What was it like there? In Africa?" she asked.

Jonah slowly shook his head. "I had never seen anything like it. The poverty, the sickness. The vision is still burned into my memory. My first response was to run, and get my wife and children out of that hell hole. Anyway, to make a long story short, as the days wore on, I watched my wife and her parents feed and care for this community. They got their supplies from a local church. Daily, they would prepare food at a small community center." He paused again. "One day it hit me, I spend my days fighting over who is going to get the BMW and the pet Maltese, and these people are happy to tear their one stale piece of bread in half and give it to the person next to them." He smiled. "My life was never the same. Within a year, I stopped practicing domestic law in favor of corporate. Corporate Law was a lot more boring, but it allowed me to go to church on Sundays with a peace of mind. I volunteered on the missions committee and the rest, as they say, is history."

"And then, your own son became a minister," she added.

"And, the other one an attorney. How ironic!" He looked at her sweetly. "How about you?"

Peggy looked down. "I'm not very interesting."

"I beg to differ," he replied firmly. He paused for a moment. "I was very sorry to hear about your husband's accident. Uriah told me about it. You and your family were in our prayers at Spring Rock for a long time."

Peggy looked up curiously. "You prayed for me?"

Chapter Forty-four

BEN ARRIVED IN the parking lot at the Sheridan Towers at six-thirty. He could use the thirty minutes, before meeting Sylvia, to pray and think about exactly what he was going to say. "It's now or never," he said out loud. He breathed in deeply and let it out hard. He just hoped he was not too late in telling Sylvia. And, he hoped she felt the same way he did. There had been a lot that had gone between them recently. Most of it involved Richard Davies. But, he hoped this evening would settle it all and his life would be changed forever.

He closed his eyes for a moment and leaned his head against the head rest. A slight tapping at his window disturbed him. He quickly opened his eyes and looked out the window. There was Sylvia with an armful of groceries. "A little help here would be nice," he could faintly hear through the glass. She was smiling.

He quickly opened the door and took all of the grocery bags from her arms. "Here, let me," he said as he leaned close to her to gather them.

"Well, thank you, kind sir."

"My pleasure," he responded. He enjoyed the way they conversed with each other.

They walked to the front doors of the Sheridan Towers without another word. They were both aware of the conversation which faced them; they just were not sure of the other's position —the tension in both of them was obvious.

When they were in the lobby and heading toward the elevator, it suddenly dawned on Ben that his hands were full of Sylvia's groceries and that he would be going up the elevator to her apartment for the first time, except of course, not considering the time he took her home when she had been drunk. But, he had not gone inside that night. His heart started beating rapidly. He was ready to enter her apartment and move into a more intimate part of her world.

The elevator carried them to her floor and they still had not spoken a word. The silence was painful. Standing outside her door, she opened her purse for her key. She slid it into lock, just as she had on the previous evening, but this time, Ben followed her in.

"The kitchen is right through there," she said pointing to her right.

Ben made his way to the kitchen, Sylvia followed him.

"You can just put all of those on the counter," her words were quick. She was nervous.

Ben set the bags down and privately took a deep breath. He, too, was more nervous than he could ever remember being in his life.

"You have a beautiful place," he said, as he took it all in.

"I like to call it home," she said with a smile.

"May I help you put these things away?" he said, gesturing to the grocery bags.

"No, they can wait," she replied. "There's nothing which needs to be refrigerated. "I know your time is valuable." She laughed out loud. "I've heard it is harder to get an appointment with the pastor of a church than it is with a doctor."

Ben laughed in return. "Only the pastors who play golf. And, you darn sure better never die on a Friday."

"I'll make a mental note of that! Would you like some tea?" Sylvia asked while she was fidgeting with a dish cloth she had picked up off the counter.

"Sure," he replied and then quickly added. "Are you sure you don't want me to put these things away for you?" He pointed to the groceries again.

Suddenly, Sylvia's demeanor seemed to change. "Is that why you came here this evening, Ben? To put away my groceries."

He took a visibly deep breath. "No."

She simply looked at him with anticipation, but he could not read her expression. Neither said a word for what seemed like an eternity.

"Well?" she finally commanded.

"Well what?"

She tossed the dish cloth on the counter and with exasperation said, "I'm not doing this anymore, Ben." She turned away from him.

He lowered his head and prayed for strength. "Sylvia."

She turned with expectation.

"You know I care about you," he said in a voice which she understood to be cold.

"No, I don't," she responded equally cold.

"I do."

I do, she thought. *Is that all he can say, "I do."* This was annoying Sylvia and she had no intention of spending her evening this way. She turned to grab the tea kettle while contemplating showing him the front door.

"I haven't seen you making any moves to show that you care," she said as she filled the tea kettle with water.

"I do care Sylvia. You know that!" Ben said firmly.

"Do I?" she said with a sarcastic tone. She placed the tea kettle on the stove and turned it on. When she turned back around Ben was standing right behind her. His eyes were intent and the muscles in his arms were rigid. She looked at him with softened eyes and said, "Ben, I don't know what to say to you anymore."

Ben moved closer. She could feel his breath on her face. He had backed her against the counter and placed his hands on either side of her locking her into the position. He moved closer to her. Their mouths were inches away from each other and he said, "What would you say to me if I told you I'm in love with you and I want to kiss you right now?"

Sylvia parted her lips as if to speak, but no words came out. Ben lowered his mouth to hers and their lips met. Moving his hands from the counter, he placed them at the small of her back and drew her against him. She surrendered every bit of opposition she had.

They kissed for a long moment and then Ben drew back slightly to focus his eyes on hers. He continued to hold her tightly against his body. "I am in love with you, Sylvia. I have been in love with you since the day I met you. Everyday that we have been apart since then I have missed you." He lifted one of his hands and placed it softly against her cheek; she tilted her head into it. "My desire for you is so deep that I think I would have missed you even if I had never met you."

Sylvia's heart was beating rapidly and she could feel his beating equally as hard. Her knees were weak and she wanted nothing more than to feel his lips against hers again. Their faces still only inches apart, she smiled that little crooked smile that always sent warm shivers through his body. Then, she lifted her arms and placed them around his neck. Dragging her fingers through his thick dark hair, she pulled his mouth back down to hers.

Chapter Forty-five

BEN SAT IN the pulpit as Ashley led the congregation in the opening hymn and the words filled every inch of his being —the old hymn was music to his soul indeed.

Love divine, all loves excelling, joy of heaven, to earth come down;
fix in us thy humble dwelling; all thy faithful mercies crown!
Jesus, thou art all compassion, pure, unbounded love thou art;
visit us with thy salvation; enter every trembling heart.

The sunlight shone through the stained glass windows on the East side of the tiny white clapboard church in the country. The rays of diffused light illuminated the faces of each of the parishioners as they sang out in harmony. Ben's heart was full of joy. He surveyed the portrait which God had so perfectly painted. On the third row back was Miss Mary in a navy blue hat encircled with a wide, white grosgrain ribbon. Standing closely next to her was her fiance, Leon Jefferson. The two would be married next week in this very chapel. Little Alex stood on the pew next to her great-grandpa looking over his shoulder to see the hymnal which he and Miss Mary were sharing. On the other side of Miss Mary stood Julia Matthews; he smiled, thinking of their deep bonds. Beside Julia was a gentleman whom Ben did not recognize, but he certainly did admire his derby hat. Ben looked three rows further back and saw Bobby Buck —his brother. Their eyes met; Ben acknowledged him. This was not going to be an easy family relation; he looked up to God for direction. Across the aisle stood Tom and Lisa Werner with their two sons. Lisa was noticeably pregnant. Ben offered up a simple prayer that God's will would be done in this difficult situation. Two rows closer and to the left Peggy

Buck stood singing with her daughter Amy and her family. Ben looked curiously. On the other side of Peggy was a gentleman whom he had only met once before. He was certain it was Gerry Jonah. It startled Ben. *Why would Gerry Jonah be at First Covenant Chapel, next to Peggy Buck?* he thought. Ben smiled as his eyes met the beautiful lady's eyes who stood in the front row, closest to him. He knew they were eyes that one day, he would see in his own children. A further scan showed that Richard Davies was nowhere to be seen. Ben prayed that Dr. Davies would be in a church somewhere, although he doubted it. But, he asked God to please bless him anyway. His eyes moved back to Sylvia; she met his eyes which spoke volumes of their private thoughts.

Finish, then, thy new creation; pure and spotless let us be.
Let us see thy great salvation perfectly restored in thee;
Changed from glory into glory, till in heaven we take our place,
Till we cast our crowns before thee, lost in wonder, love, and praise.

Ben took a deep breath and released it with great satisfaction. He smiled joyfully and thought —*all of this, for the love of Heaven!*